FEARLESS heart

BRIGHTON WALSH

COPYRIGHT

Edited by Lisa Hollett of Silently Correcting Your Grammar
Cover Design by Brighton Walsh
Cover Image: Chris C. by Wander Aguiar

Digital ISBN: 978-1-68518-023-2
Paperback ISBN: 978-1-68518-028-7
Special Edition ISBN: 978-1-68518-033-1

FEARLESS heart

Quinn Cartwright sees me as nothing more than her rival...her enemy. But I've been obsessed with her since we were teenagers. She's gorgeous and brilliant with a tongue sharp enough to cut glass...and she has no idea I love it as much as I do.

So when she needs someone to put a ring on it because of her asshole boss, I marry her without hesitation.

We draw up a contract on a napkin. This marriage might be fake, but no one in our small town has to know.

She may never see me as anything more than a playboy, but sleeping in the same bed together night after night makes me want to put my skills to use and prove just how good this fake marriage can be...

CONTENT NOTES

Please be advised that this book contains content that may be upsetting for some readers. Should you prefer detailed information for the best reading experience, please visit the author's website to view a full list of content notes.

For everyone who doesn't mind an assist—make sure your friends are charged. Ford's already on it.

CHAPTER ONE

FORD

GENERALLY SPEAKING, I didn't mind a well-placed hand on my ass.

Loved it, actually. Though, generally speaking, when said hand was on my ass, I wasn't usually at the grocery store, in broad daylight, in the view of dozens of Starlight Cove's residents and busybodies. And, generally speaking, the person copping a feel wasn't old enough to be my grandmother.

"Mabel." I raised a brow at the woman who stood next to me in all her neon-orange glory, her hair a mass of short gray curls around her head, then glanced to where she had an entire handful of my ass. "Much as I love getting felt up, Aiden and I have a little league practice we need to get to, so can you finish up?"

"What? Oh!" Mabel, Starlight Cove's gossip, troublemaker, and self-proclaimed news broadcaster, pulled her hand away—much slower than someone who was caught groping another person should have—and a sly smile swept across her mouth. She could've been anywhere between sixty-five and eighty-five—I valued my life far too much to ask—and there was no doubt she'd learned a thing or two in that time. Namely, that she didn't give a single fuck.

"Should I leave you two alone?" my brother asked dryly. Aiden—second eldest of the McKenzies—stood off to the side, arms crossed. He hadn't bothered to change out of his work clothes after leaving the family resort in the very capable hands of our baby sister. He didn't concern himself with the fact that he was going to look ridiculous in a white button-up and dress pants on the baseball mound as fifteen eight-year-olds ran circles around him and screamed their heads off.

"Hey, I gotta get it where I can," I said, winking at Mabel as she strolled away with a little shimmy in her step, her gaze still glued to my ass and not what was in front of her.

Aiden rolled his eyes and grabbed two baskets before handing one to me. "We both know 'getting it' is the least of your problems."

I pressed my lips together, not saying a word in response. Getting it? No, that wasn't a problem. Had never been. It was almost sad how predictable it had all become; I'd bet my entire life savings I'd have at least one number before I left the store.

But being interested in it? *That* was my problem—recently anyway. Though, "my" was pushing it, considering my *dick* was the one with the issue. Apparently he was no longer interested in a mindless escape. No longer at all up—

pun abso-fucking-lutely intended—for entertaining the various women in our picturesque pocket of Maine. For some unknown reason, the not-so-little bastard had suddenly become discerning. Discerning, but without an ounce of self-preservation.

Because the one woman he had become obsessed with? She'd just as soon cut him off before she ever played with him.

So, yeah. You could say my dick and I were at a bit of a crossroads, and who knew how long it would be before we were on the same page.

"Get your head in the game, man," Aiden said, snapping his fingers in front of my face. "It's no fun to win if it's not a challenge."

I focused back on my brother. He looked bored, but I knew better. When it came to competition, he was ruthless—much like the rest of us McKenzies—and he was going to try his hardest to wipe the floor with me. I'd return the favor, of course, especially when a lost bet in this family meant a fallout ranging anywhere from humiliation—there was still video floating around from senior year when I had to naked limbo outside the girls' locker room for losing at mini golf—to body modification—I was the proud owner of a pierced dick, thanks to a not-so-friendly competition with my youngest brother, Levi—and everything in between.

"Mabel would have to do a lot more than grab my ass for me to be too distracted to kick yours."

"Keep dreaming," Aiden said. "Let's lay out the rules and get started."

I scoffed and mumbled, "Of course he's gotta have rules."

"Rules make it so you won't win on a technicality."

I blew out a long sigh. "Fine. We've got ten minutes to find the best snack and meet back at checkout. Then we'll have the kids do a blind taste test after practice. The team decides who wins."

"Winner gets bragging rights, obviously," he said. "But what about the loser?"

We never bet money—besides the fact that none of us were exactly rolling in it, where was the fun in that?—and what ended up on the line varied with each competition, not to mention each competitor. But there was one thing he and I had been struggling with that I absolutely did not want to handle, so it was the obvious choice.

"Loser has to plan and coordinate the fundraiser for new team uniforms."

Aiden let out a groan and scrubbed a hand down his face.

With a grin, I lifted a shoulder. "If you don't think you'll win..."

"Fuck off. Time starts now." Without waiting for me to respond, he took off to the left with a focused intensity that was pure Aiden.

I turned in the opposite direction, set on doing the same, and nearly plowed down the person who'd been standing directly behind me. I reached out to steady them. "Sorry about—"

But my words caught in my throat when I got a whiff of too-strong perfume, one I was all too familiar with. Unfortunately. Without even looking, I knew exactly who was invading my personal space. Chelsea Dread. Yes, that was seriously her last name, and yes, that should've been the biggest red flag in existence warning me away. Alas, teenagers were idiots, and I'd been no exception.

"Oh, Ford!" Chelsea said with false surprise. "Funny running into you here. I feel like I haven't talked to you in forever!"

"Not nearly long enough," I mumbled.

Because she'd never been able to read the room, she continued on as if I were interested. "I've just been so busy lately, what with the preparations and all. I hope you're not too upset that I didn't send you an invitation."

"An invitation to what?"

She blinked up at me, her face a mask of confusion as if she didn't understand my question, and breathed out a laugh. "To my wedding, of course."

I scratched my jaw, squinting one eye as I stared down at her. "Why would I be upset about that?"

She tossed her hair over her shoulder, a cloud of her cloyingly sweet perfume smacking me in the face with the power of a two-by-four, and looked at me with pity. "I just know how hard this must be for you. Seeing me—the one who got away—moving on. Marrying someone else."

I snorted, not bothering to try to hide it. There was exactly one woman in the world I couldn't handle marrying someone else, and it sure as fuck wasn't my ex-girlfriend from high school who'd set me on my path of singledom, thanks to the horror that had been a relationship with her.

"I promise you," I said, "I am not even slightly upset about this. I'm happy for you and Larry."

"*Barry*."

"Sure."

She let out a soft, sympathetic huff and stuck out her bottom lip. "I just love how brave you're acting about this whole thing."

"Oh, for fuck's sake."

She carried on as if I hadn't spoken. "It must be hard for you to see me moving on like this. Especially when, you know…"

No, I didn't know, and I didn't need to. But Chelsea had always known exactly the buttons to push to manipulate people, and I fell right into her trap.

"Especially when what?"

She raised a shoulder. "Just knowing you're the guy women have lots of fun with before they settle down—God knows you're perfect for a good time—but you're definitely not the one they bring home. Not the one they actually *keep*."

Her words shouldn't have stung. Not when they were true. There was no denying my attributes—perpetual flirt, amazing one-night stand, consistent booty call.

Someone's forever? Not my style.

But she'd aimed the words as if they were daggers meant to kill. And I had no intention of allowing my ex-girlfriend and all-around awful human to walk away from this encounter with the upper hand. So, I did what I always did and leaped before I looked.

"I'm sure you have extra plates. Consider this my RSVP for two. I'll bring my girlfriend."

Never mind the fact that I didn't have a girlfriend. Worse, I didn't even have a bed partner, because my dick hated me, and the only woman he was interested in wouldn't give me the time of day. But that was future Ford's problem to solve.

Chelsea tipped her head to the side. "Is that what you're calling one-night stands now?"

I bared my teeth in some semblance of a smile. "Careful, you're starting to sound jealous."

She breathed out a forced laugh and narrowed her eyes, plastering on a fake smile. A viper ready to strike. "I'm not jealous! Why would I be? I've moved on from the one-and-done stage. I needed someone a bit more...permanent. And we both know that was never and will never be you."

Along with everyone else in Starlight Cove, I tended to agree with her. But something had shifted in the past couple months. Turned out, nameless bodies weren't quite as fulfilling at thirty-two as they had been at twenty-two.

"I'll send you the details." Chelsea pulled out her phone, and mine pinged with an incoming text. One of the downfalls of small-town living—once someone had your number, they had it forever. "Can't wait to meet this...*girlfriend* of yours." With a flutter of her fingers, she turned around and walked out of the store.

Well, that was just fucking great.

I didn't know how the hell I was going to get out of that one, but I had more pressing issues right now. Like beating Aiden's ass at this bet. I grabbed my phone to check the time, sure I'd blown past the ten minutes by now, but that whole hellish encounter had only lasted six. Still, four minutes wasn't nearly long enough, which meant I needed to haul ass, get creative, and call in reinforcements.

I dialed my twin's number as I headed toward the snack aisle. If anyone was going to have a winning idea on what I should grab, it would be Beck, runner of the resort diner, menu planner, and blueberry scone aficionado.

It rang twice, then, "Yeah?"

"I need your help."

"You need—"

"The clock's ticking, so I don't have time to explain. What's a good snack for eight-year-old kids? And don't fuck around. I need the *best* thing you can think of."

"Seriously?"

"Yes. Am I being unclear in my directive?" I checked the time again. "And I'm gonna need you to hurry up about it or Aiden's going to win."

There was jostling on the other end, and then Aiden's voice came across the line, "Aiden already won. You're disqualified for cheating."

"Cheating! I didn't—" I came to an abrupt halt as I turned the corner into an aisle, finding Aiden and Beck standing next to each other, Beck's phone held out between them.

"Well, well, well, if it isn't the cheater now." Aiden crossed his arms, basket filled with graham crackers, jumbo marshmallows, and about five different candy bars hanging from his forearm. Gourmet s'mores—son of a bitch, that was a fantastic idea. Not exactly the healthiest option, but we were trying to win over a bunch of eight-year-olds here, not their parents.

"I'm not a cheater," I said, pocketing my phone.

"No? Did you or did you not call Beck for help?" Aiden asked.

"Did you or did you not fail to mention that as a stipulation in the rules?" I raised a brow, and his jaw ticked.

"Doesn't matter anyway. Your time is up, and your basket is empty." He jerked his chin toward it. "Ergo, I win."

I threw my hand in the air. "This is bullshit. I didn't even get a chance to shop. Chelsea accosted me the second our time started, and she wouldn't stop talking. Are my ears bleeding?" I turned my head for them to look. "I feel like they're bleeding. I'm going to have to take a shower when I get home because her perfume is clinging to me." I lifted my shirt and took a whiff, wrinkling my nose. "*Jesus.* I've put out fires that haven't hung around this much. And now you're telling me that not only do I have to go to her wedding—with a date, by the way—but I also lost the bet, so I have to figure out fundraising too?"

Completely unmoved by my speech, Aiden shrugged. "Pretty much, yeah."

"Why the hell do you have to go to her wedding?" Beck asked.

"Long story," I said. "But just know I should win by default after having to be in that woman's presence for that long. I would've rather waxed my entire body than have a conversation with her. Would've rather stripped and run down Main Street naked during a Nor'easter, or eaten a bucket of grasshoppers, or finally allowed Mabel to—"

My words cut off as a flash of yellow caught my eye out the front windows of the store, and my dick woke the fuck up from his slumber.

"Finally allowed Mabel to...?" one of my brothers asked, but I didn't bother responding.

Quinn Cartwright stood at the flower cart just outside, her bright-yellow dress accentuating every one of her mouthwateringly lush curves. Her golden blond hair hung in loose waves down to her shoulders, and the sun made it look like a halo around her head.

But she was no angel.

An angel wouldn't enjoy tormenting me day in and day out. And she *did* enjoy it. If I didn't know better, I'd say tormenting me was the sole reason she'd moved back to Starlight Cove after more than a decade away. A decade when I'd finally been able to ignore her siren call and get on with my life. The worst part was, she had no idea the hold she had over me. Or maybe she did, and this was all part of her master plan. To see just how far the gorgeous little demon could push me before I snapped.

I pulled my phone out of my pocket, checking the time, and pressed my lips into a thin line. Yep, 5:26 on the dot.

"So fucking predictable," I muttered.

"Seriously, man? Again? This is starting to get a little creepy..." One of my brothers, again, but I still ignored them, too focused on the pain in my ass who was looking a little too much like sunshine for my liking, considering her level of pleasure seemed to be in direct correlation to how much she could irritate me on any given day.

Quinn placed her order at the flower cart—I didn't have to be a lip-reader to know it was a mixed bouquet with pink peonies—like she did every Tuesday after work. Didn't the woman have even an ounce of self-preservation? Didn't she know she needed to shake up her routine once in a while? Jesus Christ, I thought that was Safety 101.

Despite the fact that this was Starlight Cove—a tiny pocket of paradise on the Maine coast with a crown of forest on one end and a picturesque downtown on the other, where the last serious crime had been a couple of teenagers graffitiing a penis on a public mailbox—she was still a single woman who refused to deviate even a millimeter from her daily schedule. And sharp as her tongue might be, it wasn't going to scare off a would-be attacker.

She smiled at Terrance, laughing at whatever the florist said, and something tugged in my chest. That was a look I'd never been on the receiving end of from her. Scorn? Yes. Malice? Definitely. Anger, rage, frustration? Absolutely.

Happiness? Never.

It'd been a fun game we'd been playing since high school when we'd been paired up in nearly every class we'd had together all the way up until we'd competed for valedictorian. And it was something that had started right back up again her first day back in Starlight Cove. I'd been ready to bury the hatchet because I'd never had a problem with her in the first place. Quite the opposite, actually.

She, however, had not been ready to forget about the past.

We'd nearly run into each other as she strolled out of the post office. I could see an apology had been on the tip of her tongue, but she'd swallowed it as soon as she'd realized it was me and instead sent a glare in my direction. And my dick, the little bastard, had twitched in my jeans at the attention from her.

That was the beginning of the end for me and why I was currently in the middle of the longest dry spell of my life. My dick had seen her, and he was like Pavlov's fucking dog, remembering the teenage fantasies featuring her insane body that I'd jerked off to three...four...five times a day.

And now, despite the fact that we were both adults and I hadn't seen her in fourteen fucking years, nothing and no one else would do.

My brothers were still talking, trying to get my attention, but just then, she glanced up and our eyes connected. I felt the same zing of awareness I always did when she was around—a zing that said my worthy adversary was here and ready for whatever I could dish out. Ready and willing to give it right back.

She froze for half a second before narrowing her eyes on me, all joy wiped clean from her stupidly beautiful face. Then, gaze still locked on mine, she reached up and scratched her nose. With her middle finger.

A slow smile spread across my face, and I shot her a wink. A wink she returned with a scowl. Goddamn, why was pissing her off more fun than my last dozen dates combined? And why the hell did it get my dick harder, too?

Chuckling under my breath, I watched her storm away, the sway of those thick hips making my mouth water.

Two minutes ago, I'd been lost in a rant, ready to burn this day to the ground. But after that little interaction with Quinn, I felt lighter than I had since stepping foot in the store —even though I'd run into my ex, gotten conned into attending her wedding, and now had to figure out this fundraiser thing on my own.

It probably made me every bit the ass Quinn thought I was, but I couldn't deny how much I loved that my mere presence got a rise out of the unflappable Dr. Quinn Cartwright.

CHAPTER TWO

QUINN

IF THERE WAS one thing I hated, it was an overconfident man with small-dick syndrome, and the jackass I was currently working for must've had the smallest dick of all.

Unfortunately, if I had any hope of taking over this practice from Dr. Dinsmore—or Dr. Dicknose, as I affectionately referred to him—I actually had to play nice, which made dealing with his daily bullshit all the more frustrating.

At best, it was a minor inconvenience I struggled with on the regular. At worst, it had drastic and sometimes catastrophic repercussions for the patients he'd sworn to serve.

Which was the entire reason I was back in my hometown in the first place.

As much as I hated that his female patients had suffered at his hand often enough to file formal complaints, I was just grateful I was finally here and able to clean up some of his messes. And in my short time back, I'd found a metric shit-ton of them.

I knocked on the door to exam room two and stepped inside, greeting his-turned-my patient with a warm smile. "Hi, Jada. How're you doing today?"

"Hi, Dr. Cartwright." Uncertainty and defeat hung heavy in her dark eyes as she sat on the exam table, wringing her hands in her lap. Her long black locs were pulled up into a twisted bun on top of her head, and the gold dusted on her cheekbones set off her deep-brown skin. "And I guess that depends on what you're about to tell me."

I pulled out the rolling stool and took a seat, setting her chart down on the counter behind me. "Well, I actually have news, so we're coming out ahead of where you've been stuck the past several years."

Since the closest OB-GYN was a few towns over, Dr. Dicknose had been completing Jada's yearly exams—same as many of the other women in town. She'd been complaining of painful, irregular periods, weight gain, and unexplained acne for years. And for years, the tiny-dicked weasel had told her that her issues were because she was overweight or just something she had to deal with for being a female.

Even after her complaining of worsening symptoms, which now included her and her husband's inability to conceive even after more than two years of trying, he still blamed it on the fact that her BMI wasn't below twenty-five and told her if she just lost some weight, all her problems would be solved.

He'd dismissed her very real pain, brushed it aside as if it were a minor inconvenience. She'd become just another fat girl in his eyes, and he'd treated her issues as if they were the cause rather than a symptom.

I wanted to strangle the jackass, especially when a simple blood test would've diagnosed this when she'd first complained of these problems, and she and her husband could've been well on their way to a family of three.

I knew her pain all too well—literally—which only made me more frustrated. I'd been given the same runaround while dealing with the same symptoms and the same condition. Had providers brush aside my complaints and not look deeper because I wasn't a size eight. I'd spent my teenage years and early twenties in misery because no one would take me seriously, and I didn't have the kind of parents who would advocate for me.

It was what pushed me into medicine in the first place. I hated the idea that women weren't being heard or treated appropriately because their concerns were ignored.

"Okay." She nodded, the exam table paper crinkling under her as she shifted. "I'm ready to hear it."

"The results from your bloodwork came back. Your cholesterol looks great, and you're active, which is what we love to see. But the details of your ultrasound combined with some of the numbers on your bloodwork prove your symptoms have not been caused by weight and aren't something you just have to deal with because you're a woman." I winked at her. "But you and I both already knew that…"

She breathed out a laugh, her bottom lip quivering as her

eyes grew glassy. She cleared her throat a couple times, accepting the tissue I offered her with quiet thanks. Dabbing her eyes, she said, "Sorry about this." She circled a hand around her face. "I didn't realize how much I needed to hear that. After years of being told it was nothing—" her voice cracked, but she cleared her throat and continued on "—it's such a relief to know everything that's been going on isn't all in my head."

With a reassuring smile, I patted her knee. "I'm grateful I'm able to finally get you some answers."

Clutching the tissue in her hand, she inhaled deeply, then blew it out in a slow exhale. "So, you have a diagnosis?"

"I do." I nodded and reached back, grabbing the pamphlet I'd brought in and handing it to her. "You have what's called Polycystic Ovary Syndrome. You may have heard it called PCOS. It's fairly common in women our age, but it is heavily underdiagnosed because..." I huffed out a humorless laugh. "Well, I don't have to tell you why. In your case, I hope we've caught it early enough to avoid any permanent damage. And the good news is it's manageable. Now, we just need to find the right treatment plan for you..."

By the time I'd walked Jada out of the clinic, it was late, well after closing time. Alicia, our receptionist, was long gone, the front desk empty, and since Dr. Dicknose liked to do anything but work, I assumed he was gone, too. Which was too bad, really, considering the high I felt right now, confidence cloaking me as I strode down the hallway, knowing I'd helped a patient he'd been failing for years.

It was just more proof that my move back here to my

small hometown was the right one, despite the...less than welcoming reception I'd received from him upon my arrival. One would've thought I'd come to tarnish his reputation instead of trying to salvage it. The man was in desperate need of retiring—something he'd be able to do, if only he would accept my offer to purchase the practice.

I turned the corner toward my office and stopped short, nearly running straight into Dr. Dicknose himself as he strolled out of his office. He was an older white guy in his late sixties. He wasn't overly tall—just under six feet, if I had to guess, since I could look him in the eye if I was wearing heels. Which, considering how much he hated it, I tried to do on a daily basis. He kept himself fairly fit, his white hair the only real tell of his age.

As much as I loathed running into him, I wasn't about to let this opportunity slip by. Since arriving back in Starlight Cove and starting my employment here with the specific intent to eventually own this clinic, I'd tried the calm and pleasant tack. I'd tried befriending him, much as it pained me. I'd tried the we-have-history tack since he was my father's closest friend. Hell, I'd even tried bribery—not my finest moment, but at least we'd all benefited from catered meals made by the incomparable Beck McKenzie.

None of them had worked.

Apparently it was time for the zero-shits-given tack.

"Oh, good. You're still here," I said.

He jingled his keys, barely sparing me a glance. "Not for long. Have a mess you need me to clean up?"

I barely held in my snort of disbelief. The man was so

delusional, it was baffling. "Actually, I cleaned up yours. I just finished an appointment with Jada Westing."

"And?"

"*And* you've been brushing off her symptoms for years."

He rolled his eyes, swiping his hand through the air as if her problems were a gnat he could swat away. "She's overweight and constantly complained about menstruating. Much as I would love to wave a magic wand and not have to deal with the female population's monthly issues ever again, I'm afraid that's just not possible. It's something she'll have to learn to live with. Surely she's figured that out at some point in her thirty-five years."

I huffed out a disbelieving breath, my mouth dropping open as I stared at him. "She's suffered with undiagnosed PCOS for *years* because you dismissed her very real pain and couldn't be bothered to do your job. But don't worry—I did it for you. I've finally got her on a treatment plan, and hopefully it'll be enough to salvage her ability to have children."

"Oh, relax. You're being a bit dramatic, don't you think? I'm certain her inability to conceive has more to do with her weight than anything else."

I clenched my hands into fists at my sides. God, what I wouldn't give to punch this asshole right in his smug face. "I'm not sure if you are purposefully being this obtuse, or if it's a special ability reserved for me, but let me spell this out for you—my findings just saved this clinic and your ass."

He snorted. "From what?"

"At worst? A malpractice suit. At best, a PR nightmare.

That wouldn't look great, considering the reason I'm here in the first place."

That hit the bull's-eye if the tightening of his thin lips was any indication. "What is it you need, Ms. Cartwright?"

I ground my teeth together at his overemphasis on Ms. instead of Dr., a designation *he* would have demanded from anyone. "I'm done beating around the bush. We both know there's only one reason I came back and agreed to work here in the first place. I want to know what it's going to take for you to finally retire and sell me this practice."

"To put it bluntly? For hell to freeze over. I have no intention of selling this practice to you, now or ever."

Anger heated my cheeks, my face flushing. After years in a male-dominated field, I should've been used to this. Should've been ready to handle anything he lobbed my way. Especially since this man had been a fixture in my life much longer than that. But the truth of the matter was, I never *wanted* to get used to it.

"You and I both know this clinic would be better off in my hands. And so would your patients," I said through clenched teeth, trying and failing to tamp down my anger.

"What I know is that this is a small-town *family* practice, and you are a single woman in her thirties with no prospects on the horizon. What I know is that I will not have my family legacy disparaged and brought down by some kind of feminist revenge plot."

I barked out a laugh. "Oh my God. Now who's being dramatic?"

He sniffed and moved to walk past me. "My mind is made

up, Ms. Cartwright. The practice is still open to buyers —*suitable* buyers who understand and embody family values."

"Lay it out for me in simple terms. What would I need to become a 'suitable' buyer?"

He slid a disdainful glance over me from head to toe, dismissing me just as quickly. "Something that isn't in the cards for you."

"Humor me."

"A husband."

Even though I knew in my gut that had been his endgame, it didn't make hearing it any easier. Whether I had a husband should have been irrelevant when *I* was the one who had gone to med school. Who'd worked as hard—*harder* —than any male colleagues in my field to get where I was. Who'd put in the grueling hours, who'd sacrificed for this career. Having someone else's last name wasn't suddenly going to boost my credentials.

"You'd sell me the practice if I were married?"

He cleared his throat, pushing his wire-rimmed glasses up his nose and averting his gaze. "That's what I said, isn't it? But considering there's no one on the horizon for you—not a surprise, really—it's a moot point."

"Do you understand how misogynistic that is?"

He scoffed. "I'm not misogynistic! I hired a lady doctor to work at my practice, didn't I?"

I clenched my teeth over the fact that he had to signify my occupation with *lady* in front of it. Not misogynistic, my ass. "You hired me because you didn't have a choice. It was only to counteract the complaints you've received from your female patients and because your malpractice insurance was in jeopardy because of it."

"And?"

I threw my hands up in frustration. "*And* it's fucking ridiculous you can't see the issue here."

"I will not be cursed at in my own practice, Ms. Cartwright, so I think we're done here." With that, he walked down the hallway toward the front of the clinic and didn't spare me another glance.

Because I'd never been one known for holding my tongue, I called after him, "It's *Doctor* Cartwright, by the way." And then quieter for just me, I added, "You pompous, self-important, fragile little dickweed."

I stormed into my office, muttering to myself the whole way. What I desperately wanted to do was stand back and watch Dr. Dicknose burn this practice to the ground and then swoop in to build something from the ashes.

But I couldn't. Especially when I knew the lack of care his patients were receiving—had been receiving for years. I just had to find another way to make this happen sooner rather than later.

After ditching my white coat on the hook behind my door, I quickly changed into the pair of jeans and blouse I'd brought today, knowing I wouldn't have time to run back home before heading to the impromptu cupcake festival happening this evening. I had promised Addison McKenzie —youngest McKenzie sibling and Starlight Cove hurricane who was not used to hearing the word no—that I'd attend and support the bachelor auction she'd thrown together for Everly, a resident in need.

Even if Everly wasn't a friend—which she was—and I wasn't interested in helping Starlight Cove—which I was—I would have done this for Addison simply because she had to deal with five brothers every day—one of whom was a giant pain in everyone's ass, mine included. That was worth a heaping dose of sympathy in my book.

I strode down the hallway to make sure Dr. Dicknose had locked up the front when he'd left, but I stopped short when voices greeted me from the reception area.

"What'd you tell her?"

The voice was tinny, as if it was coming over speakerphone, but it was one I'd recognize anywhere, considering it'd haunted my accomplishments for the past thirty-plus years and made my stomach clench at the mere sound. My father and Dr. Dicknose were thick as thieves, even after my parents had retired down to Florida, though that wasn't a surprise. Assholes tended to flock together.

Dr. Dicknose snorted. "I told her she'd need a husband before I'd ever sell this practice to her. And you and I both know that'll never happen."

My dad laughed, the sound burrowing deep inside my heart, poking at the tender bruises he'd never let heal. "Not with the size she's at. Not to mention, she never got the memo that men don't want a wife who's more successful than they are. She's going to be alone the rest of her—" His words trailed off as Dr. Dicknose walked outside, closing and locking the front door behind him.

I took a deep breath, forcing back the sting of tears. This shouldn't still hurt. Not after growing up with my father's special kind of "encouragement." Not after the years of therapy I'd been through to move past this. To work through this. But the truth was, I wasn't sure I'd ever numb myself enough not to care.

For years, I'd tried to be the kind of daughter my parents could be proud of, even after it had become clear I'd never be a carbon copy of my mom. Not when I was four inches taller and about a hundred pounds heavier. Not when I'd gravitated toward academics rather than cheerleading. But I'd tried. *God*, I'd tried.

I'd had a full plate of extracurriculars, volunteered for any and everything I could, graduated as salutatorian. Then gone on to undergrad and med school, and now I was intent on opening my own practice.

But none of it mattered in their eyes because I wasn't a petite size six like my mom. Because I hadn't dated the quarterback. Because I'd never been prom queen or on the homecoming court. Because I was in my thirties and hadn't yet snagged myself a handsome husband.

Because I'd dared to want something more for myself than to be a shadow of my parents' former selves or someone's arm candy.

I was nothing more than an embarrassment for them, and they weren't shy about reminding me every chance they got.

I'd thought I'd be able to come back to Starlight Cove without their constant judgment since they no longer lived here, but I'd failed to account for the ties they still had to this town.

Well, fuck them.

At one time, their words would've been enough to send me into a downward spiral that would have taken my therapist and me months to get out of. Now, they only served to fuel my fire. I grabbed a tissue, dabbing the corners of my eyes and refusing to let any tears fall. Those assholes didn't deserve them.

But their words, as hateful as they were, were an excellent reminder of why I did what I did. Why I pushed on even when it was difficult. Why I wore my armor like a shield, not letting them see how much they got to me. Why I'd worked so hard to become the woman I was.

I'd been dealing with people like them my whole life, had fought and clawed my way to the top of a male-dominated field without letting anything stand in my way.

I had no intention of changing that now.

CHAPTER THREE

FORD

MY SISTER WAS a force to be reckoned with, and this last-minute festival she'd helped Beck throw together was proof enough of that. She'd also somehow talked two dozen eligible bachelors—only three of whom were her brothers—into donating their time for the auction, and she'd enlisted all the unattached parties in town to attend and spend their hard-earned money on us.

Unsurprisingly, Starlight Cove showed up in droves. But that was what this town did when it came to a good cause. And since the proceeds were going to Everly Bowman—a new-ish Starlight Cove transplant and my twin's complete obsession—in the hope that we'd raise enough money so she could rebuild her vet clinic after a tragic fire, that fit the bill.

On Addison's orders, Beck and I stood in the grass behind the gazebo as other auctions carried on to the excitement of the crowd. My sister was running this like a military boot camp, barking orders to anyone who would listen—and even those who wouldn't. She was barely over five feet tall, but she still managed to have grown-ass men eating out of the palm of her hand. Except for Brady and Aiden, anyway. The former had gotten out of this because he was already spoken for, and Luna wouldn't stand for someone else going on a date with her man. The latter...if I had to guess, I'd say he had something to hang over Addison's head and threatened to use it if she made him take part in the auction.

Unfortunately, the rest of us McKenzies didn't have an out.

Levi had already sold his soul to the devil and then gotten the fuck out as soon as possible. That only left Beck and me.

"I'm going to kill Addison for making me do this," he grumbled, crossing his arms over his chest as he split his attention between glaring at our sister and staring out at the crowd, no doubt searching for Everly.

"I figured you'd be a lot less grumpy, considering this is all for your girl."

"That's exactly the problem," he said. "*My girl* is out there thinking I'm up here for a date. All because Addison decided that was how it was going to be. Apparently she didn't get the memo that I'm not an eligible bachelor."

"No one got that memo, man. You aren't exactly transparent about your and Everly's...situation."

"Oh, so it's my fault Everly's standing out there thinking I'm selling myself off to the highest bidder, all because I didn't tell Addison I'm in love with my best friend?"

"I thought I was your best friend."

He slid his gaze to me, his lips pressed in a thin line, and I didn't even try to hold in my laugh.

"It'll be fine," I said, clapping a hand on his shoulder. "She'll find out soon enough the only thing they're bidding on is your blueberry scone recipe, and the only woman you're interested in is her."

He gestured toward the crowd where Everly stood, looking a bit lost. "And in the meantime, she's thinking the worst."

"Nah, man. Going straight to the worst is *your* wheelhouse, not hers. She's fine."

"She better be. I should've..."

"What? *You* were the one who wanted to keep it a secret."

"That was before I realized Addison's sole purpose in life was to piss me off."

"You just now realized that?"

"Oh, relax, Beck," Addison said from behind us, the eye roll clear in her tone. "Everyone who's bidding on you knows the only thing they're getting is your recipe, so your virtue is safe. You can unclench. And I promise Everly will forgive you when you tell her we're actually raising money for her." She tucked her clipboard under her arm, planted two hands on his back, and shoved him toward the steps of the gazebo. "Now, get your grumpy ass out there and earn her some money."

After shooting a scowl at Addison over his shoulder, Beck climbed the steps of the gazebo and walked out to the excitement of the crowd as the auctioneer introduced him, carefully explaining exactly what the bidders would be getting without cluing Everly in on the secret.

"You're the last one. You ready?" Addison asked without looking up, too busy making notes on her clipboard. She just needed a headset and she'd be totally in her element.

"Born ready."

She tapped the corner of the clipboard against my chest. "And *that* is why you're my favorite brother today."

"Just today?"

She lifted a single shoulder. "It changes on a whim."

"I figured Levi would be your favorite right now, considering how much cash his auction brought in."

She hummed, tipping her head side to side. "Don't get me wrong—I'm thrilled with his total. But don't think I don't know that you two have a bet going about who'll earn the most tonight. And don't think I also don't know that you've already lost one bet this week, so you're certainly not going to lose another."

I shot her a grin, no longer surprised when my sister knew even the most minuscule goings-on of our family. She was like a bloodhound with any tiny detail, especially if it concerned us. She may have been the youngest, but she mothered us to death. And by that, I meant she bossed us around like she had a doctorate in it.

"It's a good thing you've decided to use your powers for good," I said.

She nodded once. "I could make your lives a lot worse than I do, it's true. The five of you should remember that."

"I am well aware."

The auctioneer banged the gavel, calling sold for Beck's offerings, which meant I was up.

"How much do I need to beat?" I asked, stepping up to the back of the gazebo as I cracked my neck, eyes on the prize.

"If you get to a grand, you're golden."

"Consider it done."

If I had to whip off my shirt and pull a little *Magic Mike* action to make it happen, I was going to have this crowd eating out of the palm of my hand before I walked off the stage. There was no fucking way I was leaving before I hit that grand. Not when the consequence of losing to Levi was another body modification. My dick didn't need any more jewelry, and I wasn't interested in getting my nipples pierced.

The auctioneer glanced back, and a grin spread across her face as she gestured me to step forward. "And the last bachelor up for auction tonight is none other than Starlight Cove's favorite flirt, Ford McKenzie."

I strolled down the makeshift aisle, one hand in my jeans pocket as I shot a smile at the crowd. This was exactly what I needed. An escape. A distraction. A little something to forget a certain blonde bombshell with curves for days and a smart mouth I wanted to put to better use. The one who'd infiltrated my thoughts and haunted my dreams. Who'd somehow turned my own dick against me like the she-devil siren she was.

Well, no more. I was tired of jackin' the beanstalk every night, and this was my comeback...the shake-up needed for my dick and me to finally be on speaking terms again.

"You know him best for shooting a salacious grin and a

wink your way," the auctioneer continued, "but he's also good with his hands, if you know what I mean."

The crowd whooped, and I played into it, giving them exactly what they wanted. Exactly what they'd come to expect from me.

Bidding started with a frenzy, several women calling out dollar amounts and rocketing the total into the mid-hundreds within seconds. The two who were now locked in a bidding war were stunners—a brunette and a redhead with looks on their faces that said they were all too willing to spend our time horizontal.

And neither one of them did a damn thing for me.

It was official. My dick and I were in an all-out war.

The stubborn fucker couldn't even muster up a yawn at the women's enthusiasm, despite the fact that they were both objectively gorgeous.

Well, that was just great. Especially when I needed to sweet-talk whoever won this into joining me at my ex's wedding. Maybe by that time, my dick would finally agree to be attracted to someone other than the one woman who hated my guts, and I could finally fuck out some of this bottled-up tension.

The bids crept toward a thousand and then slowed. I was so damn close to beating Levi... Maybe now was a good time to take off my shirt? I just needed a little—

"Two thousand dollars!"

I snapped my head in the direction the voice had come from and narrowed my gaze. Even if I hadn't been able to see her—which I could, plain as day, as she stood wearing jeans that should be illegal, considering what they did for her full ass and those thick thighs I wanted to sink my teeth into, and a black top that swept over her curves and dipped low enough to make my dick perk up, the disloyal bastard—I'd know that voice anywhere.

Quinn, my oldest rival and the woman who loathed me and made it her mission to make my life as difficult as possible, just spent two grand to go on a date with me. She also just took away any chance I had of fucking out this pent-up tension that'd been building up inside me, all thanks to her.

What—and I couldn't stress this enough—the *fuck*.

CHAPTER FOUR

QUINN

BESIDES THE FACT that my parents were no longer here, nothing much had changed in Starlight Cove in the fourteen years I'd been gone. It still had one of the most beautiful beaches I'd ever seen. Everyone in town still knew everyone's business. And Ford McKenzie was still an insufferable ass... and hotter than any man had a right to be.

And I'd just paid two thousand dollars to go out on a date with him.

Oh my God, oh my God, oh my God.

The phrase had started running through my head since the second I'd called out my bid, and it hadn't let up in the time since. Not when Everly had gasped and asked what I was doing. Not when she'd excused herself to go in search of Beck after I couldn't come up with a plausible reason why I'd lost my mind. Not when one of Addison's helpers had come over to collect the ungodly sum of money I'd bid. And it only increased now as my gaze locked with Ford's from across the park as he stalked toward me.

He looked hot, as usual. Though that was to be expected. I couldn't recall a single time this man had looked anything less than gorgeous, and it was truly unfair. There should've been some kind of rule that your nemesis looked like a haggard old troll rather than a model peeled straight off the pages of a magazine. The bastard hadn't even had the decency to go through that awkward, cringeworthy stage in fifth grade like the rest of us.

His dark hair, cut close on the sides and longer on top, was in careless disarray. Enough stubble covered his sharp jaw that I *definitely* never wondered what it would feel like on my skin, and his full lips were curved in their perpetual state of amusement. He wore a pair of threadbare jeans that hugged his ass perfectly—not that I'd been looking—and a T-shirt that showed off the muscles he worked hard for at the fire station and being the handyman at his family's resort.

Yeah, no. This interaction wasn't happening. There was no way I was talking to him tonight. He wanted answers. I could see it in the determined set of his eyes, focused on me. But considering *I* didn't even know why I'd just done that, I had nothing that would satisfy his curiosity.

I spun around, set on heading straight for my car and getting the hell out of here, but I nearly ran into Mabel in my haste to leave.

"Quinn," she said, phone pointed in my direction like she was recording. Her phone case was bright pink, large sparkly letters proclaiming *Ask me about my favorite toy* scrawled across the back. "So glad I caught you! Mind having a quick chat with me for my watchers?"

Mabel and her fucking Facebook Lives. I'd become well acquainted with them since moving back, considering I was renting a room from her and her husband because the rental game in a town this size was abysmal. I'd hoped the reason for my first broadcast would've been when the clinic got transferred over to my name, but no. Of course not. It had to be me, looking harried as I attempted to escape the man I just spent a fortune to go on a date with. Like I couldn't get one by any other means.

Regardless if it was true or not, that was exactly how my parents were going to see it, and I couldn't *wait* to hear about it. About how my doing that looked for *them*. And there wasn't a doubt in my mind that this would get back to them, even all the way in Florida.

And now that fact was going to be forever immortalized on the internet. Fantastic.

"Actually, I—"

"Great!" She smiled sweetly at me, but she wasn't fooling anyone. She may have been Starlight Cove's Grandma—if your grandma was a horny old woman—but she was a piranha out for blood. "The viewers at home want to know what your plans are for your date with the devastatingly hunky Ford McKenzie." She waggled her eyebrows. "The views shot up when word got around about your bid."

"When word got around—" I pressed my fingers to my temples and closed my eyes. "That was ten minutes ago."

She shrugged. "Spread like wildfire. It's not every day we

see a pairing like this of two people so volatile together. So tell me, what are you thinking? Going to make him scrub our toilet with his toothbrush?" She tapped her finger on her chin, her expression contemplative. "I wonder if they make a French maid's costume for men. If they don't, you could just make him walk around shirtless and—"

"Mabel," I interrupted, absolutely not needing that visual in my head. I glanced over my shoulder, noticing Ford was far too close for my liking. I needed to get out of here, and I needed to do it quickly. "I'm late for another engagement, so you'll have to excuse me."

Without waiting for her to reply, I left her sputtering behind me and took off at a brisk walk. I might've been wearing heels, but I'd perfected the no-nonsense walk eons ago. I could run in these things if I needed to. I had half a mind to do just that, but that would only call more attention to me, and I certainly didn't need that. Especially when Ford was behind me, calling out for me to wait and drawing the gazes of everyone around us. But nope. *No.* Absolutely not. I was not going to have a conversation with him right now. Not after the day I'd had.

But, like everything with Ford, it didn't matter what anyone else wanted. When it came down to it, it was all about him.

He grabbed my wrist, his fingers brushing the delicate skin and sending a shiver down my spine, and tugged me to a stop.

"Jesus, woman, are you training for a marathon?" he asked, not even having the decency to be out of breath after jogging to catch up with me. "You have earbuds in or what? I've been calling your name."

I crossed my arms over my chest and sniffed, glancing to the side and planning my escape. "I heard you."

"Heard me and just decided to, what? Ignore me?"

I glanced up at him—he had to be at least 6'3" because he still towered over me, even when I was wearing heels—and simply raised an eyebrow in response. Because, yeah, clearly that was exactly what I'd been doing.

"What the hell was that all about?" he asked.

"What was what about?" I could play dumb with the best of them.

He huffed out a laugh and gestured behind him to where swarms of Starlight Cove residents still milled about, far too many of them pretending like they weren't watching us like hawks. "Uh, the whole you just paying as much as my first car to go out on a date with me. If you wanted me so badly, all you had to do was say so. I'm sure we could've worked something out."

I ground my teeth together, my lips pressed in a tight line. "I didn't come here for *you*. Everly is my friend, and I promised your sister I'd support this festival."

"So you decided your best option to do so was to bid on me?"

I rolled my eyes. "Don't flatter yourself. I got here late. You were literally my *last* option. Now, are we done?"

Without waiting for him to answer, I stalked off, forcing myself to act as dignified as possible and not like I was running away from the big, bad wolf. Except I hadn't gotten even three feet when my heel caught in a crack on the sidewalk. My ankle rolled, a sharp snap sounded—my shoe, thankfully, and not a bone, though it still hurt like a motherfucker—and I went tumbling backward on a gasp.

"Son of a—"

"*Jesus*." Ford lurched forward, catching me before I could fall to the ground, his thick arms wrapping around my waist to steady me. "You all right?"

"I'm *fine*." Ignoring the feel of his solid body against mine, I jerked away from him and reached down, snatching my broken heel off my foot.

And then I attempted to march off with as much grace as I could muster while wearing only one shoe. Which, admittedly, wasn't a whole lot. Especially when I put weight on my rolled ankle and gasped at the pain that shot up my leg, reaching out to steady myself on the nearest object.

Which just so happened to be Ford's chest.

It was firm and warm, solid and steady, his heart thrumming a fast rhythm beneath my hand. I yanked it back as if I'd been burned, but I couldn't move away because even the slightest pressure on my foot caused me to gasp in pain.

"Yeah, that's not happening." He stepped in front of me, blocking my path. The expression on his face was calm and casual, as if nothing in the world bothered him, but his posture was anything but. His shoulders were stiff, and a muscle ticked in his jaw as he stared at me. "In my arms or over my shoulder? Your choice."

I huffed out a disbelieving laugh as I stared up at him,

carefully balancing on one foot. "You're not going to *carry* me," I said, gesturing to myself, which only made him scowl.

"That's exactly what I'm going to do."

"I'm fine." I tried hard to hide the grimace that crossed my face when I applied the barest weight on my left ankle, but he saw it.

He raised an eyebrow, and I wanted to slap that insufferable smirk right off his stupid, handsome face. "Last chance, kitten."

"Oh my God, do *not* call me— Hey!"

Before I could even get the words out, Ford scooped me into his arms—one at my back and the other below my knees —with as much ease as if I were a couple bags of groceries and started strolling toward the parking lot.

"I gave you the option. Next time, be a little quicker on the uptake. You're normally snappier than this." He glanced down at me, his full lips quirked up at the side. "I've got you flustered, don't I? You can admit it."

I shoved against his chest, ignoring the soft feel of his T-shirt and the firmness of his chest beneath it. "Put me down!"

He tipped his head to the side. "Did you prefer over my shoulder? You should've just said so."

"I *prefer* not being carried at all. I can walk, you jackass."

"Oh, so I didn't just witness you roll your ankle?"

"No. You didn't."

His brows lifted, and he stared down at me with something that looked an awful lot like admiration. "Goddamn, woman, I can almost feel the threads of history rewriting themselves just because you declared it so."

"Shut up already and *put me down*."

"Put you down," he repeated flatly.

"Yes."

"So you can, what? Walk?"

"*Obviously*."

"Are you telling me that if I put you down, you'll be able to hustle your sweet ass to your car again like your pants are on fire?"

"I was not—" I cut off, grinding my molars together as I closed my eyes and took a deep breath. Being calm and collected was my wheelhouse. It was literally in my job description. And yet, every ounce of that flew out the window whenever I was in this man's presence. "Yes," I bit out. "That's exactly what I'm saying."

Without a second to allow me to acclimate myself, he stopped and set me down, then raised a brow as if to say, *let's see it, then*. I steeled my shoulders, preparing myself to hustle away as fast as humanly possible. But I didn't make it half a step before I stumbled, the pain in my left ankle ricocheting up my calf and stealing the breath straight from my lungs.

I gasped. "Motherfuc—"

"That's what I thought. Up you go."

This time, he didn't carry me in his arms. Nope, now I hung upside down over his shoulder, being hauled away like a sack of potatoes and feeling about as sexy as one. I pressed my hands against his lower back and pushed away, snapping my head up and glancing behind us. Probably one of my worst ideas tonight, and that was saying something.

I could've gone my whole life being blissfully unaware of

the dozen or more people who stood with their gazes locked on us, mouths agape, as they watched Ford cart me off, *over his shoulder*. One of those people was, of course, Mabel, her phone trained in our direction and a huge smile on her face.

"Are you serious right now?" I hissed to Ford, then pinched his side for good measure. "People can *see* us."

He rumbled out a low laugh, the sound reverberating through my body and tightening my nipples into stiff peaks. "A little lower, kitten."

"You're a jackass."

He shrugged, like he wasn't carrying a fully grown woman over his shoulder. "A jackass who's making sure you get to your car okay."

He strolled easily across the parking lot, holding me to him with his hand cupped against my upper thigh, his thumb enticingly close to a place that hadn't felt another's touch in longer than I wanted to admit.

That was the only reason this flurry of butterflies erupted in my stomach at the chaste touch. The *only* reason my downstairs suddenly perked up after a hibernation long enough to make even the fiercest grizzly bear jealous.

"Ford McKenzie," I spat in the sternest voice I could muster. "Put me down right this second."

He hummed low in his throat—a sound I wasn't sure I would've heard if I hadn't been pressed up against him. "I love when you say my name like that, kitten."

"Then next time I'll just call you Assho—"

Before I could get the rest of the word out, he bent at the waist and set me on my feet. With his hands on my hips, he steadied me, his eyes boring into mine. Despite the smirk on his mouth, his brow was creased, his eyes wary as he watched me. As if he was...concerned?

Tension hummed between us with nowhere to go. Not when my car was at my back and Ford was so close I could hardly breathe. Except I had to, which meant I sucked in a lungful of his frustratingly delicious scent, all crisp and clean and warm, and I absolutely was *not* thinking about what it'd be like to press my nose into his neck and inhale straight from the source.

He stepped forward, and my breath caught in my throat. What was he doing? Why was he so close that I could feel the heat coming off his body, and why the hell did I like it so much?

As I was locked in the prison of his gaze, unable to look away, he reached around me and opened my car door. Then he plucked the broken shoe from my hand and tossed it onto the passenger's seat before he brought his attention back to me. I could've sworn his gaze dropped to my lips, but it was over in a millisecond and then his eyes were focused on mine once again.

A beat passed where neither of us said anything. Was I even breathing? Who the hell knew.

Then he broke the spell when he opened his insufferable mouth and sent any ounce of attraction that had boiled up back into the depths of hell right where it belonged. "You let me know about that date, kitten. I can't wait."

CHAPTER FIVE

QUINN

IN THE TWO weeks since the auction, I'd come to the conclusion that my brief slip of sanity had all been thanks to my heightened emotions following the encounter with Dr. Dicknose, his insistence that I needed a husband to buy this practice, and then overhearing the call between him and my father. That was the only plausible excuse I had for paying an obscene amount to go out on a date with Starlight Cove's poster boy for one-night stands.

The night of the auction, Ford had followed me back to Mabel's, watching from his car as I'd stumbled into the house, trying my damnedest to make it seem like everything was fine and glaring his way when he'd opened his door and attempted to step out to help me. The last thing I'd needed was for that gossipy old woman I lived with to get wind of Ford being there that late at night. Since then, I'd traveled the full range of emotions. From irritated to frustrated to angry to, finally, acceptance.

Acceptance that I absolutely would *not* be going out on a date with Ford McKenzie, money be damned.

Initially, I'd toyed with Mabel's suggestions, thinking it would be downright entertaining to use the date to torment him. After all, if I was going to pay that much, it only made sense that I got at least a modicum of enjoyment out of it.

The trouble was, everything I came up with to fuck with him—even drawing inspiration from our extensive history as rivals—wouldn't *actually* fuck with him. The guy was as easygoing as a stoner who'd just taken his third hit, which meant that even my targeted attempts to irritate him would fall flat.

And falling flat was something I tried never to do in anyone's presence, least of all Ford McKenzie's. Which meant I absolutely was not going to subject myself not only to a date with him, but one where he had the upper hand.

As much as I wanted to make him suffer, I wasn't in the right headspace to make *myself* suffer right along with him. Not when my days consisted of working with Dr. Dicknose, where he belittled my every move and then felt it was appropriate to discuss me—namely, my appearance, my social life or lack thereof, and my eating habits—with my father any chance he got.

It was Friday evening, and I was ready to head back to my temporary home, the last patient having cleared out. Dr. Dicknose was handling closing things down and locking up while I followed Alicia outside into the warm July air. This saint of a woman had been putting up with the pain-in-the-ass doctor for three long years before I showed up. She was around my age, with dark skin and cheekbones to die for, her black hair a cloud of curls framing her face.

"Oh my God, I can't stand it anymore," she blurted before we'd even walked four feet outside. "I *need* the details!"

I slid my gaze to her, one brow cocked. "What details?"

"Oh please. The date! With *Ford*," she emphasized. "I've been waiting for you to bring it up, but I don't have the patience for that. I know you haven't gone out yet, because Mabel has been doing daily updates about it on her Lives. The buzz around town is that nothing's happened since the night of the auction when he was spotted dropping you off at Mabel's—"

Like I didn't know directly where *that* piece of information had come from...

"—and I've tried to play it cool, but I'm *dying* to hear the details. It's been two weeks. My chill is long gone. Tell me all the things!" The excitement in her eyes was unmistakable.

Excitement I was about to extinguish.

"Yeah... There's not gonna be a date."

"What do you mean, there's not gonna be a date?" She enunciated each word as if it had personally offended her.

"I mean I'm not doing it." I shrugged. "I went to the auction because I told Addison I would and because I wanted to help Everly. I accomplished both of those things. Subjecting myself to a date with Ford is not something I'm interested in."

Her mouth dropped open, and she stared at me with wide eyes. "Why the hell not?"

I blew out a laugh and shook my head. "I forget you don't

know our history. Let's just say we don't get along. You don't know what it's like when we get in the same room together."

"What I know is that guy is fine as hell, and you just paid a pretty penny to go out with him."

Too damn much, actually.

"Maybe so, but that doesn't discount that we've been at each other's throats since we could talk. Our entire high school career was basically one giant competition for valedictorian."

"Oh yeah? Who won?"

I pressed my lips together, feeling the old anger bubble up just like it always did. Honestly, it had never disappeared. How could it, when the trajectory of my entire life had been altered forever because of that irritating, annoying, overgrown child of a man?

I should have won.

I should've been the one giving the speech and having my pick of academic scholarships to amazing colleges and universities. Instead, I'd gotten a full ride, yes, but it had been to my sixth choice, and I'd replaced my dreams of Harvard Med School with something more...accessible. Read: a lower-tiered school, but one that gave me a scholarship to attend. Because God knew my parents weren't going to help, and I'd bookmarked the trust from my grandparents for other purposes—namely, owning my own clinic one day.

What pissed me off the most was that Ford didn't even *go* to college. He had all those opportunities at his fingertips, and he threw them away.

Worse, I'd done everything *right*. I'd busted my ass with AP physics, calc, and history, while he'd skated by with creative drawing, archery, and gym. Not just skated by, but actually came out ahead by taking the easy way out. And because of how the grades were calculated, an A was an A, despite the class you received it in.

Bullshit all around. Which was why I tried not to think about it. Unfortunately, that was hard to do when I couldn't seem to go more than twelve hours without seeing Ford in the flesh, our eyes connecting like magnets, no matter the distance we were apart.

Dr. Dicknose caught up with us then, apparently having heard the last part of our conversation, and couldn't help but insert his opinion. "Men aren't looking for brains, Ms. Cartwright. They want a wife who'll defer to her husband. Who'll have dinner ready and waiting for him when he gets home."

I shook my head, not even bothering to slide a glance in his direction. "The sad thing is, you're serious when you say these things."

"Of course I'm serious. Why wouldn't I be?"

"Because it's offensive," Alicia said.

He scoffed. "Everyone's so sensitive nowadays. Can't say a damn thing without hurting someone's feelings. I'm just trying to help the poor girl out. She's never going to find a husband if she keeps this up."

He said the words as if my not finding a husband was the worst possible outcome in life. I barely restrained my bark of laughter. In my experience, there were two types of men: the kind who couldn't handle a woman more intelligent and more successful than them, and the kind who felt those women were a challenge they needed to conquer.

I was interested in neither.

Alicia stopped dead in her tracks and turned her attention on Dr. Dicknose. "Did you turn on the alarm?"

"Yes," he answered without pause.

"Are you sure? I didn't hear the chirp."

"I..." He scratched the side of his head, his brow furrowed. Blowing out a sigh, he spun on his heel and headed toward the front door.

As soon as he stalked off, she turned to me with an eye roll. "*Anyway*, so you and Ford don't get along. That doesn't have to affect *other* things. All that aggression is some good fuel, if you know what I mean." She elbowed me in the side. "And he definitely isn't hard to look at."

I laughed, shaking my head. "You're relentless, but I promise you, this is for the best. He's gorgeous. I get it. It's still a no from me."

"But..."

"Seriously. It's better for both of us that I just write off what I paid and know I helped a friend in need. And now, we will all move on without the scarring that would inevitably take place should he and I have to spend any amount of time in the same vicinity."

She hooked her arm through mine, glancing back to verify Dr. Dicknose wasn't yet within earshot. "Fine. No date. But seriously, can't you just fuck him?"

Despite everything I'd done over the years to shut down that line of thinking when it came to Ford, images of the two of us together—my hands trailing over the hard planes of his chest and down the corrugated muscles of his abdomen, his gripping handfuls of my ass as he held me to him—hit me like a ton of bricks, and I nearly stumbled. Probably because my ankle was still a little tender.

Or...more probably because I'd done nothing but bury any ounce of attraction I'd ever felt for him beneath years of hostility and resentment.

I'd been stuffing it down since that very first spark had ignited when we were thirteen and I'd become keenly aware he'd developed muscles. I wasn't immune to his good looks; I didn't think anyone was. There was no denying the man was sex incarnate—his long list of conquests was proof enough of that.

But I needed to shut that down before it even got started. There was absolutely no way Ford and I would ever be a thing, for a thousand and one reasons. The most obvious was I'd bet my life savings that I didn't look like the women Ford usually spent his time with. But the most important reason of all was that I'd never be able to forgive him for taking away the future I'd planned for. The one I'd busted my ass for.

Shoving away the images of Ford and me together, I laughed, though the sound came out breathier than I intended. "No. Besides, I'm looking for someone who can commit to something more than a sandwich."

Because my day wouldn't be complete without the asinine remarks of Dr. Dicknose and because God apparently hated me, my boss caught up with us in time to add his two cents. "You're never going to find someone to put up with you forever if you don't actually put in a little effort, Ms. Cartwright. Your father and I were just talking about this last week. In our day, women spent time on themselves. Watched what they ate and actually cared about their appearances. At least wear some lipstick once in a while, for God's sake."

I opened my mouth to tell him exactly where he and my dad could shove their lipstick but snapped it shut as soon as I felt a presence at my back. My body hummed in awareness, and I knew even without looking who it was. I didn't want to examine too closely how I was so attuned to Ford that I could sense him before he even said a word, but a quick glance over my shoulder proved I was correct.

At 5'9", I was tall, especially when the heels added another couple inches, but he was taller, casting a shadow over me and Dr. Dicknose as he stepped up directly behind me. Heat poured off his body, sending shivers racing down my spine, and we weren't even going to mention the state of my nipples. They'd apparently been hijacked by the playboy himself.

No part of his body was touching mine, but I could *feel* him there, so close, I knew if I inhaled deeply, his chest would brush against my back.

I remembered exactly what it felt like to have all those muscles flush against me. All that strength bolstering me. And though I'd tried to forget, I remembered exactly how good it felt to be cradled in his arms.

When he finally spoke, his voice was low and tinged with a hard edge I'd never heard before. "If you want someone to wear lipstick so bad, then wear lipstick, Don. Things have changed a little in the past forty years. Try to keep up."

CHAPTER SIX

FORD

I WAS AN EASYGOING GUY. Generally let shit roll right off my back and left the scowling to my brothers. Life was too short to get bogged down in all that. But all bets were off when you came at someone in my circle.

And, apparently, that circle now included the smart-mouthed, insufferable woman my dick was obsessed with.

Don sputtered before pressing his lips into a flat line, his mouth pinched in a way that said he was biting his tongue. Good. The fucker's mouth could stand to bleed a bit since I was sure he didn't make it a habit of doing so around these women. That was exactly why I'd stepped in when I had.

I didn't have a doubt in my mind that Quinn could've handed Don his ass—as I'd been strolling up, I'd watched her steel herself, rolling her shoulders back and readying for battle—but with guys like him, the only thing that shut them up was having another man question them, and I was all too willing to do so.

Was it bullshit? Absolutely. But that didn't make it any less true.

Alicia broke the awkward silence, a huge grin splitting her face as she regarded me over Quinn's shoulder. "*Well,*" she said, drawing out the word. "I think that's our cue, Dr. Dinsmore. Unless you have anything else to add?"

Don's gaze darted between Quinn and me, and I cocked an eyebrow, daring him to keep digging himself into a hole. I could knock him down all day and do it with a smile.

Instead, he shook his head without saying a word and turned to leave, Alicia following him as they strolled toward their cars.

When they were several yards away, Alicia turned around and gave Quinn a huge grin and a not-so-subtle thumbs-up. "Can't wait to hear *all* about this tomorrow!"

"Oh my God," Quinn mumbled, head bowed as she brought her hands up to her face.

I couldn't keep in the chuckle even if I wanted to, and I shot Alicia a wink as she slid into her car.

Quinn took a deep breath before she turned around to face me. The woman was knock-you-on-your-ass gorgeous, and instead of getting used to it like I should've been after more than fifteen goddamn years, I got hit harder with it every time I saw her. With that ass and those lips and the thick thighs I wanted to wear as earmuffs... She ruined me, and the devil woman took pleasure in it.

It could've also been that this was the closest we'd been since the night of the auction. Though I'd seen her around town every day, she'd avoided me like it was an Olympic sport and she was going for gold.

From what I'd seen from afar—and from what Mabel had told me—Quinn's ankle had recovered quickly, so she'd probably just twisted it. Wanting to confirm it for myself, I glanced down to the soft, smooth expanse of her shapely legs.

Her skirt wasn't even close to indecent, molding to her thighs and falling below her knees, but just the glimpse of her bare calves was enough to have me sporting a semi right there in the fucking parking lot like I was fifteen all over again.

Yeah, my dick and I were still on the outs.

The fucker didn't care. Not when Quinn was now my fodder every single time I jacked off. Prior to the auction, I'd been careful, working my hardest to avoid picturing her in my fantasies. It didn't usually last, but at least I tried.

But that night, I'd fucked up. Being so close to her had put a crack in my defenses, and I'd slipped immediately.

I'd gotten home, dropping my jeans and fisting my cock as soon as I'd slammed my door shut behind me. With her scent still on my shirt and the memory of those mouthwatering curves under my hands, I'd never come so fast in my life.

The worst part of it was, I hadn't even fantasized about anything good. Hadn't pictured her on her knees, that smart mouth full of my dick, or my face between those soft, luscious thighs as I licked up the one place I knew she'd be sweet for me.

Nope.

All it had taken was remembering the feel of all those plush curves against me, her disgruntled breaths on my neck, and the way her evil little fingers had pinched my side to show her frustration.

I fucking loved that fight in her.

But that was something I abso-fucking-lutely did not need to be thinking about right now. Not when she was in front of me and I wasn't so sure my dick wouldn't stage a breakout from my jeans just to get closer to her.

"What's that all about?" I asked, lifting my chin to where Alicia was backing out of her parking spot.

Quinn shook her head, waving a hand through the air. "Ignore her. She's too new to Starlight Cove to realize how bad we are together and is very interested in our date."

Exactly the reason I was here... "Well, that makes two of us."

She rolled her eyes. "Don't worry, I'm not going to make you actually go through with it."

Her words, said so casually, should've made me happy. After all, that meant I was off the hook and could go about my business. Find someone to attend my ex's wedding with me and take a step toward getting Quinn out of my head once and for all.

But I was all fucked up inside, unable to make up my mind if I wanted to run as fast and far away as I could or crowd her up against her car, drop my face to the crook of her neck, and inhale.

"Why not?" I asked, my voice rough.

"What do you mean, why not? You *do* realize the date would be with me, right?"

"Kind of why I'm here, yeah. Gotta make you pay up on your end of the bargain."

"That's...not how this works. *I* paid for *you*, and if I don't want to go out, we don't go out."

I never thought I was a sadist. I didn't make a habit of chasing women who obviously did not want to be chased, especially by me. And yet here I was, doing just that for a woman who would rather stumble around on a twisted ankle than accept my help.

For years, it'd always been the same with us—every interaction overflowing with tension. Friction. Distrust.

And I fell right back into that familiar pattern as easily as ever.

I stepped back, bracing myself on the trunk of her car, ankles crossed and brow raised. "Oh, I see what's happening here."

I could tell by the set of her mouth that she knew exactly what I was doing—namely, goading her to the point where she couldn't help but snap back at me. And I was betting on the fact that though she didn't want to play along, she wouldn't be able to help herself. We were far too alike in that regard.

"What exactly do you think is happening here?" she finally asked, her tone sharp.

My lips kicked up at the corner because I had her. Was it toxic to crave sparring with her like this? Probably. Didn't mean I didn't love every second of it.

"It's obvious, isn't it? You're too scared to go out on this date with me, afraid it'll end up in one of our beds. I get it. I'm irresistible."

She huffed out a disbelieving laugh, eyes wide, those full lips parted in shock. "You're *delusional*. I wouldn't jump into bed with you if it was the only respite from ten thousand cockroaches crawling all over the floor."

She was a beautiful little liar, her cheeks flushed as she squared off with me, her gaze darting down to my lips, my chest...lower still.

"If that's actually true, then this date shouldn't be a problem," I said.

She snapped her gaze back up to mine, her eyes hardening. "I didn't say it was a problem."

"No? Then I'm not sure why we're not going out. Especially when it's clear you could use a little release."

I might not have been up close and personal with her these past two weeks, but even from a distance, I'd been able to see the incremental stiffening of her shoulders, the tight lines around her mouth, the pinch of her brow. With the ocean steps away, I'd have thought that would've eased some tension in her, but instead, it only seemed to increase the longer she was in town.

And I wanted to know why.

"I already told you," she said. "I'm not sleeping with you."

A slow smile crept across my mouth, and I pushed away from her car, stepping directly into her space. Her eyes flared with...something...a second before she tamped it down.

"Believe me, kitten, there'd be no sleeping involved. And I

never said anything about serving up orgasms, but it's good to know where your mind's going."

"My mind's not—" She groaned and pressed her fingers to her temples. "It's been a shitty day, Ford, and I really don't want to do this with you right now."

I glanced over to where Don's car had been parked and scowled. I knew enough from Mabel's incessant gossiping that Quinn was going head-to-head with that dickhead day after day, so no wonder she was a little tense. If I had to be around him for that long, I'd probably want to jump out a window. And I ran into burning buildings for a living, so that said a lot.

"Look," I said, softening my voice before she could throw another obstacle in my way. "It doesn't have to be a big deal. One of the volunteer firefighters is opening a new place just outside of town. He's doing a soft launch tonight, and I told him I'd stop by, see what it's all about. We'd be doing him a favor." I left out the part about me plying her with alcohol so she could loosen up a bit and relax. Fuck knew she needed it.

She narrowed her eyes, her tone laced with suspicion. "What kind of place?"

"Ever been axe throwing?"

"No..." she said, but I could tell by her expression that the thought of being in proximity to a weapon while around me was appealing.

"I see that gleam in your eye. You're thinking about murdering me, aren't you?"

"I'm a doctor who pledged her life to help others. Of course I'm not thinking about murdering you."

"Just maiming, then."

She didn't deny it, instead crossing her arms and lifting a single shoulder in a shrug. God*damn*, why did my dick get hard every time she was feisty?

"Come on," I said. "It'll be, like, thirty minutes, we'll get you a drink, you can throw some shit, and I've helped out a friend."

"And that's it?"

I scratched my jaw, not quite sure how to play this. If I didn't get in actual date-like activities, my sister was going to kill me. Addison was a little dictator on a good day, but after Quinn had bid on me at the auction, my sister had made it her mission to make sure I knew I couldn't fuck this up. Not when she was finally close to getting a permanent female doctor in town when she'd had to suffer through years of Don blaming every ailment on her period.

But I could cross that bridge when I got to it. Right now, I just needed Quinn to agree to this. So, I lied.

"Yep."

"Fine," she said on a sigh. "But if you think I'm driving anywhere with you, you're more delusional than I thought. I'll drive myself—*after* I've stopped by home to change." She opened the rear door of her car and tossed in her bag, glancing at me over her shoulder. "How'd you know where to find me anyway?"

Because it was 5:17 on a Friday night, and, as previously established, Quinn did not deviate from her schedule. This night out was no doubt going to throw off her whole weekend.

"Anyone with a working set of eyeballs and half a brain cell knows where you are at a specific time on any given day, because you do the same thing week after week, without fail," I said, unable to keep the frustration out of my tone.

"What's with the shitty attitude?" She shut the rear door and turned around, crossing her arms over her chest as she regarded me with a raised brow. "And why does my schedule concern you whatsoever?"

"I don't have a shitty attitude," I lied. There was no fucking way I was admitting that I hated the thought of anyone but me knowing where she was at any given point on any given day. I could barely admit it to myself. "I just think it would be a good idea to shake things up once in a while, so any potential stalkers won't know exactly where to find you at 6:02 on a Monday night—at the dry cleaners, by the way. And relax, we can swing by and grab your emergency late-night emotional support coffee on the way. Although this'll be your third this week. Do you really think you need another one?"

"I paid two grand to go out on a date with my sworn rival. What do you think? And you realize it's creepy as hell that you know my schedule enough to be aware when I've had two extra coffees, right?"

I reached around her, opening the driver's side door for her. "Don't flatter yourself. I know that stuff about everyone."

She scoffed. "No, you don't."

"Yes, I do. Beck is at the farmers market every Saturday morning by ten, Brady does a drive-through of the resort every morning at six, Aiden—"

"Those are all your siblings," she said as she lowered herself into her car and looked up at me with narrowed eyes.

"And?"

"*And*...you know those details about them and your... nemesis? Make it make sense."

If only I fucking could. *I* didn't understand it, so I sure as hell couldn't explain it to her.

Instead, I braced myself on the frame of the car and the open door. I didn't miss the way her gaze darted to my arms, the muscles bunching as I leaned toward her. Or how she licked her lips when I got close, like she just couldn't help herself.

"Keep your friends close and your enemies closer."

Her gaze snapped up to mine before she turned away and yanked her seat belt, latching it with more force than necessary. "Whatever, creeper."

"Yeah, well, let this be a lesson for you."

"If this is an attempted kidnapping, it's a poor choice of venue, so don't get any wild ideas."

Under my breath, I mumbled, "I've got all kinds of ideas, and you'd hate every single one."

"What?"

Louder, I said, "Might want to sharpen those claws, kitten. You're going to need them. Follow me. If you can keep up."

"Mabel's house first so I can change!" she called after me as I strolled toward my Jeep, tossing my keys in the air as I went and whistling along the way.

At her answering growl, I couldn't stop the smile from sweeping over my mouth. Tonight was going to be fun.

CHAPTER SEVEN

QUINN

I HAD no idea how the hell I'd allowed myself to be talked into this. Though, that wasn't exactly a surprise. Ford could talk a nun out of her clothes, and I had fallen right into his trap.

Admittedly, his response to Dr. Dicknose's asinine remarks had softened me toward him slightly, which was what I was blaming my lapse of judgment on and certainly not on the fact that I'd been recalling, in explicit detail, what it'd felt like to be pressed up against him when he'd carried me to my car.

Ford had followed me to Mabel's and waited for me outside while I'd changed, thankfully avoiding any interaction with anyone. Mabel and her husband, George, were out somewhere, and I'd never been more grateful for their hopping social calendar than I was then.

When I'd come out after spending way too much time deciding what to wear, I might not have been able to see his eyes on me, but I could've sworn I *felt* them. The barest caress down the curved neckline of my shirt, plunging into the ample swells of my breasts. A hungry perusal over the outline of my hips and thighs in these jeans...

My nipples were hard before I'd even slid into my car, and that heightened awareness had barely abated in the time it had taken to drive to the location. That was why I'd painted on red lipstick before I'd stepped out, needing every ounce of armor I could get.

Ford's gaze had landed on my mouth as if it had been drawn like a moth to a flame, but he didn't say anything. Instead, with a hand on the small of my back, he guided us into the building without a word.

Kick Some Axe was housed in a refurbished barn painted in a deep red about a mile out of town. With slatted wood walls, corrugated metal accents, and buffalo plaid pillows tossed on worn brown leather couches, the front room was a lumberjack's paradise.

"Hey, man." Eli, an Asian man in his late thirties with soft laugh lines around his eyes and closely cropped black hair, walked toward us. He clasped Ford's hand before pulling him into a one-armed hug. "Glad you could make it. We had a few people flake out, so I appreciate this."

"No worries. I'm happy to help. Eli, this is—"

"Dr. Cartwright. I didn't expect to see you here."

"Hi, Eli. And you know it's just Quinn when we're not at the clinic," I said with a smile.

Ford split a glance between us, his gaze assessing. "You two know each other?"

Eli nodded. "Had to get a couple stitches after that structure fire on Walker Street. She's a magician—the whole thing was painless. Don't think I ever thanked you properly for that."

"Oh, it's really no—" Before I could get the words out, Eli's arms were around me, squeezing me to him. I wasn't a hugger by nature, so I stiffened, awkwardly patting him on the back.

"Hey," Ford said, and was I imagining the sharpness in his tone? "Hands off my date." Then, as if that wasn't enough to get his point across, he hooked a finger in my belt loop at the back of my jeans and tugged me out of Eli's grasp.

Losing my footing, I stumbled back into Ford's chest with a huff, and he placed a warm hand on my waist to steady me.

"What the hell, Ford?" I glanced at him over my shoulder, ready to lay into him, but my breath caught in my throat when I found him *right there*, his warm, male scent sweeping over me, his eyes freezing me in place.

Every inch of our bodies was pressed together, my back to his front. His head was tipped down toward me, a piece of hair falling over his forehead and into his eye, and his lips were so close, all it would take was one little push up on my toes and then they'd be against mine.

Whether I wanted to or not, I couldn't stop my brain from questioning what that would be like. Would a kiss from Ford be slow and languid, easygoing and sensual...everything he embodied? Or would it be a mirror of how we were when we were together? Raw, combustible, and so charged, everyone in the vicinity would feel the spark.

Would it be over in a blink before it ever really started, or would we both crave more, unable to get enough?

"Sorry, man," Eli said, a smile in his tone. "She's all yours."

I snapped my gaze away from Ford, all too grateful that Eli had broken whatever spell I'd just been under. The night hadn't even started yet, and I was already losing myself in ridiculous daydreams. I needed to get my shit together and keep my wits about me. The last thing I needed to do was lose them around Ford McKenzie.

"I've got your pit ready," Eli said. "But first, we need to go over the rules so you don't accidentally murder each other."

Ford tipped his head toward me. "She promised she wouldn't, but you never know with this one. She's probably plotting it right now."

"You're not wrong," I mumbled under my breath, desperate to slip back into our familiar routine and shake off whatever pull I'd been feeling toward him.

After we'd been prepped and educated on the proper behavior at a place where you wielded weapons for fun, Eli led us out to the main room.

I slid a suspicious glance Ford's way when he reached over my head and held the door open for me. "Don't think manners are going to save you from getting your ass kicked."

"You can try, kitten." With a wink, he pressed his hand on the small of my back and guided me inside the space while I valiantly attempted to ignore the warmth of his skin against mine.

The main area was exactly as vast as one would expect

from a converted barn. A small lounge section was directly ahead of us where a couple people sat on a dark brown leather couch, and a short line had formed at the bar located in the back.

But the main attraction was the collection of pits that ran along the perimeter, each one separated by floor-to-ceiling metal fencing. Tape marked the floor, designating where each person should throw from, and two wooden pallet boards with black-and-red bull's-eyes painted on them hung at the far end of each pit.

The scent of freshly cut wood filled the air as dozens of people milled about. A low hum of conversation buzzed through the space, interspersed by bells ringing and cheers when someone hit a bull's-eye.

I only recognized a handful of people as we passed, though that was to be expected, considering how long it had been since I'd been back home. Ford, though... The guy couldn't walk two feet without someone calling out a hello, which he returned with a smile and a wave.

"I've got you guys set up in pit four, and I made the accommodations you requested, Ford," Eli said with a smile.

"Thanks." The single word was clipped, and Ford barely waited for Eli to finish speaking before he grabbed my hand and dragged me in the direction Eli had gestured toward.

"Let me know what you think or if you run into any issues," Eli called after us, shaking his head when Ford didn't do more than give him a wave over his shoulder in acknowledgment.

"That was rude. And why are you in such a hurry? I know

we agreed on thirty minutes, but I didn't actually start a timer, so you can relax," I said, luckily able to keep up with his long strides as he tugged me toward our pit.

"I figured we didn't have much time before you turned back into an insufferable shrew, so I better hurry up."

I rolled my eyes, but my shoulders relaxed, feeling right at home with this antagonism between us. It was a hell of a lot easier to handle than the unwanted sexual tension that'd suddenly popped up.

I squeezed his hand, still encasing mine, to get his attention. "What accommodations was he talking about?"

"Quit dragging your feet, and you'll find out."

"You know you telling me to do something makes me want to not do it ten times harder, right?"

He glanced back, flashing a smile that nearly had me stumbling. "Glad to see your claws are still sharp, kitten."

Though I tried not to show him that he got a rise out of me, I couldn't stop my brow from creasing, my lips pursing at the pet name he loved using. I hated it. Especially the way he said it, all condescending and sickly sweet. The only reason he insisted on calling me that was because he knew it pissed me off.

Our pit was located in the far corner and seemed to be the only single one in the area, all the others having double, triple, or quadruple pits lined up together. Had that been the luck of the draw or something Ford had requested specifically...the accommodations Eli had mentioned?

Ford stopped in front of a short tree stump with two axes

embedded into it. It was clear this pit had never been used, the area pristine and floors lacking any wood shavings.

As I took in the space, my gaze slid over the two targets at the end of the pit before snapping back to the one on the right. I squinted, trying to get a better look to see if it was actually what I thought it was. When I realized my eyes weren't playing tricks on me, I couldn't stop the laugh from bursting out.

There, secured directly over the bull's-eye of my target, was a picture of Ford's smiling face staring back at me.

I glanced over at him, only to find his eyes already locked on me, his lips curved up in a soft smile. He was looking at me like he'd never seen me before, and I guessed that much was true, considering how rarely I laughed in his presence.

This time, I wasn't imagining how his gaze dipped to my mouth and then stayed there. My lips tingled in response, as if his attention was a brand on me, searing me from where he stood.

And then he opened his mouth and reminded me exactly what this thing was between us, refueling every ounce of frustration I had with this unbearable man. "Since you're used to losing to me, I figured you could use any leg up you could get."

CHAPTER EIGHT

QUINN

"ARE you planning to get through this whole night without saying a word?" Ford asked, amusement clear in his tone.

Ignoring him for the moment, I stepped up to the tape, axe in hand, and cocked my arms back over my head before letting it fly toward the target. It landed with a *thwap* dead center of the now-demolished photo of Ford. I didn't know if it was the picture he'd put up or beginner's luck, but I was on fire tonight, landing all but three of my throws, many of which had been bull's-eyes.

I smirked to myself as I retrieved the axe, then tossed his words back to him. "I figured you could use any leg up you could get, so I didn't want to be a distraction."

He stood by the tree stump at the border of our pit, one hand braced on the handle of his axe. He didn't take his eyes off me as I strode toward him before swinging my axe into the stump next to his.

"Your mouth isn't the only thing that's distracting tonight

kitten. But I'm multitalented," he said, swiping a thumb over his bottom lip as he eyed me. "Believe it or not, I can do a lot of things while my hands are busy."

As if he hadn't caused a shiver to race down my spine with his words, he grabbed his axe and got into position for his turn. He probably hadn't meant them to sound dirty or flirty —or, hell, maybe he had. This *was* Ford after all—but combined with the look he shot me, his eyes molten as he gave me a slow once-over, I was feeling the heat.

If I was honest, I'd *been* feeling the heat the whole time we'd been here. Hell, the entire night since he'd stepped up behind me in the clinic parking lot. I had no idea what it was about him or why the chemistry between us crackled, but there was no denying it did. No matter how desperately I wanted it not to.

We'd spent most of our time on opposite sides of the pit, but I could still feel the tension sizzling between us. Could feel the heat of his gaze on me, following my every move, never straying from me even when faced with the not-so-subtle advances of several women here tonight. Advances he ignored entirely in favor of watching me.

And I was valiantly ignoring how much I liked it.

It obviously wasn't *Ford* who was doing this to me. I was clearly starved for any male attention at all since it'd been so long. That, and I hadn't eaten in hours, so this Manhattan Ford had bought for me had gone to my head.

He threw his axe, landing a three-point shot on the board, but it still wasn't enough to take over my lead in our race to twenty-one. And *that*...that was exactly what I needed to focus on. This ever-present competition between us—the one that had been there as long as I could remember. It was comfortable and familiar, and I slid into it easily, shoving all the other feelings away.

"Still nothing to say?" He strolled toward me, all swagger and confidence, his eyes never leaving mine. "Fine, I'll be the lube."

Of course, I had chosen that moment to take a sip from my drink, and I choked and sputtered as soon as his words registered. After several moments of coughing, I croaked, "The what?"

"*Lube*," he enunciated far too loudly, even considering the chaos around us. "Nothing to be ashamed of. Sometimes you just need it."

"Well, why didn't you say so?" Mabel asked, popping her head around the corner.

I startled at her sudden appearance, nearly spilling my drink as I jolted backward. "God, Mabel, where did you come from?"

"You should know by now that my ears are attuned to anyone discussing toys or the tools that enhance their enjoyment of them." She sniffed, and I swore she would have tossed her hair over her shoulder if it weren't so short. "It's a gift. As for your little problem, I just so happened to order a variety pack of samples for my last party. I'll give you a few later at home, Quinn—strawberry's my favorite." She shot us a wink before she scurried away, holding up her phone and focusing again on the Live she was apparently hosting for the soft launch.

"Oh my God." I stared after her, mouth agape. "Please don't tell me she was recording when she said that."

Ford stepped up right next to me and lifted a single shoulder, the move causing his arm to brush against mine. "Wouldn't be the first time."

Ignoring the hum of awareness from where our skin touched, I said, "Well, that's just great. Not only am I going to hear about it later from her, but now that conversation is going to be all over Starlight Cove by the end of the night. That's exactly what I need."

"Sounds like maybe you just need the right flavor lube, but no worries. She'll hook you up."

"You are the *worst*," I hissed. "Why the hell did you even bring it up in the first place?"

"Because it's true. Tell me we don't need social lube right now."

I glared over at him. "You conveniently left out the social part."

"I can't help what a filthy mind you have. I love it, by the way. First, the orgasms to relieve tension, and now this..."

"It wasn't just me! Mabel's ready to—" I cut myself off, dropping my head back on a groan as I stared up at the ceiling, praying for a calm that never seemed to be within my grasp when I was in Ford's presence.

"As the provider of social lube, I'm declaring that we play two truths and a lie," he said.

I slid a glance at him out of the corner of my eye. "And if I don't want to?"

"Then I'll pull Mabel over here, and she can fill in the

silence by ranking lube flavors. Since you've been staying with her, you probably know better than I do how long she can discuss that. And hey, maybe if we're really lucky, she brought a sample of the toy she has on special this month to show us."

When I'd found her rental listing during my search, I'd remembered Mabel as a sweet old lady. And while she was still sweet and old, her personality had...blossomed in the years I'd been gone. I might not have been quite so quick to rent the room from her had I known she hosted pleasure parties and sold a plethora of adult toys out of her living room. And her converted she-shed. And her trunk. And a booth down at the farmers market.

Which was all great. I loved that for her and for all the people she helped explore that side of themselves. I had a collection of my own. But I did not want to discuss it in public, and I definitely didn't want my business splashed over Facebook for everyone and their mother to see. Which was exactly why I never bought anything from my landlord.

"You wouldn't dare," I said.

He shifted so he was leaning against the metal fencing, his ankles crossed and hands slid into his jeans pockets. The epitome of a laid-back, easygoing jackass. "I assure you, kitten, I would."

I narrowed my eyes on him, trying to get a read if he was bluffing or not. But no. He wasn't. Absolutely nothing bothered this man, least of all a woman old enough to be our grandmother talking to us about sex toys. But I'd seen enough of her demonstrations that I didn't want to suffer through watching her place a toy in a bowl of water to showcase how powerful it would be on a woman's clit.

"Fine," I said through clenched teeth. "But you're first."

"Dying to know more about me, are you?" He rubbed his hands together and grinned. "Then I better make these good…"

I rolled my eyes. "Are we betting something? Or will you have lost enough for the night after I demolish you at twenty-one?"

A slow smile spread across his face, making him look a little too much like the cat who ate the canary. And *I* was the canary. "I'm always up for a bet. How about winner decides what we do after this?"

"*After*?"

"Yep."

I nearly laughed. If I had it my way, there wouldn't be an after. "And if I want to go home?"

Ford shrugged. "Then you go home. *If* you win."

"And if you win? What am I setting myself up for here?"

"Already giving up? What happened to the feisty woman who's always ready to fight to the death?"

"She wants to go home, get out of these clothes, and veg out in front of the TV before falling into an exhausted sleep." I raised a brow when Ford's only response was an intense stare down—one I could feel in all the places that should have been dormant in his presence. *Should* have been, but most definitely were not. "Well?"

Ford's eyes were dark, and though he cleared his throat, his voice still came out raspy. "Dinner."

I blinked at him for several long moments before saying, "You want to *extend* this?"

"What I want is for my sister to get off my ass. You can't tell me she hasn't been harassing you, too. If I don't have twenty missed texts from her and Everly by the time this night is over, it'll be a goddamn miracle."

Addison *had* been persistent, asking me every couple of days what my plans were and what I intended to do for this date that I'd paid way too much for. She'd even enlisted Everly to pester me, which had only made me feel worse about my original intentions to ignore it altogether.

"Fine. But when I win, we're still telling them we went for dinner."

"Deal." He agreed so quickly, I barely had time to register it before he lifted his chin toward my axe. "Can you pay attention while you're throwing, or do we need to have a time-out?"

I pulled my axe from the tree stump and got into position for my throw. "Don't worry, I can listen and still kick your ass."

While Ford stood out of my swinging range but still far too close for my liking, I lined up my shot and let the axe fly through the air toward the target. It landed with a satisfying thump. No bull's-eye, but I still snagged four points, and I couldn't stop the grin from sweeping over my mouth. What I was not prepared for was Ford's matching one as I headed toward him.

"Why do you look so smug? I'm still beating you."

"I've got my three."

"Well, let's hear them, then. I'm ready to be out of these jeans, and the faster I can make that happen, the better."

"I'm *very* good at that, kitten. You should've asked sooner. I would've been happy to Netflix and chill instead of this."

I rolled my eyes—as much for my sake as his because I refused to show or even acknowledge what his words did to me. Refused to admit the brief flicker that'd flashed through my mind of him doing just that.

His grin widened in response. It was as if he had a sixth sense for what got the biggest rise out of me, and he was not above exploiting it to his very last breath.

"Okay, two truths and a lie. I got my dick pierced after losing a bet with Levi, I've been to seven countries for Habitat for Humanity, and I never want to get married."

I nearly laughed. He didn't even *try* to make it a challenge. I already knew the last one was a truth. And I knew enough about Ford's family to know that bets between them were a sport, so the piercing wasn't too much of a stretch of the imagination—something I absolutely *refused* to allow my mind to run wild with. I shut that down tighter than Fort Knox.

"You sure you don't want to pick three different facts?"

He braced himself against the metal fencing again, his arms crossed over his chest. "Nope. I'm gonna stick with these."

I laughed and shook my head. "Then this is going to be the easiest bet I've ever won. The lie is you traveling for Habitat for Humanity. Obviously."

That smug grin of his only grew, and he shook his head slowly. "Sorry, kitten, that's a truth."

My mouth dropped open on a gasp, shocked that he'd somehow managed to trick me. Though I shouldn't have been. This was Ford after all.

"So you *don't* have your penis pierced?"

"No, I do."

Up until this point, I'd held strong and hadn't allowed my attention to drop to the front of his jeans, but I couldn't help myself now. Not after he'd confirmed it. My gaze snapped there as if it was drawn by a magnet, as if I'd be able to see the proof for myself if only I looked hard enough. What kind was it? Had he gotten it strictly for his pleasure, or was it mostly for his partner?

"Eyes up here, kitten," he said, his voice low and rough, sending a jolt of awareness through my body. "It's an apadravya since you're clearly transfixed on it. You can Google it when you get home."

"I don't care," I said immediately, snapping myself out of whatever trance he'd put me in and hating that he'd caught me. "Wait, then that means..." I blinked up at him in shock. "You actually *want* to get married?"

"Sure. Someday. Eventually... When I meet the right woman."

"But you... You're just so... Well, I mean, you always—"

He raised a single brow. "Is that your polite way of saying I'm a bed-hopper?"

There was no point in trying to soften the blow. His history wasn't exactly a secret. And though I hadn't been able to confirm it since I'd been back because tales of his nighttime activities had been suspiciously quiet, I'd heard enough thinly veiled comments around town to bolster my suspicions.

"Pretty much."

"Yeah, well." He pinned me in place with his gaze, something I couldn't quite place deep in its depths. "It's actually been a while."

Why did it feel like he was saying so much more with those handful of words than he'd shown on the surface? That couldn't be right.

This was Ford. Like the auctioneer said, he was Starlight Cove's favorite flirt and had the swagger of someone who got laid on the regular. That impression of him wasn't incorrect. It couldn't be.

But then again, I didn't think he'd be the kind of man who traveled all over the world building houses for those less fortunate, either.

I couldn't even count all the ways I'd changed in fourteen years, so why didn't it occur to me that he could've changed, too?

"Your turn," he said. "And you better make them good because your only saving grace would be if we both lose."

CHAPTER NINE

FORD

I COULD SEE the determination written in her eyes. I didn't have a doubt she wanted to win. Probably felt like she had to so this evening could end before anything came of it. But she underestimated just how much I wanted to win, too. Because even though she'd tried hard to maintain her standard level of aloofness tonight, there was no denying I was getting under her skin. That wasn't anything new between us.

But tonight, it felt different.

Without taking even a breath between her statements, probably in an effort not to give herself away, she ticked them off on her fingers. "I gave a lap dance to a male stripper at a bachelorette party, I attended my first-choice college for undergrad, and I haven't had sex in three years."

Jesus.

Fuck.

I knew she'd play hardball. I'd anticipated that. But what I hadn't anticipated was the heavy sexual undertone in her statements. It made sense, though, especially when she was trying to throw me off my game. Which meant I needed to weigh these three statements carefully, while also trying to rein in my dick's interest in them.

I tipped my head to the side, eyes narrowed on her as I ran a hand along the rough stubble on my jaw. My gaze was assessing as I stared at her, and I had no doubt she'd be able to read the heat in it if she looked hard enough.

I'd been walking around half hard this whole night, but now? After her delivering the image of her writhing in someone's lap—let's be real, I was definitely picturing it happening in *my* lap—I was completely fucked.

And the idea that she hadn't had sex in three years? Regardless of the fact that it was no doubt false—no one could go that long without it—the thought of her being so needy for it made me nearly groan aloud.

My cock pressed hard against my zipper, desperate to break free from my jeans, especially since this was the most action he had seen in months. And yes, I knew how fucking sad that was. That just a few words from her gorgeous mouth paired with the conjured-up images from them was enough to get me worked up like this, as if I was a teenager all over again.

I needed to restrain that shit though, because I was *not* losing this. Tonight was the first time she'd voluntarily been in my presence for longer than five minutes, and the fact that she hadn't yet strangled me was promising.

Thankfully, I knew one of her truths right off the bat— obviously, she'd attended her first-choice college. She was the smartest person I knew, and the only reason I'd beaten her for valedictorian had been because she had stuffed her schedule with all AP courses, while I'd decided to take it easy our senior year.

So that just left the other two...

Affecting an indifference I knew she didn't feel, Quinn took her turn, and I felt some satisfaction when she threw her worst toss of the night.

"You're good, kitten," I said as she walked back toward me. "I'll give you that. I know one of your truths right out of the gate, but the other two..." I shook my head as I stared at her, trying to ground myself in this moment and not get lost in the thoughts those other statements conjured. "It was tricky, but the lie has to be no sex in three years. I can see you letting loose at a bachelorette party after a few drinks and getting talked into giving a lap dance. But no sex for that long? Not possible."

She swung her axe into the stump next to mine. "I can assure you it is."

Her words took a few moments to register, but when they did, my mouth dropped open, and I couldn't hope to hide the emotions that crossed my face. Jesus, did that mean... "Don't tell me you haven't come in three years."

She raised a brow. "Oh, you sweet summer child. Who said I had to have a man to come? In my experience, it's a lot easier without one. They make toys for a reason."

Jesusfuck, the woman was trying to kill me. Just straight up murder me where I stood. I thought it would be a little more obvious—like an axe to the skull—but I should've known

93

better than that. She was smooth, calculating... She'd play the long game, for sure. Could a man die from lack of blood circulating? Because God knew all of mine was currently pooling in my dick.

She avoided my gaze as she said, "Since it was a draw, we should probably just call it a night, right?"

I laughed, the sound way too low and throaty to hide the fact that I was turned the fuck on by none other than Quinn Cartwright. "Nice try. We'll do a coin toss and let fate decide." I pulled a quarter from my pocket and rested it on my thumb, ready to flip. "You call it. No take backs."

As soon as it twisted in the air, she called out heads, then seemed to hold her breath. I caught the quarter in my palm and slapped it down on the back of my other hand. Then, with my eyes locked on hers, I lifted my palm and watched the emotions flit across her face—excitement, nerves, and trepidation—and knew how it had landed without even looking down.

Group text with Brady, Aiden, Beck, Levi, Addison

5:48 p.m.

ADDISON:

Why am I hearing reports that you literally dragged Quinn through Kick Some Axe, Ford?

Um, hello?

I'm gonna need a check-in

Like, immediately

And what's this I heard about lube???

Text thread with Everly

6:11 p.m.

EVERLY:

How are things going with Quinn? Are you having fun? Is she?

Group text with Brady, Aiden, Beck, Levi, Addison

6:23 p.m.

ADDISON:

I swear to god, Ford, if you've scared off Quinn, I will literally murder you

LITERALLY

Levi will help me bury the body

There's a bare patch of land close to where Beck and Everly's place will be

That way, your twin can visit your dead ass

I'm not a monster

But I'm also not joking

I need Quinn here

In Starlight Cove

Taking over the clinic

NEED

I'm tired of the old jackass doctor blaming everything on my period

BECK:

Ford, text Everly back.

I mean it.

ADDISON:

What about me?

Shouldn't he text me back??

BECK:

You're on your own. Everly's mine to worry about, and she thinks this is all her fault since the money was for her. I don't want her feeling guilty when we break ground for the house and clinic next week.

Fix it, Ford.

AIDEN:

I thought we agreed we wouldn't blow up the group text with stupid shit.

LEVI:

obviously that's not true

BRADY:

Since there's no emergency and there was mention of murder, I'm muting this until tomorrow for plausible deniability.

ADDISON:

HELLO!

There IS an emergency!

If Ford scares off the one good doctor we've had in this town in my lifetime, I'm going to make every single one of you come with me to my future appointments

Then you can listen to that idiot tell me that bleeding from my vagina once a month is the reason for an earache

Or a sinus infection

Or the fucking flu

All because my uterus sheds its lining every 28 days

Does that sound fun to any of you?

Does it???

LEVI:

Jesus

AIDEN:

Ford. Make it stop.

ADDISON:

If it's painful for you guys to hear about it, imagine how it feels for me TO ACTUALLY LIVE IT

That's why I need Quinn

And why I never should've let Ford go out with her

FORD:

Appreciate the vote of confidence, little D

And shit, I'm out of pocket for an hour, and you all lose your minds? Wtf

ADDISON:

Don't call me little D

And we're losing our minds for good reason

Your history speaks volumes

FORD:

I already told you I'm not typing out little dictator in every text. And considering what you just did for my ego, little D stays, little D.

ADDISON:

Like you need any help with your ego

Now I need an update!

Tell me how it went

Do you still have all your fingers or did she get friendly with the axe?

FORD:

Yes, I still have all my fucking fingers

ADDISON:

Hurry up and get back to the resort so you can tell me everything

FORD:

Can't. We're going to dinner.

ADDISON:

Wait, what?

No, seriously

WHAT?

She actually agreed to this??

Like, of her own free will???

Where are you taking her?

Ford?

Hello????

Text thread with Everly

6:46 p.m.

FORD:

I think Quinn probably had more fun than me, considering she handed me my ass. We're heading to dinner now.

EVERLY:

Dinner too?!? I like it! Makes me feel better about how much she paid to help me. Try not to goad her too much. You might actually have a good time. :)

CHAPTER TEN

QUINN

THE RESTAURANT FORD drove us to was one of my favorites, a tiny little hole-in-the-wall with amazing Italian. Since I was still a little tipsy, my two choices had been riding with him and picking my car up in the morning or extending our time at Kick Some Axe to allow my buzz to fade. And given that I wanted this night to be over as soon as possible, I chose the lesser of two evils.

As we walked toward the entrance, he stared at me, his brow raised. "How do you want to play this?"

"What do you mean?"

"Should I request two tables, or...?"

"Why would you request two tables?"

"I wasn't sure if you'd, like, burst into flames if you sat with me."

"Oh my God." I elbowed him in the gut, relishing in his sharp *oof*. "You are such a pain in my ass."

With a chuckle, Ford lifted his hands in surrender before

reaching out to open the door for me. "Just want to make sure you're comfortable. For all I know, you stashed one of those axes in that luggage you call a purse and will have no qualms using it on me later."

I rolled my eyes. "I already told you I'm not murdering you."

"Yeah, well. I have a younger sister. I know how quickly a woman can change her mind, so I didn't want to take chances."

Without dignifying him with a response, I walked straight up to the hostess stand, not bothering to make sure he was following. "Table for two, please."

With a smile, the hostess grabbed two menus and led us toward the back of the restaurant. I'd been here several times since moving back, but for some reason, the restaurant felt more romantic tonight than I remembered it being. It was quiet and cozy, only about a dozen tables inside, and nearly all of them were full. Candles flickered on each table, and that, combined with the low lighting, provided a warm ambience I normally loved.

Normally.

However, normally, I wasn't with Ford McKenzie, infamous flirt and all-around playboy, and my defenses were solid and secure...something he'd carved a chink in tonight.

I reached for my chair, but Ford beat me to it and pulled it out for me. When I stared at him, mouth agape, he simply raised a brow in response. I didn't know why, but I hadn't anticipated he would be the kind of guy who'd open doors or pull out chairs for his date.

In fact, I'd sort of assumed he'd be the kind of guy who fucked in the back seat and then swung by a drive-thru for dinner. But if there was one thing tonight had taught me, it was that my original assumptions of Ford might not all be accurate.

Somehow, during this brief interaction with him this evening, Ford had shaken the foundation that everything I thought about him was built on. Years of preconceived notions and assumptions had fractured right down the middle, and I was left floundering.

"Well, this wasn't on my bingo card for the night," our waitress said with a smile as she walked up to our table. With a name tag reading *Emily*, she was a short white woman with dark hair cut in a severe bob, and I recognized her as someone who'd been a couple years behind us in school. "I never thought I'd see the day where you two weren't at each other's throats."

"I assure you," I said, "we are still at each other's throats."

"Don't let her fool you," Ford said with a smirk. "I'm growing on her."

"That's good for me, because I'd rather not clean up any food fights." She laughed. "Speaking of, do you guys know what you want?"

I came here often enough that I didn't even have to look at the menu, and by Ford's raised brows at me, it seemed the same for him. After giving Emily our orders—including a glass of wine for myself because, fuck it, I needed it—we were once again alone.

Ford stared at me from across the table, something deep

in his gaze I hadn't noticed—or been aware of—before. "Okay, so growing on you might've been a stretch, but at the very least, I think maybe you don't hate me anymore."

"I never *hated* you. I just...didn't like you. Which isn't my fault, by the way. You're very annoying."

Ford barked out a laugh, drawing the attention of a few of the diners. "I love that you never pull your punches with me. You're the only one in my life besides my family who does that, you know."

"It's because you've got everyone else wrapped around your finger."

"That's because I'm very charming." He grinned when I only rolled my eyes in response. "But I also don't see you doing that with anyone else."

"What? Not pulling my punches?"

"Yep. It'd be a cold day in hell before you told someone to fuck off, but you've probably flipped me off five times this week alone."

He wasn't wrong. I'd been conditioned to people please... to make myself as small as possible so as not to be too much of a burden. But for some reason, I had no issue doing the opposite with him.

I shifted in my seat, wondering where the hell my wine was, because...yeah. That was exactly how I was, and I sort of hated that Ford had been able to read that about me.

A slow smile spread across his face, and seriously, how was it fair that this man was so freaking hot? Like, drool on yourself, walk into a pole, trip over air because you can't stop staring hot.

"Don't worry, kitten," he said. "You don't have to say anything, because I already know I'm right. Which tells me that you might not like me very much, but you're comfortable around me, at the very least."

Shaking my head, I huffed out a breath and glanced down. Uh...no. The last thing I felt tonight was comfort. Heat, arousal, irritation...yes. All of that, in spades. But comfort? Not even a little.

"So..." he said, drawing out the word. "About this no sex for three years thing..."

I snapped my gaze to his. He was leaning back in his chair, casual as you please, as if he hadn't just brought up sex at dinner. I glanced around the restaurant, worried someone had overheard him. But whether intentionally or not, the hostess had put us at a table away from prying ears, thankfully. Because God knew what shit was going to come out of Ford's mouth before the end of the night.

"Oh my God," I hissed at him. "Why are you still caught up on it? It's not that difficult."

He snorted. "Speak for yourself. I think my dick would literally fall off."

I rolled my eyes as I reached for my glass of ice water, forcing myself not to imagine his dick. I'd seen hundreds— maybe thousands. His wouldn't be anything special, apadravya piercing or not. "As a medical professional, I can assure you it would not. Next topic, please."

"Fine, but remember you asked for this." Leaning forward, he braced his forearms on the table, pausing only long enough for our waitress to drop off my glass of wine and leave. "Have you ever considered recreating your *Magic Mike* lap dance? Because I volunteer as tribute." He tipped his head to the side as he studied me. "Or do you only pull it out in bachelorette situations? If so, I can probably get one of my brothers to pop the question by next week. Fuck knows Beck's foaming at the mouth for it."

"I'm not giving you a lap dance."

"Maybe not in real life, but don't doubt for a second I won't be imagining it tonight." He tapped on his temple, his mouth tilted up in a smirk.

I refused to let his words get to me. This was what Ford did. It wasn't *me*, specifically. His flirt game was on point 24/7, regardless of who was on the receiving end of it, and I needed to remember that.

Desperate to get the subject off sex, I asked, "How about you? You seriously build homes for Habitat for Humanity?"

"Is that so hard to believe?"

"Uh...yeah. Kind of. You don't exactly give off the selfless vibe."

He lifted a single shoulder. "If people don't care to look hard enough to see past the surface, I don't care what they think."

I couldn't help but envy him that. I'd crafted my entire life around what other people thought of me, and it had become suffocating.

"So, what? You just like to make people think you're a lazy jackass who gets everything handed to him?"

"Are we talking about people or you, specifically?"

"Both."

"Before tonight, would you have actually thought something different even if I'd told you otherwise?"

I had enough self-awareness to admit the answer was probably no... Okay, there was no probably about it. For a very long time, I'd had Ford neatly placed inside a specific box in my mind, and it was jarring to suddenly realize maybe he didn't belong there.

That maybe, for years, I'd been wrong about this annoying jackass.

Instead of admitting that to him, I asked, "When did you get started with them?"

I didn't know what it was about that question, but Ford's entire demeanor changed in a blink. He was no longer leaning toward me, instead shifting back in his chair. His body language said he didn't have a care in the world, but the expression on his face told another story entirely.

"About ten years ago. After my mom died."

I'd been away at college when Mrs. McKenzie's accident had happened, and I'd had no reason to come back home for the funeral. I'd never been particularly close to any of the McKenzie kids—I'd never been particularly close to anyone, actually—unless one counted a near-obsessive rivalry with Ford. But everyone in Starlight Cove knew she was a kind woman who'd adored her family.

I'd never had that kind of relationship with either of my parents, so I couldn't imagine the level of grief Ford and his siblings had faced after losing a parent who actually loved and cared for them.

"I was sorry to hear about your mom," I said, softening my tone.

Ford shrugged. "It was a long time ago, but thanks."

"Is your dad still around?" Interestingly enough, I hadn't seen Mr. McKenzie at all in the time I'd been back, which was weird, considering the size of Starlight Cove. Come to think of it, I also hadn't heard anything at all about him.

"Barely." Before I could ask him to elaborate, he asked, "What about your parents? They moved to Florida, right?"

"Yeah, thankfully, or I wouldn't be here right now."

His brows lifted as if he hadn't been expecting that. Though I wasn't surprised he didn't know just how volatile our relationship was. No one did. My parents were very careful about that—had to keep up appearances, so they'd made sure to berate me only in the privacy of our own home. To everyone else in town, they were the perfect couple, the perfect parents, and we were the perfect family.

"You wouldn't have moved back to Starlight Cove if they were still here?"

"Definitely not."

"So, you're not close."

I laughed. "Um...no."

"I sense a story there."

Before I could answer, our waitress showed up with our entrees. After placing our meals in front of us, she asked, "Can I get you anything else right now?"

Ford glanced at me with a raised brow, and after I shook my head, he said, "We're good. Thanks."

"I'll check on you in a bit," she said before leaving us alone once again.

She'd barely walked three steps when he gave me an expectant look, obviously wanting to continue our conversation.

I twirled some of my pasta, gathering a bite, and shrugged. "There's no story. I'm not the daughter they wanted, and they have no problem reminding me of that every chance they get."

Ford's face clouded over with what looked an awful lot like anger. "Seriously?"

"Seriously."

"What, becoming a doctor isn't good enough for them?"

"Not really. They're more of the mentality that Dr. Dicknose is."

Ford coughed, sputtering on the bite he'd just taken. After drinking some water, he asked, "Doctor *what*?"

"You heard me." I picked up my wineglass, smirking at him over the rim. "You didn't think I could work with him every day and not have a derogatory nickname for him, did you?"

"I didn't really think about it, but it fits." Ford speared a bite of his seafood lasagna. "And what's their mentality?"

Thank God I was on my second drink of the night so I could affect a nonchalance I definitely didn't feel. Lifting my shoulder in a shrug, I said, "That I need to have a husband to be of value, and since they're certain I won't find anyone who wants to be with me, I'm basically worthless."

Ford's mouth dropped open as he stared at me. "What the *fuck*?"

"Yeah."

"And you *chose* to work with him? Why?"

"Because I was promised a chance at purchasing the clinic. That's something that would take another decade at least in a bigger town. When I got the call asking if I'd be interested in taking a position here with that as an opportunity, it felt like it was meant to be." I blew a breath out slowly, shaking my head. "But if this awful month has shown me anything, it's that he has absolutely no intention of selling it to me unless I suddenly show up married one morning."

"What a complete shithead. Addison always told me that guy was an asshole." He pressed his lips in a tight line, his jaw flexing. I'd never seen Ford anything but cool as a cucumber, but this was getting under his skin, no doubt realizing just what his sister had been putting up with at the hands of the doctor. "You know what? I think this calls for a little street justice."

A grin kicked up the corner of my lips. "I *have* been tempted to slash his tires on more than one occasion."

"Now I see why you've needed the extra late-night emotional support coffees the past couple weeks. It makes the run-in with my ex look like child's play."

"Your ex?"

"Chelsea Dread. You remember her?"

It was hard to forget a bitch like that. I didn't like to fall into the catty female stereotype and preferred to support women and lift them up rather than tear them down, but that sentiment didn't extend to Chelsea. She'd been the epitome of a mean girl in high school, and she'd made my life a living hell every chance she got. All because Ford and I had always seemed to be paired together in any classes we shared—an extra-special little punishment that'd lasted nearly all four years.

Why she'd been jealous of me when *she'd* been his girlfriend, I had no idea. Little did she know, we'd spent the entire time at each other's throats, and I'd had to stop myself from strangling him just to shut him up.

"I may have a vague recollection..." I said.

"Yeah, well, just be glad it's only that. She cornered me in the grocery store a couple weeks ago. She's getting married and doesn't think I can handle it because I'm apparently still hung up on her."

"Are you?"

He laughed. "Fuck no. Which pisses her off, I'm sure. But I had to make sure she knew that, so somehow I got myself wrangled into attending her wedding with my *girlfriend*."

"You have a girlfriend?" I couldn't keep the surprise out of my voice.

"No," Ford scoffed. "So you can see my problem. Now I just need to find someone who pities me enough to go."

A flash of him attending this wedding with someone else made the bottom drop out of my stomach, and I had no idea why.

"Oh please," I said. "You haven't had a single pity date in your entire life. Women are lining up for a chance to go out with you—hell, you had three of us willing to *pay* for it—so it shouldn't be hard."

"Actually, I was planning to sweet-talk my auction date into it, and, well..." He lifted his brows and gestured to me. "Besides, a one-off date is going to do fuck all to prove I don't give a shit about who she's marrying. I dodged a bullet with that one. What I need is a relationship."

Around a bite of my scampi, I said, "Sounds like what we both need is a spouse."

Ford was quiet for a long moment, and when I finally glanced at him, his eyes were calculating. He braced a forearm on the table and leaned toward me. "You said you've thought about slashing Don's tires, but you need to think bigger, kitten. How about instead of that, you take his practice?"

I breathed out a short laugh. "Well, that's not gonna happen unless I get a husband, and I don't see any of those around."

"Uh, hello?"

I tipped my head to the side, brows drawn. "Hi?"

"*I* need a semi-permanent date for this wedding. *You* need a husband. *We* should take care of our problem together and just get married."

If I'd been drinking when those words came out of his mouth, no doubt I would have spewed it across the table. I stared at him, openmouthed. "You're kidding me."

"Not even a little. If you're really serious about this, you've gotta commit to the bit."

I breathed out a laugh. "Commit in the form of marriage... That's what you're suggesting?"

He lifted a single shoulder. "If that's what it takes."

"Marriage...to *me*." I gestured to myself just to be clear.

"Why not? Might as well get the first divorce out of the way."

"And you don't think Dr. Dicknose is going to get suspicious that we've had a rivalry for years, and, as far as he knows, I hate everything about you, yet we're suddenly in love enough to get married?"

"As far as he knows, you paid two grand to go out on a date with me. And I think you're underestimating the power of my sex appeal."

"I need you not to be a pig right now."

His eyes danced as he chuckled, the sound low and smooth, sending a shiver through me. "I'm not trying to be. You're giving him way too much credit. He's the exact kind of douchebag who'd think this is all his doing. You finally took his advice...put on some lipstick...and nailed down a husband."

"You're seriously serious."

"I seriously am." He lifted a brow, his voice taking on a taunting lilt. "But this *is* out of your weekly schedule, so it might be too spontaneous for you to consider. And I get it. You're probably worried you'd fall in love with me if we went through with this."

I scoffed. "I would *not* fall in love with you."

He raised a brow. "Then what's the problem?"

The problem was, this was deceitful. It was taking the

easy way out—although God knew being married to Ford, real or not, wouldn't be easy. But fuck, I'd been struggling along the "right" path, the *harder* path, my entire life, watching as others skated by and got ahead while I worked myself to the bone and came up short.

It'd happened in high school with my AP classes and being booted for valedictorian because Ford had snuck by with an easier course load. It'd happened numerous times in med school when I'd thoroughly busted my ass doing things exactly as they were supposed to be done, while others took the shortcut. Hell, it happened when I had agreed to come back and help Dr. Dicknose to right this sinking ship instead of standing in the shadows and waiting for it to implode before sweeping in and playing the savior. And look where those had gotten me... Angry, resentful, and no closer to achieving my parents' love or respect.

So why the hell wasn't I taking those shortcuts too?

Would it really be so bad to be married to Ford for a brief stint of time when it would end with me realizing my lifelong dream of owning my own clinic? When I could finally prove to my parents—prove to everyone—who didn't think I'd make anything of myself that I had?

"So, what?" I asked. "You'd marry me so I could buy the practice? And I'd just have to go with you to Chelsea's wedding? That's it?"

"Well, we'll have to be a devoted couple for a while to pull this off. How long do you think it would take to convince him?"

"I would like to say it wouldn't take anything to convince

him because he told me this was his stipulation, but I've known him long enough to know that he's not going to roll over that easily."

"Think you can get it done in a couple months?"

"Maybe? Probably..."

Ford pulled out the napkin from under his drink. "Got a pen?"

I dug around in my purse and handed one over to him. He immediately started writing on the napkin, then he pulled out his phone and thumbed to something before writing a date.

He turned the makeshift contract around to face me, pressing his finger just over the date. "You've got eight weeks to convince him to sell it to you as a married woman."

"And then what?"

"Then we get a divorce or an annulment and go about the rest of our lives. Easy peasy."

Somehow, I didn't think it would be quite so *easy peasy*. But...my knee-jerk reaction wasn't a no. I stared down at the napkin, where Ford had written "no take backs" and signed his name below it, leaving space for mine.

I didn't know if it was the culmination of my time here in Starlight Cove, or listening to Dr. Dicknose berate me day in and day out, or the fact that I was two drinks in, or that Ford was turning out to be someone other than who I'd thought he was, but I found myself agreeing before I could stop myself. For once, taking the easy way out.

I grabbed the pen from him and signed my name below his. "I'm in. Let's get married."

CHAPTER ELEVEN

FORD

I COULDN'T BELIEVE Quinn had actually said yes.

Nothing about her would've led me to believe she would. She didn't jump into things like this lightly—hell, she didn't jump into *anything* lightly. She and I were complete opposites in that, her preferring a detailed map before she took a single step, and me preferring to just start and figure it out along the way. Which was why, when I'd seen an opportunity—a *tempting* opportunity to sate my interest in her once and for all, while also getting back at my ex—I'd taken it. Without thought.

And even though I'd had two days to get used to the idea, I was still shell-shocked. But considering I'd just come off a twenty-four-hour shift at the firehouse and then headed straight to One Night Stan's, I hadn't really had time to dwell on what Quinn and I would be doing tomorrow.

While I usually liked a little downtime immediately

following a shift, I wasn't going to bail on my entire family celebrating Beck and Everly as they broke ground today on the section of the resort property that would eventually house their forever home and the brand-new vet clinic.

It wasn't often all six of us were together, and close to never for something not involving the resort. Even then, it was usually only once a month because Addison refused to allow Levi to skip that mandatory budget meeting, no matter how much he complained. My youngest brother preferred solitude, even from us. It hadn't always been that way, but as he'd gotten older, he'd withdrawn more and more. And God knew solitude was a far cry from whatever the hell this was.

"Oh! I forgot to tell you guys that Harper's gonna be back soon," Addison said before sticking out her tongue in a failed search to find her drink straw, completely oblivious to how everyone's attention swiveled to Levi to gauge his reaction.

Years ago, when Harper had spent her summers here, she, Levi, and his best friend, Chase, had been thick as thieves, but something had happened in the past ten years, because we couldn't even say her name without him scowling a hole in the ground. And he sure as shit wasn't interested in talking about it.

"I need another drink," Levi mumbled and stood, turning toward the bar without hesitation.

"One for me too, please!" Addison called after him.

"Let me know when she's going to be here, so I can clear some space on my calendar," Luna said from where she sat in Brady's lap. "The girl loves my massages."

"Who doesn't?" Brady asked.

"That reminds me—I wanted to book one with you," Everly said, shifting in Beck's lap to face Luna. Everly and Beck had been so sickeningly sweet in the past couple weeks, and if I didn't love my twin so goddamn much, I'd need to be drunk just to witness it.

"You just let me know," Luna said, tipping her drink toward Everly. "First one's on the house."

"You're sweet, but I don't want to take advantage. And after witnessing what I did the other week at the farmers market, I *really* don't want Brady to bite my head off for undervaluing you."

"Brady wouldn't fucking dare," Beck said—growled, really.

"Relax, Beck." Brady curled an arm around Luna's waist, tugging her back into his chest. "She doesn't do that anymore, because she knows what's waiting for her at home if she does."

"Ew...that sounds like sex stuff." Addison scrunched up her nose. "I thought we talked about that. If I have to hear it from you, you have to hear it from me. Is that what you want?"

"Fuck no," Beck, Brady, Aiden, and I said in unison. As far as I was concerned, our baby sister was a virgin and would forever stay one, and I was sure my brothers felt the same.

With a laugh, Everly asked, "When will Harper be here?"

Levi was nearly to the table and stopped dead in his tracks at the mention of Harper's name, a muttered curse leaving his lips. No one else seemed to be aware, but I watched as his jaw ticked twice before he finally seemed to steel himself and continue toward us. He set Addison's drink down harder than necessary before dropping into his seat with his own glass.

She shot him a bright smile and turned back to Everly. "Sometime in the next couple weeks to do a follow-up on her last article. She's not sure the timing yet, because she's going to tack it on to another assignment, so it may be last minute."

Everly's gaze flitted between Addison and Levi. "Do we not like Harper?"

"Of course we like Harper!" Addison said, her voice cranked to ten. The girl got loud as hell when she was tipsy. "She's part of the reason the resort's not in the red for the first time in a decade."

Everly tipped her chin toward Levi. "Then what's with the scowl?"

I was well versed in avoiding topics I didn't want to discuss with my family. Hell, all of us were. And there was no denying Levi absolutely did not want to go down this path. He never did, and believe me, I'd tried.

So I played the nice brother and threw him a bone— probably not one he would have chosen, but beggars can't be choosers. "That's probably because he's still feeling a little tender, thanks to his most recent lost bet."

He shot me a look that wavered between gratitude and irritation, but he and I both knew discussing whatever body jewelry he was currently rocking was the lesser of two evils.

"Um, I need more details, please," Luna said, dividing a look between Levi and me.

"We had a bet going over who would get the highest bid at the bachelor auction. Loser had to get a body modification."

"What, like a tattoo?" she asked.

"Not what he chose," I said, unable to hide my smirk.

"Oh my God!" Addison hissed. "Did you get your nipples pierced?"

"Not sure you want to know this, sis," he said.

"That feels like a no. So, you mean..." Everly's brows lifted before she flitted her gaze down toward Levi's lap.

"Dude, what the fuck?" Beck snapped.

Levi held up his hands. "I didn't say a damn thing. Blame your twin for bringing it up in the first place."

"Well, I don't wanna hear anything more about it. I don't care what the hell you do to your junk as long as it doesn't keep you from finding a wife," Addison said. "If we want to capitalize on this avenue and have weddings become the next major draw of the resort, I'm gonna need to use all of you as guinea pigs. Which means, whichever one of you"—she pointed a finger, bouncing it between Brady and Beck—"gets married first, it has to be at the resort. Swear it, or I'll kill you."

Brady blew out a long sigh. "You can't threaten an officer of the law, Addison."

She scoffed. "Oh please. You're not Sheriff McKenzie right now. You're just my stupid older brother. And when you get married, you're going to do so at the resort. Luna's okay with it. Aren't you, Luna?"

Thank fuck the attention was off me because I wasn't sure I could keep a straight face with this line of conversation. If only Addison knew she was pointing at the wrong brother... But it would at least allow me some leeway to save my ass from her wrath when she inevitably found out I was actually the first to get hitched.

Not wanting to tempt fate, I pushed back my chair and stood with my bottle of beer. "I'm gonna grab another."

It didn't matter what I said, because Brady and Addison were now in a full-blown argument over where his and Luna's nonexistent wedding would be taking place and didn't pay any attention as I slipped away.

I hadn't even gotten three steps before the door to One Night Stan's swung open and in walked none other than my future bride. This was nowhere near her normal routine, so she had probably heard about Beck and Everly's celebration tonight and had decided to swing by. People had been stopping by to congratulate them all night, so Quinn wouldn't be the first. But for some reason, I hadn't expected to see her here.

Or, rather, I'd hoped she wouldn't be here.

The last thing I needed was for my family to realize prematurely what was going on between us, because someone would inevitably try to talk me out of this. I might regret that at some point, but I'd never let that stop me before. Not when I took off to Iceland on a whim or went skydiving in Pensacola or headed to Idaho for the weekend to

BASE jump off the Perrine Bridge. Had any of my siblings known about those beforehand, they all would've tried to talk me out of them. But I didn't want to be reminded of the reasons this was a bad idea. I never did.

Quinn wore one of those flirty fucking sundresses that she practically lived in and that I foamed at the mouth for. I swore she wore them for the sole purpose of driving me out of my goddamn mind, all thanks to the way the hem brushed her soft thighs, teasing at everything she was hiding beneath.

I whipped my gaze back to where my family was still bickering, confirming they hadn't yet seen her. Barely allowing her inside the space, I marched up to her, wrapped an arm around her waist, and tugged her toward a shadowy alcove in the back where we could stay out of sight.

"What the hell, Ford? Do you *mind*?"

With another quick glance back at my family, I turned my attention to her. "What are you doing here?"

"Excuse me?"

"I said, what are you doing here?"

"And I said, what the hell?"

"You can't be here."

"I assure you, I can." She moved to step around me, but I blocked her path.

"No, you can't." I ran a frustrated hand through my hair, shooting another look over my shoulder to make sure my family was still occupied. "I don't want my family to know about what we're doing."

She blew out a disbelieving laugh, her eyes flitting

between mine. "What do you mean, you don't want your family to know about this? It was *your* idea in the first place."

"Uh...no, it wasn't. It was *your* idea. You're the one who said we both needed a spouse."

"And *you're* the one who said we should get married. Clearly, we're both idiots, because this is never going to be believable if all anyone ever sees us do is fight."

"I can promise you, kitten, I'm not going to have any problem making it believable."

She scoffed. "Somehow I doubt that. Of the two of us, it's you I'm worried about. I'm quite a divergence from the women you usually go for."

"How would you know what kind of women I usually go for? You haven't been here for over a decade."

In a dry tone, she said, "I took a wild guess that the women don't usually look like me."

With the way she'd said it, somehow I didn't think she was suggesting that no other woman besides her had been able to get my dick to so much as twitch since she'd waltzed her sweet ass back into Starlight Cove and made me crave every lush inch of her. She'd said it like it was a foregone conclusion that I wouldn't be attracted to her or her insane body that'd been starring in my fantasies for weeks—*years*.

"What the fuck is that supposed to mean?" I snapped.

"Whatever, never mind," she said, waving me off. "Get out of my way so I can congratulate Beck and Everly and—"

"Tell me to prove it."

She blinked up at me, frozen for a moment. "What?"

I took a step closer to her, backing her into the wall. I

inhaled deeply, taking in her subtle citrus scent, my dick perking up at that nominal tease. Caging her against the wall with my hands pressed on either side of her, I leaned forward until our mouths were an inch apart. "Tell me. To prove it."

We were so close, her breaths ghosted over my lips, and her gorgeous, full tits brushed against my chest with every one of her inhales. My cock grew so hard, I was afraid I'd pass out from lack of blood to my brain. Fuck me, the things this woman did to me without even trying. Scratch that. She managed that while *actively* trying to piss me off. But for some reason, that only made me hotter for her...*harder* for her.

She licked her lips, and I couldn't stop my gaze from dropping to them. I wanted to suck on that plump lower lip and trace the Cupid's bow at the top with my tongue. Wanted to finally know what that mouth felt like against mine. Wanted to know what she tasted like so I could torture myself with a memory the next time I wrapped my hand around my cock and came to thoughts of her.

Then she uttered two words that might as well have been a gunshot for how my body reacted. "Prove it."

With a groan, I cupped her face, sliding my fingers into her hair and tilting her chin up toward me, and took her lips with mine. This kiss wasn't soft or sweet. It wasn't tentative or unassuming...there was no buildup. It was all-consuming from the start. Passionate and hungry and a little angry—everything we seemed to be when we were together.

I swept my tongue into her mouth, moaning low when she opened for me without hesitation. She fisted the front of my shirt, tugging me closer, and I didn't even try to hide what she was doing to me. I didn't care if she felt how fucking hard I was. How much I *ached* for her.

"You feel this?" I wrapped an arm around her waist as I kissed my way across her jaw, down her neck, grinding my cock into her so there was no question what I was talking about. "Don't tell me I'm the one who won't make this believable. All you have to do is *breathe* and I'm hard."

I brought my lips back to hers, inhaling her breathy little moan as she panted into my mouth, her tongue sliding against mine. I wanted to pull her closer and shove her away at the same time because she shouldn't feel this good. She shouldn't taste this good. We shouldn't be this good together, but there was no denying the truth.

I couldn't get enough of this irritating, insufferable woman. She drove me wild with a need I'd never known, turned me into a simpering idiot with a few insults from her luscious lips, and I couldn't get enough.

By the time I pulled back, we were both breathing hard, and *fuck me*. Had I ever experienced a kiss like that before? One that made me desperate to fuck right where we stood? One that felt as good as sex in and of itself?

Without giving me a chance to say a word, she pushed against my chest with one hand, forcing me to step back. She raised those fingers to her lips, her eyes wide as she stared up at me. Her face was flushed, her eyes brighter than I'd ever seen them, and I had the insane urge to put that look on her face every day for the rest of our lives.

Then, like a switch being flipped, she seemed to come

back to herself. She dropped her hand and rolled her shoulders back, looking every bit the woman who didn't take any shit, save for those swollen lips and mussed hair, both of which were courtesy of me.

"Since this was your idea, you can figure out how to tell your family," she said, her voice raspy. "I'll see you tomorrow."

Without giving me a chance to respond, she turned and stalked off. And because I could never let her have the last word, I followed after her.

"That's not how it happened, and you know it."

"What I know is this was all your idea," she tossed over her shoulder.

This fucking woman...

"Oh, you *wish* it was my idea," I said. "Have you already forgotten?"

"Forgotten how much you begged for it? Not hardly."

"Tell yourself whatever you need to, kitten, but I know the truth."

"All you know are your delusions," she said as she pulled open the front door and flew outside without a backward glance.

I couldn't decide whether I wanted to go after her or drown my sorrows in an entire bottle of tequila, because *fuck. Me.* I wasn't so sure I was going to survive this marriage.

With a growl of frustration, I headed to the bar, getting the bartender's attention immediately. "Tequila. And make it a double."

He was a transplant to Starlight Cove—someone I hadn't

seen around before. His brows lifted as he poured me the drink. "Trouble with an ex?" he asked, chin lifted toward where Quinn had stormed out.

I breathed out a laugh. "I wish it was only that," I said under my breath. Then louder but not enough to carry, I added, "Actually, she's about to be my wife."

CHAPTER TWELVE

QUINN

I'D NEVER SPENT a lot of time daydreaming about my wedding.

As a little girl, I'd never played dress-up with a makeshift veil on my head crafted out of a dish towel and pretended to be a bride. But even if I had, I definitely wouldn't have imagined Ford McKenzie as my groom. Nor, in my wildest dreams, would I have imagined him strolling up the steps of Bayhaven town hall toward me and looking obscene in his dark gray suit pants, white dress shirt with the sleeves rolled up to display his drool-worthy forearms, all topped off with a freaking vest.

Looking good had never been Ford's problem. It was effortless for him, much like everything else, regardless of whether he was wearing his usual uniform of a T-shirt and jeans or his actual uniform at the firehouse.

But this? This was downright unfair.

Especially when the memory of our kiss still bubbled

under my skin, haunting me every single second since I'd walked out the doors of One Night Stan's.

"Did you wear this hoping for a better kiss than last night's?" he asked as he came to a stop directly in front of me, his voice a low rumble that absolutely scrambled my insides.

"What?" I shook my head, forcing myself out of my Ford stupor, and glanced down at my outfit. I wasn't wearing anything special. Just an old white sundress covered with tiny lavender flowers that I'd pulled straight from my closet because I wasn't going to buy something new for this farce. "What's wrong with what I'm wearing?"

"I didn't say there was anything wrong with it." He allowed his gaze to sweep over me from head to toe, his thumb brushing a slow path across his bottom lip as he looked his fill.

That simple move drew my attention to his mouth, which was the last thing I needed, considering the reminders of what he'd done to me with it last night had been stomping around in my brain like a marching band since it'd happened.

"But I also can't promise I'm not going to take full advantage of that first kiss with you as my wife." He lifted his eyes to mine as he said the last two words, his gaze heated, and there was no good explanation for the way my stomach dipped and swooped like I was on a roller coaster.

This was *Ford*. The guy who practically subsisted on one-night stands. Whatever we had between us wasn't going to change that. And no matter what kind of feelings he managed to bring out in me on top of the ever-present desire to strangle him, I needed to remember that.

The reason I was here—the entire purpose behind my going through with this insane plan in the first place—was for the clinic. To realize my dream and to become the doctor the people of Starlight Cove needed and deserved. One they could count on.

"You ready?" he asked, tipping his head toward the town hall doors.

I absolutely was not.

This was, without a doubt, the dumbest thing I had ever done in my life. Which, granted, wasn't all that difficult to accomplish, considering my history of never stepping even a toe off the safe path. But I was determined to see this through. Once I made up my mind, I was locked in. I planted my feet like a tree and refused to budge. This would be no different.

I just had to keep reminding myself that this was only a means to an end. There would be nothing permanent about my marriage to Ford.

I took a deep inhale before blowing it out slowly. "As I'll ever be."

In Maine, there was no waiting period to receive a marriage license, and I didn't know if that was a good or a bad thing. It made everything easier for us, but how many other fake couples had made an appointment for a false wedding just like we had? Had filled out the same paperwork, walked the same steps down the empty corridor, stood in front of the same judge with no intention of their vows being real at all?

It took six minutes. Three hundred and sixty seconds until, suddenly, I stood facing Ford, about to become his wife. Everything up until now had been a blur, just a low hum of voices in the back of my mind. But, as if my brain knew this was the important part, it tuned in as the judge spoke.

"The contract of marriage is not to be entered into lightly, but thoughtfully and seriously and with a deep realization of its obligations and responsibilities. If anyone can show just cause why this couple should not be lawfully joined together, let them speak now or forever hold their peace."

She paused for a brief moment, but since the two people standing in as witnesses were town employees who didn't know us from Adam, we were in the clear.

The judge turned toward Ford. "Ford, will you take Quinn to be your wedded wife, to love her, comfort her, honor her, and keep her, forsaking all others, for so long as you both shall live?"

"I do," he said without hesitation.

"Quinn." She turned to me with a smile. "Will you take Ford to be your wedded husband, to love him, comfort him, honor him, and keep him, forsaking all others, for so long as you both shall live?"

I felt like I was having an out-of-body experience when I responded on autopilot, "I do."

Ford seemed to have no such hang-ups as he looked down at me with a grin and waggled his eyebrows. Meanwhile, I was attempting to swallow down this lump of nerves that had lodged itself in my throat.

"Please join hands and repeat after me," the judge said. "I,

Ford McKenzie, take you, Quinn Cartwright, as my lawfully wedded wife. I promise to love, honor, and cherish you for as long as we both shall live."

Ford must've read the look on my face as the pure terror I was feeling, because he squeezed my hands twice and tipped his lips up into a smirk. "I, Ford McKenzie, take you, Quinn Cartwright, as my lawfully wedded wife. I promise to love, honor, and cherish you—and get you as many late-night emotional support coffees as you need so you don't turn into an insufferable harpy—for as long as we both shall live."

At his words, I pressed my lips into a thin line, meeting the amusement in his eyes with a glare of my own. Oh, he wanted to play? I could play.

The judge chuckled under her breath before turning her attention to me. "Now, Quinn, please repeat after me. I, Quinn Cartwright, take you, Ford McKenzie, as my lawfully wedded husband. I promise to love, honor, and cherish you for as long as we both shall live."

"I, Quinn Cartwright, take you, Ford McKenzie, as my lawfully wedded husband. I promise to love, honor, and cherish you—and keep you humble by handing you your ass at every possible opportunity—for as long as we both shall live."

Instead of irritating him like I'd hoped, my words only seemed to make Ford's smirk grow wider, turning into a full-blown grin.

"Did you bring rings to exchange?" the judge asked.

It was one thing we hadn't talked about, so I wouldn't have been surprised if he hadn't remembered this part, but I reached into my dress pocket to pull out the ring I'd purchased for him. "I have one."

"Got it," Ford said at the same time, holding up what looked like a plastic-wrapped package.

I tried to get a better look at what he had in his hands, but he just stared at me with a cocked brow while he ripped open the package and pulled out whatever was inside.

"Perfect," the judge said. "Ford, please place the ring on Quinn's finger and repeat, with this ring, I thee wed."

I glanced down when Ford took my left hand in his, distracted momentarily by the gentle way he held it, his callused fingertips lightly tickling my palm. The soft touch stunned me so much it took me a minute to notice the gigantic ring he held, topped with a huge rock.

Made of candy.

It was a ring pop, green and gaudy. I used to love those when I was a kid but probably hadn't had one in twenty years.

"With this ring, I thee wed," he said, his eyes locked on mine as he slid the massive candy ring on my finger. Then, softer and just for me, he said, "Your real one is coming, but I didn't want to show up without anything. I didn't know how to make a ring out of watermelon Jolly Ranchers, so I figured a watermelon ring pop was a good substitute."

It took a moment for his words to register, but when they finally did, my mouth dropped open in shock. In high school, I had practically lived on watermelon Jolly Ranchers. They were my favorite study snack, and I was never without them, no matter where I was. But how did he—

"Quinn, please place the ring on Ford's finger and repeat, with this ring, I thee wed."

I swallowed and held his left hand, not even trying to hide the questions swimming in my eyes as they searched his for answers I wasn't going to get. "With this ring, I thee wed," I murmured, sliding the black band on to Ford's finger, grateful I'd guessed his size correctly.

Ford dropped his gaze to where I pushed the ring on to his finger, his brows lifting. "Silicone?"

I couldn't read anything from the tone of his voice, so I just shrugged. "I know it's not very expensive, but they're supposed to be the best option for firefighters."

He continued to stare at me without saying a word, his gaze weighted and heavy, and I shifted under his scrutiny. I had no idea what he was thinking and couldn't read anything in his stare. All I knew was my stomach was a swarming mass of riotous butterflies, and I didn't know why.

"Now the good part—the kiss," the judge said with a wink.

Oh shit.

Would it be weird to refuse to kiss the groom? Probably. But after what had happened last night, I honestly didn't trust myself around Ford. Not with these butterflies running rampant inside me.

I'd assumed he would be a good kisser, especially given his extensive experience. But I hadn't been expecting *that*. From the moment he'd delved his fingers into my hair and cupped my face, covering my lips with his own, my body had come alive in a way it never had before.

The judge continued, "Inasmuch as Quinn and Ford have consented together in wedlock and pledged their vows to each other, by the authority vested in me by the state of Maine, I now pronounce you husband and wife. Ford, you may kiss your bride."

Time slowed then as Ford stepped into me and lifted his hands to my face. He slid his fingers around my nape, his thumbs pressing lightly under my jaw to tip my face up toward his. Then he leaned down until his lips hovered just over mine and said, "No take backs now, wife. Just remember I warned you..."

I didn't have a second to think—hell, I didn't even have a second to *breathe*—before his mouth descended on mine. This kiss was slower than the one last night. Softer, sweeter... and yet not any tamer. Without thought, I reached up and gripped his forearms, opening my mouth to his seeking tongue and tasting him all over again.

I'd had kisses before. Most of them less than mediocre, but there were a few good contenders in the mix.

But there had never been anything like this... Never anyone like Ford.

He kissed me like I was the only person in the world. Like I was oxygen and he was gasping for breath. Like I was a feast in the middle of a desert.

He kissed me like I was *actually* his wife.

And I had no idea what to do with that.

CHAPTER THIRTEEN

QUINN

WELL, evidently I was a married woman now, and I hadn't yet completely lost it. Okay, so I'd had a minor freak-out when Ford had handed me a key outside town hall and said he'd see me at home because...*what*?

Home?

A home we'd now, apparently, share...

Somehow during all of this, I hadn't stopped to think about the details. Like the fact that husbands and wives generally lived together, and we certainly weren't going to do that in Mabel's extra bedroom down the hall from where she hosted sex toy parties.

Which was how I found myself sitting in my car outside Ford's cottage, in the dark, and unable to move. My moving in here made the most sense, even if his place looked small enough that I wasn't sure I wouldn't accidentally smother him in his sleep in the first week, not to mention the weeks after while we kept up this farce.

What the hell was I *doing*? What were *we* doing? It was one thing to dive into this when I knew there was nothing between us but simmering animosity, but after that kiss last night...after our first kiss as a technically married couple? I knew I wasn't the only one who had felt those sparks. The feel of exactly what those kisses had done to Ford had been proof enough of that.

The front door opened, and there he stood. "Are you waiting for an invitation, Mrs. McKenzie?" he asked, backlit by the porch light as he strolled down the front steps of his cottage toward me.

"It's Cartwright," I snapped, angry at myself more than him but unable to curb my snippiness.

He was close enough now that I could see him clearly, even in the dark of night, as he eyed me. "You're not taking my last name?"

"Uh...no," I said, gathering my purse and the bag I had in the passenger seat. "This is going to be a blink of a marriage, so I'm not going through all that. Changing names is a giant pain in the ass. If this were forever, it would be a different story, but we're not talking about forever. We're talking about for now."

It was the same thing I'd been repeating to myself since we'd said I do, but it hadn't seemed to lessen this giant boulder filling up the entirety of my stomach.

After a deep breath, I stepped out of the car and finally allowed myself to take him in. He'd changed out of his wedding attire—thank God—but this wasn't any better. He wore a fitted SCFD T-shirt that molded to his chest and biceps and a pair of gray sweatpants that left very little to the imagination and showcased a whole lot of him.

A whole fucking lot. Sweet fancy Moses riding a bicycle, there didn't appear to be anything little about *that*.

He chuckled under his breath and snapped his fingers in front of his crotch. "Man, Beck really is onto something..."

I shot my gaze up to his. "What?"

"He and Everly read romance books together. He swears they're like manuals and more men should take note. And your ogling proves romances are basically law—gray sweatpants really are like lingerie for men, aren't they?"

I refused to take his bait about the sweatpants—but he was absolutely right, because sweet Lord in heaven, they should've been illegal on Ford and his not-so-little friend— and admit he'd caught me drooling over him. So instead, I asked, "You read romance?"

"Hell yeah, I do," he said, taking my bag from my hand and shouldering it. Then, with a wink, he added, "The filthy ones are my favorite."

Romances ranked right up there with cozy mysteries for me, so I'd read my fair share of them—had a well-worn copy of *Being His Good Girl* stuffed in my bag, in fact—so I could only imagine what constituted filthy in Ford's mind.

"You got any more?" he asked.

I snapped my gaze to his, wondering if I'd mentioned the dog-eared copy of one of my favorite books out loud.

"Bags," he clarified. "Is it just this sad little thing, or do you have more?"

"One more in the back seat."

"*Two* sad little bags." He opened the back door and grabbed it. "You travel light."

That was true. I'd sold most of my possessions before the move to Starlight Cove since I didn't know where I'd be staying or how long I'd be staying there.

I shrugged, following him up the stairs to his cottage. "I still have a few things at Mabel's place, but I didn't want to chance being there any longer than I had to be in case I ran into her. But you and I both know that only buys us a couple hours, max, and she's going to be on this. I hope you're prepared to tell everybody tomorrow."

"I'll never be ready to have my ass handed to me by my baby sister."

"Addison will be mad?"

"Oh, she's going to lose her shit, for sure. But she won't be the only one. I'm sure your landlord will have something to say about it. I'm surprised you managed to keep this from her in the first place."

I shrugged. "I left while George was sleeping and Mabel was hosting a Pleasure Party."

"A Pleasure Party, huh? You ever go to one of those?"

"Nice try, but I'm not talking to you about my sex toy collection."

"You have a whole collection?" he asked, not hiding the interest in his tone. "Not gonna lie, I love a good assist."

I forced myself to ignore the images those words conjured up, knowing I needed to keep myself in check, now more than ever. Rather than answer him, I just pinned him with a glare before glancing around at what would be my home for the foreseeable future.

It was bigger than I'd thought it would be but smaller than I'd hoped. Directly off the front door, a small seating area housed two oversized chairs that faced the wood-burning fireplace bracketed by floor-to-ceiling mostly bare white bookshelves. A small galley kitchen sat on the opposite side of the room. Through glass-paned French doors was the bedroom, and from my vantage point, I could just make out a sliver of the en-suite bathroom.

It was cozy and quaint, if a bit impersonal. And it was a bonus that I was only steps from the beach. Even now, I could hear the crash of the waves against the shore, and I knew when it was light enough outside to see, I'd have an unobstructed view of the ocean from the front porch. All things considered, it could have been a hell of a lot worse.

There was just one problem...

"Why is there only one bed?"

Carrying my bags, Ford strode toward the bedroom and shot me a raised brow over his shoulder. "Not sure if you noticed this, kitten, but this isn't exactly a mansion. I've done my best to fix it up over the years, but I can't add square footage. Were you hoping for two twins?"

"It'd be better than this," I said, gesturing to his king-sized bed.

While it wasn't anything fancy, it was, surprisingly, made. A light gray duvet covered it, and four huge pillows were stacked at the head of the bed, a piece of paper resting on top of the pillows on the left. Right next to where Ford was placing my bags.

I walked toward him, glancing down at the paper, my brows lifting when I realized what it was. "Did you need help reading your test results? I know data isn't your strong suit."

I'd had to carry both our asses in statistics when we'd been paired together for group projects, and I wasn't above reminding him of that.

After setting down my bags, Ford shifted so he could lean against the wall, his arms crossed as he stared at me with amusement. "Those are for you, kitten. I thought you might be curious."

"Why would I be curious about your test results?"

He lifted a single shoulder. "I figured my wife had a right to know her husband has a clear bill of health. You know, in case you can't keep your hands off me tonight."

I rolled my eyes, but I couldn't stop the sudden flash that came to me thanks to his words, Ford pinning me beneath him as he took my mouth, slipped between my thighs, and—

"Oh my God, I'm *not* sleeping with you."

"I don't know, wife, it looks to me like you've got yourself all set up on that side of the bed. Which is, obviously, directly next to *my* side of that very same bed."

I opened and closed my mouth several times, but I was at a loss for words. Which was never a good thing in this man's company.

"*And...*" he said, clearly waiting for something from me.

"What?" I snapped.

"Do you have anything to tell me?" He gestured to the paper on my side of the bed.

I rolled my eyes. "You're not getting mine because they're three years old, and I didn't bother keeping them when they were clear and I wasn't having sex."

"What about birth control?"

My *God,* this man was irritating. "I already told you, I'm not sleeping with you, so you don't need to worry about it."

He hummed low in his throat and shook his head. "Don't you think our birth control method is something a husband would know? What do I say if one of my siblings asks?"

"You think one of your siblings is going to ask about birth control," I said flatly.

"Who knows. I'm just trying to be prepared here." He shrugged. "But if you want to allow people to poke more holes in our story, then..."

Goddammit. I hated that he was right.

"Fine," I gritted out through clenched teeth. "I have an IUD."

His brows hit his hairline, and I rolled my eyes, reading his surprise over the fact that I had one when I hadn't had sex in so long as clearly as if it were written across his forehead.

"IUDs are used for more than just birth control." I scrubbed a hand over my forehead, letting it drop as I exhaled a deep sigh. Fuck. I didn't want to tell Ford my medical history—especially because it made me feel vulnerable...something I hated to be in his presence—but he had a good point about knowing these kinds of details about each other. "Which I guess is something a husband would know about his wife. I have an IUD because I have PCOS, and it helps with my periods. Sometimes..." I muttered the last word under my breath.

He nodded, satisfied. "There. That wasn't so hard, now was it? We're both clear, you have an IUD, and we're officially sleeping together..." Then, softer, as if he didn't want to admit it, he said, "Even if it's not the way I want."

I studied him, my brow furrowed as I tried to get a read on him, but I couldn't. And I was tired of his games. "And what way is that?"

From the second Ford's eyes landed on me, his gaze a bit unfocused as if he was lost in a fantasy, his tongue making a slow path along his bottom lip, I knew I'd made a mistake by asking. Knew I'd fucked up as he walked slowly toward me.

"One thing you'll come to learn about me, kitten, is that I'm not picky. I'd be happy with you under me. On top of me. In front of me while I take you from—"

I leaped toward him, closing the distance between us and clamping a hand over his mouth. I wasn't sure I could take it if he finished that sentence. Holy shit, it was roasting in here, my cheeks flushed, thanks to the heat and definitely not because a matching fantasy had popped up in my mind after each scenario he'd stated.

"I'm not doing any of that," I snapped before removing my hand from his mouth. "I can't believe you don't have a couch."

"No couch, sorry. But I do have these fluffy barriers you can use to protect yourself," he said, gesturing to the huge stack of pillows on the bed. "If one of my hands or my dick should attempt to make contact with you at some point during the night, just shove them back on my side of the bed. They tend to have a mind of their own when you're involved."

"The only thing I'd use a pillow for in the middle of the night is to smother you in your sleep." I forced the words out, though they lacked their usual sharpness, because there was no stopping the thoughts now.

Imagining us lying together in the dark, working our way through each of the scenarios he'd presented... My breath quickened with every thought that floated through my head, my nipples tightening in response and my cheeks flushing even more. Whether because of curiosity or reflex, my gaze dropped to the front of Ford's sweatpants, and there was no missing the prominent bulge there—definitely larger than it had been when I'd first shown up. And I hated myself a little bit that I'd given in to temptation and Googled his piercing last night, which meant I could picture it...

Ford stepped closer to me, his hand going to the flare of my hip, his thumb slipping beneath the band of my sweatshirt to sweep against the soft curve of my stomach. "You're thinking about it, too, aren't you, kitten?"

Too?

My gaze snapped to his as my lips parted, and I stared up at him, trying to gauge if I was reading too much into that single word.

But without my voicing the questions flitting through my head, Ford answered them anyway. "Yeah, I was thinking about it. But that's not anything new. It's basically all I do where you're concerned."

"You've...thought about me like that?"

He huffed out a humorless laugh. "More times than I can count."

The heat pouring off his body sent shivers racing down my spine, and the side of my breast brushed against his arm with every breath I inhaled.

It wouldn't take anything to have his lips on mine again. Just a few scant inches and then—

But no. We couldn't do this. This marriage wasn't supposed to be real, which meant I absolutely was not going to fuck my husband.

I turned away from him and busied myself by grabbing the test results to set them aside. My gaze snagged on the date at the top and rolled my eyes. "If you think an old test is going to reassure me of anything, you're wrong."

"Who said it was an old test?"

"Um, I did? I can read, and this says it's from April."

"And?"

"*And*? What do you mean, and?"

Ford just looked at me with raised brows as if the answer to this should be obvious. My mind scanned through a dozen possibilities, but it kept coming back to the same one. If what he was saying was true—that this wasn't an old test, just the last one he'd needed to take—that meant Ford hadn't been with anyone in months.

Not since I'd moved back to Starlight Cove.

CHAPTER FOURTEEN

FORD

EARLY THE FOLLOWING MORNING, I sat in the diner at that month's mandatory family meeting, all my siblings surrounding me while we discussed the latest report for the resort. Addison was no doubt saying something incredibly important like what my next projects on the docket were. And Aiden probably had an update on the budget that I should be paying attention to, especially since the little league team the resort sponsored needed new uniforms, and we'd have to foot the bill if we didn't raise enough at a fundraiser—one I still needed to come up with.

Yet, even with all that shit, I couldn't focus on any of it.

Not when I couldn't drag my attention away from the matte black wedding band on my left hand. A matte black, *silicone* wedding band. Those weren't exactly mainstream— even if all the married guys at the fire station wore them— which meant Quinn had actually researched this. For *me*, not just some guy who was standing in as her husband.

That probably meant nothing. Quinn was the kind of person who researched absolutely everything down to the letter, so this was just par for the course with her.

But then, why did it feel different?

I didn't know how much longer it would be before my siblings noticed the new piece of jewelry I was rocking, and I knew things would go over better if I came clean before they could comment on it. God knew Addison was already going to lose her mind when she found out.

So, when we had a lull in the conversation, I figured there was no time like the present.

Around a mouthful of blueberry muffin, I said, "Thought you guys might want to know I got married yesterday."

"Ha-ha," Addison deadpanned. "We don't have time for your jokes today, Ford."

"Who said I was joking?" I held up my left hand, flashing the black band toward them.

My pronouncement was met with silence that lasted three...two...one...

"*What do you mean, you got married?*" Addison shrieked. "*To who?*"

Well, this was going to be fun...

"Quinn."

"*Quinn?*" Again with the shrieking.

"No matter how loud you say it, it won't stop being true. She moved in last night."

Addison's mouth dropped open as she stared at me, eyes wide. "*What do you mean, she moved in last night?*"

I glanced to my brothers, but they all gave me *you're on*

your own, man looks. "I'm not sure what you want me to say here..."

She slammed her hands on the table and pinned us each with a glare. "I want to know why I'm the only one who's having a reaction to this! This is just like when the whole Beck and Everly thing came to light, and everyone else—" She gasped, turning accusatory eyes on my brothers. "You all *knew*? And you little assholes didn't tell me?"

I held up my hands, ready and willing to throw my brothers under the bus if it would save my ass from her wrath. "Don't look at me. I didn't tell anyone."

"And don't think we aren't gonna talk about that as soon as everyone leaves," Beck grumbled under his breath. Then, louder, he added, "I wasn't sure, but I overheard something he said at One Night Stan's."

Aiden shrugged. "He borrowed the computer in the main inn and left open a web page on Maine marriage requirements."

When everyone turned their gazes to Brady, he just lifted his mug to his lips. "I'm the sheriff. It's my job to know shit, especially sneaky shit people are trying to get away with."

"I wasn't trying to get away with—"

"I can't believe every one of you knew before I did," Addison said. "*Again!*"

"I didn't know," Levi said.

Addison scoffed and waved a hand through the air. "You don't count. You never go anywhere."

Brady cleared his throat and held up a copy of the *Starlight Cove's Gazette*. On the front page was a large picture of Quinn and me under a headline that read *Starlight Cove's Favorite Rivals Get Hitched*, byline by none other than Mabel. "Actually," he said, "it looks like the whole town knew before you."

The picture taking up half of the front page was a shot of our first kiss—how Mabel managed to get a picture of that, I had no idea, though I hadn't exactly been paying attention to anything other than Quinn's lips against mine. While we'd traveled thirty miles to another town specifically to keep this quiet as long as possible, we'd clearly underestimated Mabel's investigative reporting skills.

Below the main picture were two smaller ones—both of Quinn and me. One from the back as I'd held her in my arms and carried her toward her car after she'd rolled her ankle following the auction. My head was bent down toward hers, making it look like we were having an intimate conversation. And the other at Kick Some Axe when I'd tugged her away from Eli, her back pressed to my chest as I held her to me with a hand curved around her waist. Her head was tipped back, resting on my chest, and mine was lowered toward her. And though I knew she'd been asking me what the hell I was doing while glaring daggers at me, from this vantage point, it looked like we were about three seconds away from fucking right there in front of everyone.

Jesus, was it getting hot in here?

With a gasp, Addison snatched the paper from Brady and stared down at it with wide eyes. "Holy shit, I can't believe it's true. You"—she shot a glare at me—"got *married*. To Quinn.

The one woman besides me in this entire state who doesn't fall for your bullshit?"

"So it would seem."

Addison huffed out a breath. "Seriously? That's *it*?"

I shrugged, glancing at my brothers once again, but they were still no help. "Yeah? What else do you want me to say?"

"Um...I don't know? How about you tell me what kind of backward reality I've stumbled into?"

"Not backward...just reality."

"When did you decide to do this? Better yet, how did you manage to talk her into it?"

"How do you know I was the one who talked her into it?"

"Oh *please*. This has Ford written all over it. I just want to know how much you had to drug her to get her to agree." She gasped. "Oh my God, you're blackmailing her, aren't you?"

"No, I'm not fucking blackmailing her. Jesus, Addison."

She scoffed. "Oh, like it's that much of a stretch with you two. I seriously don't understand what's happening. Every time I see you two together, you look ready to claw each other's eyes out."

"Or rip each other's clothes off..." Brady piped up over his cup of coffee.

Aiden glanced at him with a raised brow. "Weird thing to notice about our brother, man..."

He shot Aiden a scowl. "It's my job."

"Okay, Mr. Small-Town Detective," Addison said with a snarky edge to her voice. "Tell me what the hell is going on here, then, because none of it makes sense."

"What do you mean, none of it makes sense?" I said,

shifting in my seat. While Quinn and I hadn't explicitly laid out that we weren't going to tell other people about our little make-believe marriage, it sort of went unsaid. And if my family got in on this? *Fuck me.* "Quinn and I actually had a wedding yesterday."

"Oh, I don't doubt your wedding," Addison said, eyes narrowed on me. "I doubt your *marriage.*"

She was too damn close to the truth, and I was sweating now for a whole different reason than the thought of fucking my wife. "Why the hell would I be in a pretend marriage?"

She crossed her arms over her chest. "That's what I'm trying to figure out."

"You two *were* just arguing at One Night Stan's," Levi said.

I shot him a glare. I'd helped that little shit out so he wouldn't have to talk about Harper, and this was how he repaid me? See if I saved him from the wrath of our siblings ever again.

"Right before he grumbled to the bartender that she was about to become his wife," my traitor—I mean, twin—said.

"Wait..." Aiden said, his attention pinging between our siblings. "He ran into Chelsea a couple weeks ago and got conned into going to her wedding. He wouldn't actually go as far as to marry Quinn just to have a date to that, would he?"

Well...it sounded stupid when he said it like that.

As one, they all turned to face me, gazes scrutinizing, before turning back to one another, all of them nodding.

"Yeah, he'd definitely do that," Aiden said.

They were acting like *I* had been the deciding factor here, when I was just a willing participant. Quinn was getting far more out of this than I was.

"Hey!" I snapped. "It's not even mostly for me!"

Addison spun on me with a gasp. "So you admit it!"

Motherfucker.

I pressed my lips together in a flat line, refusing to say anything else because I was only going to dig myself deeper into this hole.

"Wait a second..." Brady said, tapping a finger on the counter. "Could this have anything to do with Dr. Dinsmore's backward philosophy about women?"

"What do you mean?" Addison asked. "I know he's a misogynistic asshole, but how is that relevant here?"

Brady lifted a shoulder. "I may have heard around town that the only reason Quinn agreed to take a position at the clinic was because Don's close to retiring, and it went without saying that she'd be first in line to purchase it."

"Don would fucking hate that," Aiden said.

"Hate it enough to put some bullshit stipulations on it," Brady said. "Like that Quinn had to be married before he'd consider an offer from her."

Beck turned to me, shaking his head. "Never saw the marriage of convenience trope for you, man."

"What the fuck," I whispered to no one in particular. It'd taken them less than ten minutes to put it all together. We were wasting our time with this resort when clearly they should've been out solving crimes.

Addison gasped, her eyes darting between Beck and me. "Oh my God, we're *right*."

"No," I said without hesitation. "No, you're not right." I glared at all of them, hoping they understood the unspoken threat threaded through my words. "I'm *married*. To *Quinn*. That's all you need to know. Got it?"

"Okay, got it." Addison shot me an exaggerated wink and a thumbs-up. "So, how does this all work? For the love, please tell me you have a plan for keeping your...*activities*...on the DL while you're married."

I shot her a scowl and snapped, "I'm not going to fuck someone else while I'm married to Quinn. Jesus."

"Does *she* know that?" Addison asked. "Better question, is she going to give you the same respect?"

Considering it had been three years since the last time Quinn had had sex, I didn't think I needed to worry about it. But that didn't stop the thought of her with another man from twisting something in my gut, a knot in my chest tightening until it felt like I could barely breathe.

I rubbed a hand over the spot, trying to ease the ache to no avail. "I don't fucking know. We didn't talk about it."

"You didn't *talk* about it?" Addison asked, eyes wide. "Well, then I guess I don't have to be mad at you for not including me in this, because it's clear you were both thinking out of your asses and didn't bother to take anyone else into consideration."

"Oh, I'm sorry, Addison," I said, heavy on the sarcasm, "that *my wife and I* didn't take *your* feelings into consideration when *we* decided to get married."

"*Fake* married," Levi piped up from the back.

"Damn," Beck said. "That sounds really fucking weird."

"The weirdest," Brady agreed.

"Can't believe he's the first one of us to get married," Aiden said, shaking his head. "Didn't see that one coming. What kind of alternate dimension have we jumped into?"

"One where we all have to work together to make sure this marriage doesn't go off the rails," Addison said. "I'll do whatever I have to to make sure Quinn can take over for that asshole, including making sure you two can pull this off."

She turned her attention to our brothers. "That means you're all helping as well. From now on, we're on Team Quord."

"What the fuck is a Quord?" Levi asked.

"You know, Quinn plus Ford," Addison said. "Like Brangelina or Bennifer. I could've flipped it, but I figured 'Finn' would get confusing."

"Oh, but Beverly doesn't?" Beck asked with an eye roll.

As I'd told him, that was the only logical name pairing for Beck and Everly, and he needed to get over the fact that his couple name was that of an old woman.

"We're going to make this happen." Addison stood, gathering up her iPad and the folders she'd brought in. "And I just want to make it very clear to the rest of you assholes that you'd better tell me before you get married—real *or* fake. Or I'm never speaking to you again."

Aiden's brows lifted. "That's a little drastic, isn't—"

"*Never*," she cut in, hand raised. "*Again*."

"You don't need to make anything happen," I said. "In fact, I'd appreciate it if we could just rewind the past fifteen minutes and pretend this conversation never took place."

"Too late!" Addison said, striding toward the door. "Already on it."

"I'm out, too," Levi said, tipping his chin toward me on his way out.

"I hope you're ready for this, man," Brady said, clapping a hand on my shoulder as he headed toward the front door.

"Don't think your new nuptials are going to get you out of figuring out the fundraiser for the uniforms," Aiden said before following Brady out of the diner.

With a groan, I braced my elbows on the counter and dropped my head into my hands. "*Fuuuck.*"

When I finally lifted my head, I found Beck staring at me, arms crossed and an unreadable expression on his face.

"What's that look for?" I asked. Which...yeah. That was a dumb-as-fuck question because what *wasn't* that look for?

"I just want to know why you didn't tell me."

It was a fair question, considering Beck and I told each other everything. He knew me better than anyone in the world—sometimes I wondered if he knew me better than I knew myself. And that was exactly why I hadn't wanted to tell him before I'd gone through with it, worried he would have found a way to talk me out of it.

It was the same reason I never told him before I went off on one of my impromptu adventures. I always told him everything he wanted to know, but not until *after* the fun had been had.

"Because I thought you'd try to talk me out of it."

He scoffed. "For good reason."

"Maybe, but we're doing this for a good reason, too. The

jackass she works for refuses to even consider an offer from her unless she's married. You should hear the shit he says to her. I'll be lucky if I get out of this without Brady arresting me for assault and battery."

"And what are you getting out of this?"

"A date to Chelsea's wedding."

"And?"

"And...I get to show up with a smoking-hot woman on my arm who happens to be my wife."

Beck leveled me with a look. It was his big-brother look. He didn't pull it out often—hard to do when he was only sixteen minutes older than me—but when he did, I knew I was in for a lecture.

So I saved him the trouble and held up a hand, the other going into my pocket to rub my thumb over our napkin contract. "No lecture needed. We both know what this is and what this isn't."

"Yeah? So she knows you've been obsessed with her since you were fifteen and her table partner in chemistry?"

"I'm not—nor have I ever been—obsessed with her. Jesus."

Beck glanced down to my wedding ring before lifting his gaze back to mine, his brow raised as if to say, *aren't you?*

CHAPTER FIFTEEN

QUINN

BY THE TIME I pulled up outside Ford's cottage—*our* cottage, for the foreseeable future—it was after seven. I'd been done at the clinic for a couple hours, and while I'd run a few unscheduled errands and drove around town for far too long, I couldn't delay the inevitable any longer.

When I'd woken up this morning in Ford's bed—a place I never thought I'd be—I hadn't anticipated finding him so close. Although that was a gross understatement. Ford wasn't just close—he'd been curled around me, his chest pressed against my back, knees tucked up under mine, and his arm slung possessively around me, hand spread wide over the soft flesh of my stomach as if he was afraid I was going to try to sneak out.

Which, to be fair, was exactly what I'd done.

I'd slunk away to the clinic and spent the day submerged in work. I'd taken longer than usual with each patient, and when there hadn't been any appointments for me to see, I'd tackled the outdated filing system Dr. Dicknose still used. Alicia told me they'd purchased a new program years ago but hadn't yet transitioned to it, so I'd made that my project this afternoon and had started inputting patients into the system.

But I couldn't put off the inevitable any longer.

I grabbed my purse and headed toward the cottage, steeling myself for our unavoidable encounter. Opening the front door, I scanned the area for any sign of Ford, exhaling a deep sigh when I didn't immediately see him. He wasn't on shift today—he'd given me his schedule so I knew when he wouldn't be coming home, and I'd ignored the unease in my stomach over everything that could possibly go wrong for him during those two twenty-four-hour shifts each week—but maybe he was with one of his siblings? His Jeep was out front, but maybe Addison had him working on a project for the resort... Maybe he'd be gone for a while, and I would be asleep by the time he got home.

Was 6:30 too early to call it a night when you were only thirty-one? Probably, but what else was I supposed to do?

It wasn't that I didn't want to be around him.

Okay, so it wasn't *only* that I didn't want to be around him. More, it was that I didn't trust myself around him. Sweet-talking people into getting what he wanted was Ford's specialty, and I'd always loved denying him that.

But if these past few interactions had proven anything, it was that my body did not agree with my brain. While my brain was putting on the brakes, my body was ready and all too willing to do whatever the fuck Ford suggested, especially if it involved his lips on mine.

I hung my purse on the hook by the front door before making my way into the bedroom, shedding my cardigan as I went. I was just reaching for the hem of my sundress when the bathroom door flew open, startling a scream out of me.

"Jesus, kitten!" Ford said. "You scared the shit out of me. Did you forget I live here?"

"No, I—" My words cut off as I turned to face him.

He stood in the doorway of the en-suite bathroom, his hair wet and chest bare, clearly having just gotten out of the shower. Without my permission, my gaze tracked over every naked inch of him, following a droplet of water as it trailed over his body. From his shoulder, down his chest and then the ridges of his abdomen, before disappearing into the towel that hung so low on his hips, his Adonis belt was on display and a shadow of hair was visible at the bottom of his happy trail.

If I thought gray sweatpants showcased what Ford was packing, they had *nothing* on a thin piece of white terry cloth. It was doing very little to hide anything, least of all the monster between his legs.

Holy.

Hell.

I couldn't drag my gaze away, especially when I swore his cock twitched at my attention.

"Quit looking at me like that, wife, or I'm going to stop trying to hold this towel up and show you what your horny eyes do to me," Ford said, his voice so low and deep and rough that my body responded immediately, a shiver working its way through me, my nipples tightening as heat pooled between my legs.

And *no*. Absolutely not. That wouldn't be happening. Not today, not ever.

This was exactly why I'd avoided coming back to the cottage. But I needed to figure out a way to handle whatever was between Ford and me, because I wasn't going to avoid coming home for the next eight weeks or however long we were in this sham of a marriage.

"I don't have horny eyes," I said, finally finding my voice. "And I didn't think you were home."

"Well, I am," he said, taking a step toward me. "And I was right."

"I do *not* have horny eyes."

"You do, but I wasn't talking about that…" He smirked at me while I diligently attempted to look anywhere but at him, doing my damnedest to keep my horny eyes to myself just so I wouldn't prove him right. "Addison definitely lost her shit. Especially when she saw the newspaper."

I exhaled in relief, grateful for the change in topic. This morning's paper had been a surprise for me, too. But, even better, it had shocked Dr. Dicknose into silence, while Alicia had squealed her excitement, swearing up and down she'd known there was something going on between us, but she understood we'd wanted to keep it a secret.

That was nowhere near the truth, but I was going to let her fill in whatever story she wanted to, so long as it made this marriage plausible.

I didn't know whether I wanted to hug or kill Mabel for

splashing our nuptials all over the front page of Starlight Cove's newspaper, but I couldn't deny that it gave our marriage outside credibility that Ford and I wouldn't have been able to achieve on our own.

"Yeah, that was a surprise to walk into this morning," I said. "Apparently I spoke too soon when I said Mabel didn't have a clue."

"As long as Dicknose saw it, that's all that matters, right?"

"Right. I just thought we'd have more time to get used to things before Mabel spread our business to the whole town. I swung over there after work, picked up the last of my things, and told her I was moving out."

"How did she take it?"

"You would've thought she won the lottery with how much she was smiling at me. She sent me away with a lifetime supply of strawberry-flavored lube. The bag's in my trunk."

Ford barked out a laugh. "Better that than her not believing this. Let's just hope she doesn't figure things out as quickly as my siblings did."

I snapped my gaze to his, careful to keep my wandering eyes above his shoulders. "What do you mean by that?"

He grimaced and ran a hand through his wet hair, causing another water droplet to fall, but I absolutely was not going to get distracted by that one. "They know what's going on."

"What do you mean? *How*?"

"Because they're fucking Carmen Sandiego? I don't know. Between the five of them, it took them like fifteen minutes."

"Shit..." I breathed, closing my eyes and rubbing my temples. This was the last thing we needed if we had any hope of our coupling passing as reality. "Are they going to keep it quiet?"

"Oh yeah." Ford nodded. "Addison's all over it. She wants Dicknose out of there as much as you do, so she's willing to do anything to help."

"Well, that's a relief."

Ford was still standing there in nothing but a towel, so I busied myself with the bags I hadn't bothered unpacking last night. I'd never been more grateful for procrastinating because it gave me the perfect activity to avoid looking at him.

After grabbing one of the bags from my side of the bed, I strode over to the dresser, where Ford had cleared a couple drawers for me. I started tossing items in without much care to how they were arranged. I could fix it later. As long as it kept my attention off the nearly naked, extremely gorgeous man—who happened to be *my husband*—I didn't care.

I could hear Ford shuffling behind me, but I refused to even glance his way, though my body seemed to be acutely aware of his movements, regardless. Goose bumps had erupted on my skin just from the soft breeze of him walking behind me, and was I seriously getting turned on from someone *walking past me*?

God, maybe Ford had been right, and three years actually was the breaking point. Hell of a time to figure that out...

I spun around, intent on grabbing the other bag, but instead landed face first into Ford's warm, solid chest.

He steadied me with a hand on my hip, the other still clutching his towel in place. "Easy, kitten, I'm not gonna bite."

But then his gaze raked over my upper body, sweeping down the column of my neck, across my nearly bare shoulders since I'd shed my cardigan, and down into the serious cleavage I was showcasing in this dress. When he lifted his eyes to mine again, they were molten, the unspoken *unless you want me to* hanging heavily in the air between us.

"Would you put on some clothes, please?" I snapped, sidestepping him to grab my last bag and storming back to the dresser before I did something I'd regret. Like tracing those water droplets with my tongue or tugging that towel right off his waist and telling him to put his money where his mouth was. Because that was the thing—Ford was an excellent flirt, but that didn't mean he actually wanted to act on this when it came right down to it. Hell, I'd seen him flirt with Mabel more times than I could count, and I was fairly confident he didn't want to bang her.

Too late, I realized what I'd stashed in this bag—the sex toy collection I didn't want to discuss with Ford. It wasn't a collection so much as a couple prized toys—one in particular that always, *always* got the job done—but still... It was not something I wanted to take out in his presence. Hoping Ford wasn't looking, I grabbed one of them and shoved it into the drawer.

Or that was what I attempted to do anyway.

In actuality, I missed the drawer entirely in my clumsy attempt to keep Ford's attention off me and threw my Rose toy on the floor, where it proceeded to roll across the wood planks before coming to a stop against Ford's bare foot.

Oh my God.

Oh my fucking God.

My cheeks flamed, whether from the embarrassment of my toy being out in the open or the fact that Ford was still standing there looking like sex on a stick, I didn't know. It didn't matter.

I was prepared and waiting for Ford's mocking voice to reach me, his teasing, taunting words to break this tension between us so we could get back to the status quo and fall into the antagonistic relationship we'd always had.

But I wasn't prepared for him to reach down and pluck the toy from the floor, holding it between his fingers as he slowly stalked toward me, his eyes never leaving mine. "You should take better care of your toys, kitten. You can't just throw them around."

I leaned back, bracing my hands behind me on the dresser. My breaths were coming too fast, my breasts heaving with each one, and there was no way Ford didn't notice. Not with my double D's practically shoved in his face.

"Give it back," I said, but my voice came out softer than I'd intended.

"What if I want to see how it works?" he asked. Then he glanced down, finding the on button and pushing it. Nothing happened.

Because I'd worn out the charge the night we'd gone out to dinner.

I'd come home, headed straight for the shower—living

with two senior citizens really put a damper on solo fun—and made myself come in under two minutes to memories of Ford's kiss. But one hadn't been enough, and I'd worked myself through two more before I'd been sated enough to quit.

With a single brow raised, he said, "Had a lot of tension to work out lately?"

I didn't bother responding. He knew the answer as well as I did. The tension between us crackled like lightning, illuminating an attraction I'd always kept shoved down deep.

He reached around me and set the toy on the dresser, then he braced his hands on either side of my hips, caging me in. With his thumb and forefinger, he pinched the material of my dress. "You drive me fucking crazy in these little dresses, did you know that? Have me hard as a fucking rock every goddamn day while I imagine everything you have underneath it."

I swallowed thickly. "I hate to tell you this, but you'd be disappointed by my plain white underwear."

"Oh, kitten, I can promise you I won't be disappointed by anything that's under there. But I wasn't talking about your panties. I was talking about that ass I want to sink my teeth into and those thighs I think about wrapped around my head ninety-five percent of the day."

I froze, caught in the snare of Ford's gaze, trying to read if he was being truthful or if this was just another one of his games. Something he did for the sole purpose of tormenting me. Flirt with his wife, crank her so tight with need she was desperate for release, and then turn away with a grin, knowing her toy was out of charge and she couldn't go to anyone else to fulfill her needs.

He must've read the skepticism in my expression, because he said, "Tell me to prove it." An echo from One Night Stan's when he'd turned my world upside down with just a kiss.

But Ford wasn't talking about just a kiss.

And if I thought my world was tipped on its axis after only having his lips on mine, I knew this would be so, so much worse.

"What are you suggesting?" I managed to get out through a dry throat.

"You want the censored or uncensored version?"

"Uncensored," I whispered.

"You sure?" he asked, stepping even closer until I could feel the thickness of him against my thigh.

Unable to speak, I simply nodded.

"I want to fuck you, kitten. Badly. I've wanted to for a long fucking time. But now that I'm wearing this ring?" He held up his hand, showing me the black band. "I want it even more. It's my job as your husband to release this tension that's been tying you up in knots. My job to make my wife come harder than she ever has before."

He was so close now, my achingly hard nipples brushed against his chest with every rapid inhale, his cock thick and hard against my thigh, and I desperately wanted to reach down and feel it. Wrap my fingers around him and see just how much I affected him.

"Tell me to prove it, wife, and I'll sink to my knees right here and eat your pussy like it's my last fucking meal. And then I'll break that dry spell of yours and fuck you until the neighbors know exactly who's making you scream."

Oh my God.

My legs were shaking, my stomach twisted with a mix of excitement and nerves, and I wasn't even going to mention the state of my panties. Soaked was an understatement. I could probably come right now with just a brush of the material against my clit, so God knew what Ford would be able to do to me.

That was the only logical explanation I had for why I skipped right down the path I'd already been down and uttered the two words that had sealed my fate two nights before. "Prove it."

CHAPTER SIXTEEN

QUINN

I BARELY GOT the words out before Ford yanked my underwear down my legs, lifted me up onto the dresser, and then dropped to his knees in front of me. *Oh Jesus*. It'd been so long since anyone had done this to me, and with Ford between my thighs, it felt a little like I was diving straight into the middle of the ocean without a life jacket.

He cupped my ankles, sliding his hands up my calves, over my knees, to the insides of my thighs, his touch soft and delicate...almost reverent. Then he shoved my legs wide to make room for his shoulders as he settled between them, his eyes glued to what he'd just revealed.

Ford turned his head to sink his teeth into my thigh and groaned. "Knew you'd be this pretty," he said, flipping up my skirt so he had an unfettered view of where I ached for him. "And I fucking knew that pussy was going to be soaked and ready for me. I've waited *years* for this. Tell me you're going to let me taste it, kitten. Tell me you're going to let me slide my tongue inside this gorgeous cunt and finally put me out of my misery."

Though I had no idea how, I managed to choke out a soft, "Yes."

He hummed and brushed his nose along my inner thigh, tracing it over the crease where my leg met my body, and *holy hell...* My clit throbbed in anticipation of what he was going to do, his breaths teasing me with every exhale, and I was desperate for him to put his mouth on me.

But Ford took his time and played his usual game. Reveling in tormenting me and driving me wild just because he could. He ran his hands along the insides of my thighs, not stopping until he framed my pussy between them, then he used his thumbs to spread me open for his hungry gaze.

"Look at that needy little clit." He brushed a featherlight touch over it, and I shuddered out a moan.

"Ford..." I panted, no longer in control of my words or my body. No longer caring how desperate I sounded. I *was* desperate. And I needed exactly what he'd promised me. I threaded my fingers through his hair and gripped tightly, silently begging him to get on with it already.

"We're going to play a game, kitten." He looked up at me, eyes full of something I couldn't quite name. "It's called, *Let's See How Many Times My Husband Can Make Me Come.*"

He didn't wait for a response—which was good since all my snarky replies had evaporated into thin air the second he'd tossed my panties to the side—before he threw my legs over his shoulders and dove in. He licked up my seam, the flat of his tongue making a slow path from my entrance to my clit as if he didn't want to miss a single inch of me. As if he wanted to lick up every drop. As if he was *savoring* me.

I gasped as he groaned into my pussy, the vibrations sending shock waves through me and pushing me that much closer to my climax. I was already close, my body having been primed and ready, not to mention how long it'd been since I'd had another person's attention on me.

I glanced down, overwhelmed by the sight of him between my thighs, his hair gripped in my fingers, his eyes locked on mine as he fucked me with his tongue. This big, strong man, who could have any woman he wanted eating out of the palm of his hand, was on his knees for *me*.

"Give it to me, kitten," he said, flicking his finger over my clit. "I want to know what my wife tastes like when she comes."

His words combined with the skilled way he worked my clit was all it took, and I exploded against his mouth, my orgasm ripped from me before I even knew what was happening. My moan was soundless as my body shook and quaked, the ripples rolling through me until I was nothing more than a puddle on top of his dresser.

But Ford didn't stop.

Instead, my orgasm only seemed to spur him on even more, his tongue working harder against my clit as he slid two fingers inside me and pumped them deep.

"Oh God. Again?" I asked, breathless, my body somehow both sated and yet still strung tight, desperate for more.

"Yes, again," he said, his fingers curling inside me. "Come

on, wife, give your husband another one. This time, I want to feel this greedy cunt squeezing my fingers."

This marriage wasn't even real—hell, I didn't even *like* him. So why did it turn me on so much to hear him refer to himself as my husband?

With one hand braced behind me on the dresser and the other gripping Ford's hair, I shamelessly ground myself against his face as he worked me toward my second orgasm of the night. My body was tightening, seeking another release even though I'd just come down from one. But Ford had opened the floodgates, and my body was as greedy as he said it was, desperate for whatever he could give me.

I rocked my hips in time with his thrusting fingers, lips parted as I watched him devour me. His mouth covered my pussy, his tongue working in quick strokes against my clit as he pumped those fingers deep, and *God*, I needed to come again. I groaned, the sound needy and wild.

"Fuck." His lips brushed against my clit as he spoke, his fingers working me toward my peak. "You want it so bad, don't you, baby? Want to come all over my fingers and my tongue."

"Yes," I breathed.

"But we're not going to stop there, are we? Before the end of the night, my wife's going to be coming all over my dick, too. This pretty pussy's going to take every inch of me while you scream for more."

His words shot through me like wildfire, and I tipped my head back, moaning toward the ceiling as the orgasm roared through me. Ford's answering groan only sent me higher, and I pulsed against him through my release.

But yet still, somehow, I ached for more. Ached for him to make good on every one of his promises.

While I was still trying to catch my breath, Ford stood, scooping me straight off the dresser and into his arms. I yelped and gripped his neck as he strode toward the bed before dropping me onto it.

"I want this *off*," he said, pushing the hem of my dress up and over my hips.

I froze, the old thoughts I'd spent years rewriting with the help of a therapist creeping in. It was one thing to have him eat me out while the majority of my body was covered. It was another thing altogether to be spread out on a bed for him, completely naked, with the July sun still shining brightly despite the hour, lighting up every square inch of our bedroom. Especially when the man who was seeing it looked like...*that*.

He climbed over me, bracing himself on either side of my shoulders as his gaze pinned me in place, his brow furrowed as if he could read my thoughts. His pupils were blown wide, his face flushed, lips still shiny from the two orgasms he'd given me with his mouth.

"If you think I don't want to see every inch of my wife's body the first time I fuck her, you're sorely mistaken." He sat back on his heels, his towel long gone, and draped my thighs over each of his, spreading me wide for him. Then he pressed his whole palm against my pussy, rubbing in slow circles and gathering all my wetness before gripping his shaft. "You see how much I want you, kitten? I'm hard as a fucking rock because of you."

I finally allowed my gaze to drift down his body, coming to rest where he stroked himself. And holy fuck.

Holy. Fuck.

I was woman enough to admit that I'd been wrong when I thought Ford's cock wouldn't be anything special. It was long and thick—so thick, I knew I'd have to work to take him all the way inside—with a silver barbell vertically through the flared head, precome leaking from the slit. And somehow, it looked infinitely better on him than in any of the pictures I'd seen online. I'd never imagined, or even fantasized about, being with someone with a pierced penis. But I couldn't deny the way my pussy pulsed at the sight. How would that feel against me...*inside* me?

"Those horny eyes are going to get you fucked, wife."

I snapped my gaze up to his, my face flushing as I shifted on the bed. I didn't know what Ford and I were to each other anymore. Didn't understand this sudden need I felt for him. But there was no use denying it anymore—I *wanted* him to fuck me. Desperately.

And, apparently, so did he.

"You believe me now?" he asked, his hand gripped tight around the base of his shaft, as if he was holding back an orgasm that had come too soon. "You believe me when I tell you you're fucking gorgeous and you make me so goddamn hard?"

Unable to deny it when the proof was staring me right in the face, I simply bit my lip and nodded.

"Good. Now take off that dress and show me what I've been fantasizing about since I was fifteen."

CHAPTER SEVENTEEN

FORD

AS SOON AS the words were out of my mouth, I wished I could snatch them back. Especially because of the look on her face. It was too much, too soon, and those kinds of confessions had no place in whatever the hell Quinn and I were doing. Married on paper, spouses in name only...

But I was about to fuck her like she was *mine*.

Not allowing her a chance to respond, I helped her strip off that cute little dress that had starred in more fantasies than I could count before unhooking her bra and tossing it to the side. And then I looked my fill.

"Jesus Christ, you're beautiful," I said, voice scraped raw.

And she was, all soft and inviting. From her hair spread out against my pillow to the slope of her jaw to those full lips and the lush curves of a body she'd been taunting me with for more than a decade. A body I'd dreamed about plenty but somehow still managed to get wrong because every filthy fantasy I'd concocted of her didn't hold a candle to the real thing.

"These tits have had me losing my fucking mind." I cupped them, groaning at how they spilled over my hands, and bent my head to suck one dark pink nipple into my mouth. I swirled my tongue around the tip, my cock twitching at her answering moan. "You like my mouth on you, kitten?"

She hesitated for a moment, then finally whispered, "Yes," as if she didn't want to admit the truth aloud.

But she still had a ways to go until she was as far gone as I was. I ached to be inside her with a need that was unmatched —to finally feel her under me, around me, consuming me.

Sunlight shone in through the windows, and I took full advantage of her spread out before me, cataloguing every inch. With her legs draped over my thighs, arms bent and hands resting beside her head, her pussy open and waiting for my dick, she looked like a feast prepared just for me. Ready and waiting for me to devour her.

"If you had any ideas that this would be a one-time thing, get those out of your head right now." I peered up at her from where my lips hovered over her nipple, and I scraped my bottom teeth over it. "I'm going to need a hell of a lot more than once to get my fill of you."

I swept my hands over her body, wanting to touch every single soft inch of her. Wanting to grip her tight while I fucked her through one orgasm and straight into the next. Fucked her so hard she screamed my name when she came.

My cock pulsed at the thought, and I sat back on my

heels, wrapping my hand around the base to stave off the orgasm that'd been breathing down my neck since my first taste of her pussy. I was hard as stone and aching with need, desperate to slide inside her.

But I needed her just as desperate for me.

Her pussy was still wet from the two orgasms I'd given her, her lips flushed a deep, dark pink, her clit swollen and needy. I swept the head of my cock through her slit, gathering her wetness before circling my barbell around her clit. She shuddered in response and bit her lip as she fisted the sheets on either side of her head, her body arching toward me.

"You like that?" I asked, unable to tamp down the self-satisfied lilt of my voice.

"I don't hate it," she said, her words stilted.

I chuckled under my breath and kept my touch featherlight, just the barest brush of my cock against her, until she was rocking her hips, tilting them toward me and attempting to get closer. But I wasn't ready to give her what she wanted just yet, so I kept it up, stroking her pussy but never sinking inside, driving us both wild.

And then, finally, she groaned, pressing her head back into the pillow as she pinched her eyes shut.

"You need something, kitten?" I'd intended for it to come out teasing, but my voice was rough, my need for her bearing down on me. She had me tied up in fucking knots, so desperate for her I could barely see straight.

"Stop asking questions you already know the answers to," she snapped, glaring up at me. "Yes, I need something, so would you do it already?"

"Do what?"

She dug her heels into my ass and reached down, sinking her nails into my thighs. "Stop teasing and fuck me."

"Well, all you had to do was ask..."

She opened her mouth, no doubt to snap back at me, but before she could, I settled my cock at her entrance and pressed just the tip inside her, groaning at the feel of her around me. She was tight and so fucking hot, I nearly came before even really getting inside her.

"*Oh shit*," she breathed, staring up at me with wide eyes while she gripped my thighs as if she needed the anchor to keep herself grounded.

I couldn't decide where I wanted to look more, so I split my gaze between her face, watching the expressions flit across it as I filled her, and her pussy, groaning as it stretched around my dick and took another inch of me inside her. "*Fuck*, kitten."

My cock was already throbbing with the desperate need to come, and I hadn't even gotten halfway inside her yet. She was tight enough that I had to work for it, so I braced my hand on her lower stomach, extending my thumb down to swirl circles around her clit, relaxing her even more so I could push a little deeper.

"Oh God," she said, fingers digging into my thighs. "Fuck, you're big."

I breathed out a pained laugh as her pussy rippled around me. "Why doesn't that sound like a compliment?"

"Because it's not. *Holy hell.*"

"How much more can you take, kitten?"

"There's *more*?" She snapped her head up, eyes huge as she stared down between us to where I disappeared inside her. "Oh Jesus. I should've known you'd try to murder me with your giant cock."

I breathed out a laugh, my dick throbbing as her cunt squeezed around me. "Not even halfway in yet, wife. But you wanted my cock, so you're going to take it." I continued to stroke her clit, pressing my other hand to the inside of her thigh and opening her up even more so I could ease farther inside. "There you go. Open up for me, baby. Be a good girl and let me all the way inside this pretty pussy."

"Ford," she panted, cupping one of her breasts and teasing her nipple, her other hand sliding down to join mine against her clit.

And motherfucking *hell*, there was no stopping me now. Not when my name passed those pretty lips while I was buried inside her and she guided my fingers with her own, showing me exactly how she like to be touched.

With a groan, I pushed forward, sliding the rest of the way in and settling my hips against the cradle of her thighs. "Look at you," I rasped, staring down to where we were joined. "Oh *fuck*, look at you."

She was obscene like this and so fucking gorgeous as she took me all the way in, her pussy spread wide around my shaft, her needy clit exposed completely.

"Oh my God, oh my God," she chanted, her eyes glazed as she stared up at me with something that looked an awful lot like awe. "God, you feel..."

"What, kitten?" I asked, pulling out slowly before sinking inside her again. "Tell me."

She moaned, hips rocking in time to my slow thrusts. "So good. Why is it *so good*?"

"Because this pussy was made for me." I held her hips, digging my fingers into her soft flesh and loving how her body gave against my grip. "Now let's see if I can make you scream..."

Holding her still, I snapped my hips forward, setting a steady rhythm that dragged my barbell against her G-spot with every thrust. Her eyes were glazed, fingers working frantically over her clit, her pussy tightening around me with every stroke.

"That's my good girl. Rub that pretty little clit for me. Make yourself come all over my cock so I can fill you up."

That thought alone had my balls drawing up tight, ready to explode. I'd never once fucked without a condom—hadn't thought much about it, to be honest, because it was just a fact of life. But for reasons I couldn't articulate, I was desperate to spill myself inside her. Desperate to sate my need inside my wife and see her filled with my come.

"Quinn," I managed through gritted teeth.

"Almost," she panted. "Almo—"

She didn't even get the word out before she bowed off the bed, her head pressed back into the pillow, eyes closed as she screamed her release.

"Fuck yes, there it is. Christ, you look beautiful coming all over my cock like a good girl. Such a good fucking girl." I groaned, thrusting one last time and settling as deep inside her as I could, her pussy squeezing my shaft as she came.

I couldn't take it anymore and finally loosened the control I'd held on to so tightly. With a groan of her name, I exploded inside her, my orgasm ripping through me. I dropped my head to her chest, panting through my release, distantly aware of her fingers running through my hair.

It felt so good—*she* felt so fucking good—I didn't allow myself to second-guess what we'd done or worry over the fact that this was supposed to be a fake marriage but I'd just fucked my wife into oblivion.

And I had no intention of stopping anytime soon.

CHAPTER EIGHTEEN

QUINN

THE BLUEBERRY FEST was being held downtown, near the park, with vendor offerings ranging from pie to wine to scented body products and everything in between, all befitting the blueberry theme.

Even though it was a beautiful late July day, if I had it my way, I would've avoided attending this altogether. But since Ford had a booth—a dunk tank fundraiser he'd come up with for the little league team I'd had no idea he and Aiden coached—Addison had cornered me yesterday and told me I was going whether I wanted to or not. And I'd come to realize that when Addison had her mind set on something, there was no use arguing with her.

Besides, she'd had a point when she'd said Ford and I needed to keep up appearances to make everyone buy this coupling—especially when Dr. Dicknose still refused to entertain any discussion of my purchasing the clinic. Little did she know, this coupling was more real than I'd ever intended, and I didn't know what to do about that. It had been plaguing me since the night Ford and I had slept together—both literally and figuratively—and I'd fallen asleep with him curled around me, my mind and emotions a jumbled mess.

So...I'd avoided. Him, yes. But more specifically, sex.

It had been easy at first... I'd been sore—like, holy shit, *had my hymen actually grown back and he just devirginized me again?* sore—so that was a plausible excuse to skip another round with Ford and his magic peen. Then he'd had a twenty-four-hour shift at the firehouse—one that had, surprisingly, kept him busy around the clock with various calls and emergencies, which meant he'd crashed as soon as he'd gotten home. After that, our schedules hadn't synced up for a few days, so that was an unplanned but welcome reprieve.

Then I'd had to get creative.

First, I'd told him I was too tired to do anything but crash after rearranging the furniture in the cottage. Then I said I thought I might be allergic to his shampoo, so he shouldn't get too close to me. Then I'd blamed it on a stubbed toe.

The excuses were weak at best, and the worst part was, he saw right through them. Immediately.

Instead of pushing, he allowed me my space. But anytime I was around him, I could feel his eyes on me, heavy and weighted, brushing over my skin like a caress, and I hated how much I liked it. How much I'd come to crave it in such a short period of time.

In public, he played the doting husband, bringing me

lunch at the clinic or carrying my bags for me when Addison had forced us together for errands. And he somehow always knew when I had an exceptionally challenging day and needed an emotional support coffee, delivering it to me without my having to say a word.

When he did those things, I was confused all over again, wondering if he was doing this because he wanted to or because it was expected of him as my fake husband.

While we were at home, he gave me space. On his days off from the fire station, he busied himself with projects around the resort and then crashed hard at night... On *his* side of the bed.

And in between it all, he ate me up with his gaze, not bothering to hide the fact that he was eye-fucking me every chance he got. It was clear he knew exactly what I was doing, and he was just biding his time until I finally gave in.

But I couldn't.

I didn't know what the hell was happening between Ford and me, but I wasn't so sure I wanted to figure it out. Not yet.

As sad as it was, our relationship was probably the most consistent and safe one I had in my life. I knew what to expect from it and him. I had acquaintances, sure. And *hey, how's it going* friends like Everly and even Addison, but none who'd worked their way into my inner circle and past the walls I'd erected long ago. Walls I'd learned to put in place to protect myself.

Antagonistic as it was, Ford's and my relationship was a pleasant reprieve from what I was used to, and I wasn't quite ready for that to change. Not when my only other true relationships were with my narcissistic parents who'd kept me on my toes my entire life as I guessed what they needed from me in an attempt to avoid ridicule. Getting married without telling them *wasn't* the way to do this apparently, as my mother not so gently pointed out when she'd called in a fury last week.

"About time you got here," Addison said, pulling me out of my thoughts. She hooked an arm through mine and turned us around, steering us in the opposite direction.

"So we're going this way, then?" I asked on a laugh.

"Of course we are. Your *husband* is this way." She glanced around then lowered her voice and tipped her head closer to mine. "Honestly, it's like you two *want* to get found out. I thought we were going for gold here. I can't have another yearly appointment with that weasel-faced fuckhead, Quinn. I *can't*."

I snorted at her descriptor, but her words, blunt as they were, were exactly the reminder I needed. There was more at stake here than my libido. My ultimate goal to own Starlight Cove's clinic was going to have a real impact on this community, and I couldn't allow myself to get derailed from it, no matter how magical Ford's cock was.

"I'm working on it," I said. "But Dr. Dicknose is dragging his feet."

"Um, first of all, *love* the nickname," she said, guiding us past the vendor booths and toward the east side of the festival. It was late and everything was beginning to wind down, but plenty of residents were still out wandering around. "Second, how's he dragging his feet?"

I blew out a frustrated sigh. "Every time I bring it up, he finds an excuse to cut the conversation short or avoid it entirely."

"Well, maybe it's not malicious. Maybe he's just being an idiot, like usual. In the meantime, you need to keep up the act. Which reminds me..." She reached into her pocket before slipping something into my hand.

I glanced down at it, then back to her. "What's this?"

"A key."

I rolled my eyes. "Yeah, I got that. A key for what? Where'd you get it?"

"From Aiden, who got it from Mabel. It's for the Pleasure Palace."

I scrunched my nose at what Mabel had named her she-shed where she sometimes hosted parties featuring the toys she sold, still not used to it even after living with her for months.

"Okay... Why did Mabel give this to him? What was he supposed to do with it?"

Addison waved her hand through the air. "That woman is constantly trying to get my brothers laid. It's disturbing, to say the least."

"Well, that's...something I wish I didn't know."

"Doesn't matter—it's not the point."

"What exactly is the point? You want me to find a girl in the crowd for Aiden and slip this to her so they can get in a quickie?"

"Um, *ew*?" she said, scrunching up her nose before

shaking her head. "Wouldn't matter anyway. Anonymous sex isn't really his style."

I held up the key between two fingers. "Focus, Addison."

"Right." She stopped walking and turned to face me, hands on her hips. "It's for you to sneak away with your husband... *Obviously*. I don't care what you two do in there as long as there's no bloodshed. Just make the escape look good —like you can't keep your hands off each other. We want the entire town talking about it, so good old Dickie won't have a choice but to believe it."

Well, that was just fantastic. I needed to have a pretend quickie with my pretend husband who was *actually* my husband and whom I'd *actually* had amazing and not at all pretend sex with and was now avoiding. That clusterfuck explanation pretty much summed up exactly how difficult this was going to be.

I glanced behind Addison, my gaze immediately connecting with Ford's. Even with all the commotion going on around his booth, his eyes were trained on me, and a shiver slid down my spine at his pointed attention. He was enclosed in the tank, shirtless and sitting on the levered stool, as people tried to hit the target. His hair wasn't wet, but that didn't mean anything with how hot it was outside; he could've easily dried off, thanks to the sun. And even though the festival was winding down, the kid currently tossing balls at the target looked determined as hell, so I wasn't so sure Ford wouldn't be dunked at least once more.

Worse, I wasn't sure I'd be able to handle a shirtless, dripping wet Ford. Especially when he was looking at me like *that*. Like he was replaying every second of our night together. Like he was remembering exactly how it had felt to be inside me. Like he wished we didn't have these layers of clothes between us.

His gaze did unspeakable things to me, and I wasn't so sure I was strong enough to resist them. Thank God we were in public.

CHAPTER NINETEEN

FORD

MY WIFE HAD BEEN AVOIDING me like the plague, and I was tired of it.

She'd given me every excuse in the book to escape being near me. It had made sense at first—I had no doubt she was sore when mine was the first cock she'd taken in three years. But the longer it went on, the more ridiculous each excuse got until it was clear exactly what she was doing.

Now, she stood off to the side next to my sister, wearing one of those flirty fucking dresses. The kind that drove me damn near feral with my need to have her. Worse, it was the same one she'd been wearing the first night I'd fucked her. The hem kissed her thick thighs, the neckline dipping low enough to give me a glimpse of those gorgeous, full tits, and I was *done*.

I was done playing this bullshit game, and I was done waiting. Quinn wanted me just as much as I wanted her—I'd woken up so many times to her, still sleeping but grinding herself all over my dick, my name a whimpered plea on her lips—and I wanted to know why she was punishing us both by not giving in to what we both clearly wanted.

And if I had to fuck the answers out of her, so be it.

I had five minutes left of this dunk tank fundraiser—a last-minute idea I'd pitched to the Blueberry Fest coordinator with a promise to fix her front porch steps if she'd let me slip in for free—and then I was going to grab Quinn, drag her back home, and we were going to work this out, one way or another.

"Come on, Bobby." Aiden clapped from the sidelines as one of the kids on our team wound up, ready to throw his attempt to dunk me. "You're our last hope. Send him down!"

"You should be the one in here, you asshole," I said for his ears only.

"Your idea, your ass in the tank. Those are the rules."

"You and your fucking rules," I grumbled under my breath.

I wasn't sure how much we'd raised so far, but there had been a steady line of people attempting to dunk me. Luckily, I'd only been taken down a handful of times, and it was hot enough out that I dried off quickly. While I didn't want to do this every day, it was fun watching the kids on the team practice their throws and cheer one another on, even if it was at my expense.

Scary as it was, I was a stand-in father figure for some of these kids, especially the ones like Bobby, who lived with just his widowed grandmother. When the resort first sponsored the team and I started coaching it with Aiden, I hadn't realized just how...fulfilling that would be.

I also hadn't realized just how many memories it would dredge up.

As a kid, I'd had a father, but I hadn't had a *present* father —still didn't, actually. No one to cheer for me at games or play catch in the backyard. Brady had been that person for me and the rest of our siblings, because our dad was usually passed out on the couch by noon. Hell, Brady was *still* that person, because our dad didn't care enough about us to step foot outside Cottage Thirteen even to say thank you for the shit we dropped off at his door to make sure he was taken care of. He'd sequestered himself there ten years ago after Mom had died at sea in a storm, and we hadn't seen heads or tails of him since.

So yeah...now that I was able to be that someone for a kid who needed it? It was rewarding in a way I hadn't anticipated.

Which was why, when Bobby's ball connected with the target and sent me down, I wasn't even mad. I dropped into the water and surfaced to the cheers of the crowd. I shook the hair out of my face and watched as Aiden—that traitor— lifted Bobby onto his shoulder. The kid raised his arms above him in a victory V, his grin aimed my way while his grandma laughed from the sidelines.

But that wasn't the smile that had me snared. That achievement belonged to my wife.

Quinn, now standing alone, looked on, just the subtlest curve to her lips as she watched this all unfold, and I couldn't

BRIGHTON WALSH

wait another second. Couldn't be smart or methodical about this. Couldn't plan out the best way to approach it.

I was *done*. And whether she wanted to or not, we were working this shit out right now.

Without bothering with a towel, I slipped out of the tank and stalked toward her, uncaring of the fact that I was dripping along the way. My swim trunks were bogged down with water and hanging damn near indecently low on my hips, but I couldn't focus on any of that. Not when I had a mission in mind.

As soon as Quinn realized what I was doing, her eyes went wide, and she started backing up. "Ford..." she called to me, a warning in her voice as she held a hand out in front of her. "What are you doing?"

"I'm greeting my wife. Aren't you happy to see me?"

She shot a frantic gaze around, no doubt realizing that all eyes were on us. This was our first public event as husband and wife, which meant we had to play this up. We had no choice but to be *on* in front of half the town.

And I damn well was going to take full advantage of that when she'd been icing me out at home.

The closer I got, the narrower her eyes grew until she hissed in a low voice, "Don't you dare..."

"Aw, don't be like that, kitten," I said, eating up the space between us. "You know you want a hug and kiss from your brand-new husband."

"Stop it. You're going to get me all wet."

"Good. That's always my goal." Finally to her, I cupped

204

her ass in one hand and hauled her up against me, lifting her straight off the ground.

Fuck, it felt good to have her in my arms again. I had no idea what she was doing to me, no idea why I craved her so much. No idea why I felt this constant hunger to touch her, but I did. There was no use denying that anymore.

With a yelp, she threw one arm around my shoulder and reached back with the other, trying to tug at the bottom of her dress as she wrapped her legs around my waist. "Seriously? The hand on my ass is a little excessive, don't you think?" she snapped in a low voice. "You better not be giving everyone a show of my panties."

I pressed my mouth to her ear, tracing my bottom lip along the shell. "Believe me, kitten, no one gets to see your sweet ass and that pretty little cunt but me."

A shudder racked her body, and I pulled back to look at her. Her lips were parted, cheeks flushed and eyes bright, and she could play that she was mad all she wanted, but I knew her expressions well enough to know, without a doubt, this wasn't anger. This was desire, thick and undeniable.

"Everyone's watching," I murmured, tipping my face to hers. "Time to kiss me, wife."

"You are such an ass," she hissed.

I pressed my lips to the underside of her jaw, forcing her to tip her head back, and carried her through the crowd, uncaring of the murmurs around us as we went. I was desperate to get her someplace semi-private so I could finally get my fill of her. "An ass you loved enough to pledge the rest of your life to. Are you going to kiss me, so all these people know how desperately you want me?"

"I hate you," she whispered, but the way she stared at my mouth, licking her lips as if she was just waiting for my kiss, belied her words.

"No, you don't. You love this game we play. Tell me you want it." I scraped my teeth over her earlobe and pressed my lips to the shell. "Tell me you want it, wife, and I'll give it to you."

"Everyone's looking," she said, even though her eyes never strayed from mine. "Just kiss me already."

She could blame it on whatever she wanted so long as she gave me the permission I needed. Without hesitation, I pressed her up against the nearest building, pinned her to it with my hips, and took her mouth with mine.

Christ, it'd only been two weeks since I'd last tasted her— and a fucking lifetime before that—so how did her lips on mine already feel like coming home?

She opened for me and groaned into my mouth, her arms tightening around my neck as she slid her tongue against mine. *Fuck.* I hadn't thought this through before I'd shoved her against this wall. I was hard as a fucking rock while wearing swim trunks that left absolutely nothing to the imagination. Worse, I'd loosened my restraint, the only thing that had been keeping me in check. And now that it was gone, I needed to fuck her. Badly.

"Ford," she panted, tipping her head back when I dragged my mouth down the column of her neck. "We can't do this here."

Distant sounds of the crowd filtered to me, kids yelling and playing, and I definitely wasn't interested in giving them this kind of show.

"You're right, but we're doing this somewhere, and we're doing it *now*. You've got me all fucked up, so desperate for you, I can't even smell your goddamn shampoo without getting hard." I gripped her hip and pressed myself against the cradle of her thighs, groaning when I felt her heat through my soaked trunks. "And with the way you keep trying to grind that pussy down on me, you feel the same."

Her cheeks flared bright red, her eyes flashing with that fire I loved so much. "Don't tell me what I feel."

"Am I wrong?" I asked. "Tell me I'm wrong, kitten, and I'll set you down and meet you back at the cottage, where you can keep feeding me your bullshit excuses just to avoid this thing between us. Tell me, and I'll jack it in the shower with your soap just like I have been for the past two weeks. Tell me," I urged. "And don't fucking lie."

With a glare, she snapped her mouth shut, pressing her lips into a thin line. Not saying a damn word.

"That's what I thought. Now find me someplace and do it quick because I'm tired of the games. I told you this wouldn't be a one-time thing. I need to fuck my wife."

My words seemed to spur her on, and she glanced around, her eyes brightening when her gaze landed on something behind me. "I have a key!"

I glanced behind me to see what she was looking at. I'd managed to walk us to the area where residences started to bleed into downtown, houses interspersed with small businesses for another block or so. And right on the cusp of that area was Mabel and George's home.

My brows flew up to my hairline. "You want to fuck in Mabel's house?"

"God no," she said, then lifted her chin to the right of the house. "But I have a key to her she-shed."

Mabel's Pleasure Palace—dubbed the smut shed by locals —was where she hosted some of her sex toy parties, and I could only imagine what lay within those walls. But I didn't care. Not when I was thirty seconds away from being inside Quinn again.

So, with her legs still wrapped around me, I took off in that direction, forcing myself not to flat-out sprint.

"You're seriously going to carry me there?" she asked, the barest hint of amusement in her voice.

"You're damn right I am. The only reason I'm going to let you down is to bend you over, flip up that little skirt, and sink inside the pussy I haven't been able to stop thinking about since the last time I fucked you."

Quinn shuddered in my arms, and I picked up my pace, my need to be inside her a constant thrum in my cock. When we got close, she fumbled in her pocket before pulling out the key in triumph and unlocking the door.

I didn't hesitate to step inside and kick it shut behind us. The space was small, and though I'd never seen the interior, I couldn't be bothered to pay attention now. Not when I had tunnel vision for my wife.

I set her down in front of a narrow table that ran the length of the front window. There were no blinds or curtains, meaning everyone who walked by on the path ten yards away would be able to see clearly inside. But I couldn't be bothered to worry about that. Not when Quinn was standing in front of me, looking as if she'd stepped straight out of one of my dirty dreams.

I *had* gotten her wet, the front of her dress clinging to her full tits and that soft belly and those fucking thighs I wanted wrapped around my head. The pale purple sundress was one of her favorites—mine, too. I could barely drag my eyes away whenever she wore it.

She was a goddamn wet dream come to life, and she was *my wife.*

A wife I hadn't fucked in two weeks because of some bullshit she'd concocted in her head to keep us apart. Well, I was done. *Done.* I wasn't going to let her avoid the inevitable any longer.

I spun her around so she faced the window and flipped up that flirty little skirt, taking in the lush curves and scrap of lace she wore underneath. "Jesus Christ," I muttered, running my finger along her ass beneath the pale blue lace. "Who'd you wear these for, wife? Were you hoping I'd see them?"

"No," she snapped at me over her shoulder, that fire shining bright in her eyes. "I wore them for *me.* Women can wear lingerie for themselves, you know."

I chuckled under my breath. "I might believe you if you weren't tilting your hips up to get me to touch you."

And I wanted to. *Fuck,* I wanted to. Over the past two weeks, I'd jacked off in the shower to thoughts of her more times than I could count, like I was fifteen all over again.

Though my hand had been a satisfactory substitute while my dick was on strike...now? After I'd been inside the tight little heaven she had between her legs? *Nothing* compared to that.

"You've run the show for two weeks, and I've let you, but I'm done." I dug my fingers into the soft flesh of her ass and pressed my lips to her ear. "I'm going to fuck you in here, kitten. Right in front of this window so anyone walking by can look in and see that I couldn't wait to get my wife home before I had to be inside her perfect cunt."

Her reflection stared back at me, making my dick even harder. Her eyes were glazed, her attention transfixed on the people walking along the sidewalk, cheeks flushed as she dug her teeth into her bottom lip. She *liked* that idea. And I'd bet anything she was wet as hell.

"Is that what you want?" I asked.

A slight hesitation, then a whispered, "Yes."

"You don't have to be embarrassed with me, kitten. I want to know everything that turns you on. Everything that gets you off, including the idea of getting caught. You like that, don't you? Like that there's a possibility someone will look this way and know how good you're getting fucked."

She shuddered against my chest as I reached around and cupped her full tits, brushing my thumbs over the hardened peaks. "*Yes.*"

I ran my lips over her shoulder, sucking at the spot that had her moaning my name last time. "But first, I need to check something."

"What?" She arched her hips, rubbing her ass against my cock.

"I'm going to reach into those panties and see if your pussy's wet. And if it is? Your ass is getting spanked because you've been denying it what it needs. Now put your hands on the table and let me see."

With only the briefest pause—no doubt her stubbornness over giving me an inch—she did as I said, a shudder working its way through her body. And if I had any question about whether having my palm crack on her backside was something she'd be into, the wiggle of her ass as she tried to get closer to me told me everything I needed to know.

"You know what I think I'm going to find, kitten? I think I'm going to find you've made a mess of these cocktease panties. That your needy little cunt has soaked all the way through."

Slipping my finger under the lace edge, I guided it down the generous curve of her ass and then between her legs, groaning when I felt just how wet she was. I slipped my finger inside her, pumping slowly before pulling it out and sucking it clean with a groan, tasting just how much she wanted me.

"I fucking knew it." I smacked my palm down hard on her ass, her answering moan and the pinkening of her cheek sending a shock wave straight to my dick.

"How long has this pussy been craving me?" I asked, dropping my hand between her thighs once more and pressing my fingers tight to her clit. "How long have you needed your husband's cock?"

With her head hanging between her shoulders, she shifted against my hand, trying to work my fingers in some kind of rhythm, but I didn't budge. Not yet. It was torture for us both, but I needed her answer. For *both* of us, because I had little doubt she'd been lying to herself, too.

Finally, she whimpered and shook her head. "Don't make me say it."

I chuckled under my breath, slipping two, then three fingers into her pussy and groaning when she tilted her hips, trying to take me deeper. "Whether you say it or not doesn't stop it from being true. Now tell me."

"The whole time," she whispered.

"That's what I thought." I pumped my fingers into her, my cock growing harder with every whimper that left her lips, every flutter of her pussy around me.

She groaned and dropped her forehead to the window. "Please, Ford."

"What, baby?" I scraped my teeth along her neck, sinking them into the juncture of her shoulder. "What do you need?"

"Take my panties off and get inside me."

"I don't think so."

"What—"

"A little scrap of lace isn't going to keep me from your pussy, kitten." I slipped my fingers from her and slid her panties to the side, groaning when she angled her hips back and gave me an unobstructed view of her. She was dark pink, swollen with need, and so wet, it glistened on her inner thighs.

Shoving down the front of my trunks, I pulled out my cock and swiped the head through her slit, coating myself in her wetness and teasing her clit with my piercing. "You're going to keep these soaked panties on while I fuck you, so you remember what happens when you deny us. My wife's pussy deserves to be taken care of, and I'm the one who gets the privilege. So quit punishing us and give us what we both want."

"Yes," she breathed, and I couldn't wait another second to be inside her. Had waited too fucking long already.

I notched myself at her entrance and thrust into her, sliding deep on a groan. Fuck me, she was tight, her body molding to mine like it was made for me.

Like *she* was made for me.

"You feel this?" I gripped her hair and tugged her head back. Pressing my lips to her ear, I pumped into her and reached around with my other hand, fingering her clit in fast circles. "You feel how fucking good we are together? How much your pussy wants this? How much I fucking *crave* you?"

"*Yes.*"

"No more denying this, wife. No more bullshit excuses."

"No more," she agreed, her hands flat on the window as she panted, tipping her hips to allow me deeper inside her.

"That's what I wanted to hear." I flicked her clit to the rhythm of my thrusts, shifting my hips until I found the perfect angle to slide my piercing over that spot inside her. As soon as I hit it, she jolted and her walls fluttered around me, a loud moan falling from her lips.

"There it is, kitten... There it fucking is. Now be a good girl and come all over your husband's cock. I want to feel exactly what I do to you. Want to know how good I served my wife's pussy."

"*Oh my God.*" She dropped one of her hands to join mine as we stroked her clit in increasingly fast circles. Her pussy tightened around me until she sobbed out a moan. With her head dropped back on my shoulder, eyes clenched shut, she came in a whole-body shudder as she screamed her release loud enough there was little doubt those walking by could hear.

"That's it, baby. That's my girl. That's my good fucking girl." I clenched my teeth as she pulsed around me, nearly taking me over the edge with her. But I wasn't done yet. Not by a long shot. "Look at you. So fucking gorgeous coming all over your husband's cock."

"*Ford,*" she choked out, the waves of her orgasm still rippling through her, but it was clear she still wanted more.

Pressing my hand between her shoulder blades, I pushed her facedown on the table. Our groans filled the space when the new position allowed me even deeper inside her.

"*Fuck.*" Faintly, I worried about hurting her. About taking her too hard, especially after so long, but given her breathy moan when I thrust deep and her pleas for *more, God yes, more,* I couldn't stop. Couldn't stop the snap of my hips, the tight grip of my fingers on her ass, my hand fisted in her hair, tugging her head back to look at me.

I needed her to know she was *mine.* For however long this lasted between us, she was mine. Mine to take care of. Mine to make come. Mine to fuck.

Mine.

"Give me another one, baby. Just one more. Come all over me and show me what's mine."

She pressed a hand between us and strummed her clit, her fingers slipping down to where I was pumping into her, and I had to grit my teeth against the urge to come. But then she was looking back at me, lips parted, cheeks flushed, eyes glazed and filled with something more than desire. Those eyes fluttered closed as she tightened impossibly around me and then burst, her pussy squeezing my dick as she found her second release.

"There you go, kitten. You come for me so fucking well. The next time you get it in your pretty little head that we shouldn't do this, I want you to remember just how hard you came all over my cock."

Her soft little whimper paired with the flutter of her pussy around me sent me over the edge. Unable to hold back any longer, I settled deep and spilled myself inside her, losing two weeks of frustration in her perfect body.

With my forehead pressed to her shoulder, I matched my panting breaths to hers, all the while wondering if I could make this fake marriage last longer than the six weeks we had left. Because fuck knew I wasn't ready to be done with this. Wasn't anywhere near done with her.

CHAPTER TWENTY

QUINN

A WEEK LATER, I sat on the small set of bleachers at the ballpark where Ford and Aiden ran little league practice, along with a smattering of parents and a few nosy onlookers. My attendance here had been another of Addison's *suggestions*. And by that, I obviously meant demands. The girl had made it her personal mission to make sure Ford and I were seen everywhere together, all the while acting like a couple in love.

After last week's...incident, I wasn't sure we needed to worry about it. Ford and I had, in fact, been the talk of the town, just like Addison wanted. And Mabel hadn't hidden her smugness over the fact that we'd used her Pleasure Palace to sneak off and have some fun. She wasn't even upset Aiden hadn't used it as she'd hoped, so long as it had gotten used.

I'd never met a person—her age or otherwise—who was so invested in the health and enjoyment of people's sex lives, but more power to her.

And there was no denying Ford's and my sex life was healthy. That may have been the only part of our relationship that was, but I wasn't going to complain. I was getting regular D for the first time in years, and I wasn't mad about it. Especially when that D was attached to someone who knew exactly how to use it.

The two-hour little league practice was nearly up. I'd watched Ford—and Aiden, but let's be real...my gaze mostly stayed locked on my husband—interact with the kids, being his usual carefree self. He was exactly as I'd expected him to be—kind, funny, goofing off with the children, and not taking anything too seriously.

What I did *not* expect was the softer side of him and just how good he was with the kids. Or how much it would make me want to melt.

In the dugout, he knelt in front of one of the kids. With blond pigtails braided over her shoulders, Cassidy was one of only three girls on the team. She'd just struck out—again—and though no tears streaked her face, I could tell it was taking everything in her not to shed them. Her bottom lip quivered, her eyes bright and glassy, and I wanted to wrap her up in a hug and tell her everything would be all right. That she didn't have to be strong all the time, but as that was something I hadn't yet mastered in my life, my advice would've fallen flat.

This was...just who I was. Who I'd conditioned myself to be after years of sly abuse at the hands of my parents. I'd always been the aloof one. The one people thought was snobby or stuck-up, but it'd been my barrier. And I'd perfected it in my thirty-one years, using it as a shield from those who didn't think I could do something. Or worse, who actively tried to knock me down.

But it turned out Cassidy didn't need a hug from me or false words I didn't actually take to heart. Not when she had Ford.

I sat directly behind them, close enough to hear his words, though I wasn't sure anyone else could.

"You know you did awesome, right?" he said.

"I didn't do awesome. I struck out twice!"

"Striking out is all part of the game, Cass. Even the pros do it."

"Not as much as me." She folded her arms over her chest, brows drawn down and her bottom lip stuck out in a pout.

"You know they miss more balls than they hit, right?"

"They do?"

"Yep...they usually hit fewer than a third of what's pitched to them. And they're out there making millions every year. So we're going to give ourselves a break for not playing as well as they do, all right?"

"Okay," she said, though her voice was wobbly, and those tears she'd been trying so hard to hold back rolled in two fat drops down her red cheeks.

"Today was just one day in a whole lot of them. We all have off days. But the point is that you show up and try again. That you don't give up if it's something you love." He reached up, swiping away her tears with his thumbs.

I wasn't so sure I hadn't turned into a puddle right there on these uncomfortable bleachers, because holy shit. *Holy shit*. What I wouldn't have given to hear that kind of pep talk as a kid. Or, hell, as a teen or even an adult.

The people I'd surrounded myself with—my parents, especially—were more inclined to point out all my flaws. For as long as I could remember—the first time happened when I was six and fumbled a step in my dance recital—they'd focused on everything I'd done wrong.

They also liked to remind me exactly how my fuckup would affect *them*. How their friends would view them if I didn't get straight A's, didn't graduate as valedictorian, didn't go to Harvard Med School. It didn't matter what I *did* accomplish. That paled in comparison to their expectations.

Their words were never about lifting my spirits and encouraging me to do better. To try again. It was always about how disappointed they were. How I could've done better. How embarrassed they were to have me as a daughter.

So I'd resorted to giving those talks to myself. The problem was, my words weren't always the kindest where I was involved. I had a lot of grace for my patients and for the few people I considered friends or even acquaintances.

But for myself? Hardly any. I was a perfectionist, and nothing was good enough for my standards. Not even my best.

"You ready to get back out there with your team?" Ford asked the little girl. "They need you in the field. No one catches a pop fly like you do."

Swiping the back of her hand over her eyes, she nodded and bumped her fist against Ford's when he held his out to her. She picked up her glove and ran to her position on the field, shooting her teammates a bright smile, her spirit clearly lifted.

Ford stood then and glanced over at me, his ball cap low over his eyes, and shot me a grin. Butterflies erupted in my stomach at the single, inconsequential glance.

I'd just finally acknowledged that it was okay to enjoy our bedroom activities. That it was perfectly acceptable to allow him to make me come since he seemed to have a knack for it and did so amazingly. And we *were* married, after all, so it wasn't like either of us could get it elsewhere.

But now? After witnessing that?

I was beginning to worry I might actually *like* my husband.

"YOU MIND if we stop someplace on the way home?" Ford asked, driving us away from the ballpark. One of his hands rested on the steering wheel, the other on my thigh, his thumb brushing over my skin. His fingers were tucked absent-mindedly beneath the hem of my sundress, and this was not good. Not good at all.

"Sure," I said, trying to keep my voice even. Pretending like I wasn't freaking out on the inside over my shocking realization on the bleachers.

How the hell had this happened? How had I *let* this happen? He was supposed to be my rival. My nemesis. The one person who'd challenged nearly every high school success I'd had, who'd made the planned dominoes of my future to land off track, caused so many of those early disappointments and so much harsh criticism from my parents... And he was starting to get under my skin.

Worse, I was beginning to wonder if I'd been wrong about him all along.

Had he always been the guy he'd shown me these past few weeks as his wife? The guy who laughed freely, who offered himself up on a silver platter in the name of a fundraiser, who gave a pep talk to a disappointed eight-year-old... The guy who brought his fake wife flowers and ice cream and emotional support coffees and subtly but firmly put Dr. Dicknose in his place anytime he was around.

"Shouldn't take too long," he said. "Bob called during practice and left a message that the new uniforms are ready. And then we can pick up some Chinese on the way home."

Which was, unsurprisingly, what I'd been craving all week, though I couldn't remember ever actually voicing it. But Ford was more astute than I'd given him credit for, especially when it came to me.

He pulled into the parking lot of Bob's Sports Shop and put his Jeep into park. "You want to stay out here or come in?"

I unbuckled my seat belt, knowing if I waited in the car, I'd just fixate on everything that had been knocking around in my brain, and that absolutely was not a good use of my time or focus. "I'll come in. I want to see these uniforms you willingly got dunked for."

"Yeah, they better be fucking amazing, or I'm gonna be pissed." His laughter belied his words as he climbed out of the car and strode around to my side, meeting me at the hood. Without hesitation, he grabbed my hand, linking our fingers together as if it were second nature, and guided us inside.

Bob's was a small, family-owned shop. A glass case full of varying trophy styles took up the far wall behind the counter, and racks filled up the rest of the store, showcasing several uniform offerings.

"Ford," an older white man with a bald head and a wide smile greeted him. "Looks like you got my message."

"Hey, Bob. You got the goods?"

"Sure do. And they're real beauts." He opened up a box and pulled out a royal-blue jersey. It had their team name in bright white on the front and an embroidered *19* below Starlight Cove Resort's logo on the back. "I think you made an excellent choice with these. The kids are gonna love them."

"That they are," Ford agreed, running his fingers over the embroidery, a smile tipping up the corners of his mouth. "What's the damage?"

Bob shuffled through some papers before announcing the total, and my eyes nearly bugged out. But Ford just nodded as if he'd been expecting it. The thing was, I knew exactly how much the dunk tank fundraiser had made, and it only covered a little more than half of the total.

"You want the rest of this on the resort's tab?" Bob asked, handwriting a receipt like we were back in 1953.

"Nah, put it on this." Ford plucked a credit card from his wallet and slid it across the counter toward Bob.

And goddammit. *Goddammit.*

The hits just kept coming.

Why did he have to be a genuinely good guy...a truly kind person? And why did I have to suddenly become aware of it?

I knew I should be happy about this. Happy about the fact that I was beginning to actually like—not just tolerate—my husband, but I feared that would only complicate things further.

I was already married to the man. And God knew we were compatible sexually. What happened if we clicked on an entirely different level? What happened if we slipped into something neither of us had planned for or expected when we'd agreed to this marriage on paper only?

What kind of tangled web would that weave?

CHAPTER TWENTY-ONE

FORD

AFTER A LONG SHIFT at the firehouse, I strolled up the front steps of the cottage. It had been busier than usual—among others, we'd had a call for a possible heart attack that turned out to be an intense panic attack, a carbon monoxide leak, and a three-car collision on the highway. I was exhausted and ready to crash, but I wasn't about to do that before I got in some time with my wife.

I unlocked the door and stepped inside, my ears perking up at Quinn's voice coming from the bedroom.

"Well, he obviously sees something in me, or he wouldn't have married me," she said, her voice strained.

Brow furrowed, I set my keys on the counter and strode toward the room, stopping just inside the doorway. Quinn's back was to me as she hung her head, defeat cloaking every inch of her. And I wanted to know who the fuck was making her feel that way.

She didn't say anything for long moments, but whoever

was on the other line was giving her enough of an earful that I could hear the murmur of it from where I stood, even without the call on speaker.

"No, I'm—" She breathed out a frustrated sound and tipped her head back to stare at the ceiling, her hand curled into a fist at her side. Her shoulders were rigid, her entire body tense, and I'd had enough.

I slipped into the room and walked up behind her, my steps faltering at Quinn's next words.

"My relationship with my husband is none of your concern, Mother. I promise that what we do or don't do is not meant to embarrass you."

This was her *mother* who was speaking to her like this?

Quinn had alluded to not having a great relationship with her parents, but I'd assumed it was in the typical *they irritate me, but I love them* kind of way. Not in the *they berate me and tear me down every chance they get* kind of way.

I stood close enough now that, even without the call being on speaker, I could make out every word Mrs. Cartwright said, her tone shrill and harsh.

"You're the most ungrateful child I've ever met. After everything we've done for you...after your father got you that job...and this is how you repay us? Flaunting yourself around town like that... Even if it was with your *husband*. You should be mortified. It's no wonder you don't have any friends when this is how you behave."

What. The. *Fuck*.

With my mouth set in a grim line, I reached up, ready to snatch the phone away and give that bitch a piece of my mind when three beeps sounded, indicating she'd hung up on her daughter.

Instead of getting mad like I'd expected, instead of lashing out like she would've done if I'd been on the other end of that phone, Quinn just tossed her phone on the nightstand and pressed her fingers to her forehead, her shoulders curling forward.

I'd never wanted to comfort someone more in my life. I wanted to wrap my arms around her, squeeze her tight, and remind her just how fucking amazing she was.

But I knew Quinn well enough to realize she wouldn't want any outright coddling. In fact, I was pretty sure she might knee me in the junk if I tried.

So instead, I cleared my throat to warn her of my presence and smacked her ass before she could turn around.

She gasped, spinning to face me, a hand on her chest. "Ford!" Her cheeks were flushed, her brow pinched, and I hated her mother for making her look like that. Hated that she'd put that strain on my wife's beautiful face. "You scared me."

"Sorry, kitten," I murmured, tipping my head down to hers and pressing a kiss to her lips.

She was stiff for a few moments until, finally, she rested her hands on my chest and melted into me. With a soft hum of contentment, she opened her mouth, sliding her tongue against mine. She felt so good in my arms, so right as I held her to me, gliding my palms over her body.

After long moments, I pulled back with a couple small

kisses and looked down at her. "Sounds like you've had a shitty night so far."

She breathed out a laugh. "The shittiest."

"I have the perfect antidote for that," I said before jumping backward and landing on my back on the bed, arms folded behind my head. "Climb on up, wife."

She grinned but shook her head. "Shitty night, remember? I'm not in the mood for sex."

"I never said anything about sex. I just want you to come over here and sit on my face for a little while."

"Pretty sure I'd smother you."

"And I'd die the happiest man on the planet if your pussy was the last thing I tasted. Now, take off those panties, straddle my shoulders, and sit on my face."

"Be serious," she said flatly.

I raised a brow. "Do I look like I'm joking?"

"Ford..."

"Kitten. Someone made you feel like shit tonight. Let me make you feel good."

I couldn't do a whole lot when it came to her parents, wasn't sure how to support her in that, but I could do this. I could do this all fucking night.

She bit her lip, indecision written all over her face. But she slipped her hands beneath the hem of her dress, slid her panties down her legs, and stepped out of them. And then she stood there in one of those little sundresses, her pussy bare beneath it.

I didn't even try to hide the hunger in my gaze as I

watched her climb onto the bed, her legs going on either side of my hips as she straddled me just like I told her to.

I slipped my hands under the skirt and gripped her hips, digging my fingers into her flesh and urging her higher. "Come on, wife. It's been a whole day since I've had a hit of your pussy, and I'm starting to have withdrawals. Climb on up here and give me a taste."

With her hands braced on my chest, she looked down at me, one brow raised. "Are you sure you want me to do this?"

"I'm rock fucking hard just from the thought of it, so yeah. I want you to do this."

Apprehension was written on her face, but after a glance behind her at the giant hard-on I was sporting, she seemed to be reassured. Because, finally, she shuffled her way up my chest until her knees were on either side of my head, and she hovered over my mouth.

"I didn't say hover." I smacked her ass, her body jerking closer to me. "I said *sit*. Now be a good girl and give me that cunt."

Without waiting for her to comply, I reached up and gripped her hips, guiding her down onto my face. At that first taste, I hummed into her pussy, opening my mouth and gliding my tongue over her, from her entrance to her clit and back again.

She gasped, her hands flying to the headboard as she stared down at me, eyes wide. With her ass cupped in my hands, I devoured her, grinding her down onto my mouth because I wasn't sure I'd get my fill otherwise. I fucking loved how she tasted, loved how she smelled, loved that awed look of rapture on her face as I took her exactly where she needed to go.

"Ford," she breathed, starting to rock her hips against my face and finally losing herself in her own pleasure.

I groaned against her, desperate to tell her how gorgeous she looked like this. How much I wanted her to come...that I needed to taste it. How badly I wanted her to fall apart for me.

But because my mouth was full of her pussy and there was no way I was stopping until she came down my throat, I just gripped her ass tighter, swirled my tongue faster, and worked her quickly toward a well-deserved orgasm.

She arched her back, one hand gripping the headboard, the other speared in my hair, and I wanted to see this view every day for the rest of my life. Wanted to watch as my wife bit her lip and looked down at me, her eyes glazed over, lips parting as she tightened her thighs around my head. As she moaned low in her throat while I worked her over with my mouth. As she kept our eyes locked together when succumbing to her pleasure and coming all over my tongue.

But I wasn't going to get to enjoy this for the rest of my life. I wasn't even going to get a year.

Nearly half of our agreed-upon time was already gone, the weeks flying by far too fast, but I was damn well going to enjoy every second I had left with her.

CHAPTER TWENTY-TWO

FORD

ON OUR ONE-MONTH ANNIVERSARY, I sat with my wife on the resort's secluded stretch of beach. The moon was high and bright, the ocean calm as the waves lapped at the shore, and a bonfire crackled in front of us.

It might've been romantic, if not for the death glare Quinn was shooting me. Or the constant bickering of my siblings as they, as well as Everly and Luna, sat next to us following an intense game of charades. An intense game wherein Quinn and I fought to the death on opposing teams, and Addison nearly beat Levi over the head with a stray rock because he wouldn't correctly guess her clues.

"I still can't believe I got paired with someone who couldn't guess a teapot," Addison grumbled to no one in particular.

"Jesus Christ, Addison." Levi dropped his head back and groaned to the sky. "This again?"

"Yes, this again! This *forever.* I'm never going to let you live this down. A five-year-old could've guessed that. I even acted out the short and stout!"

"That means fuck all. If you don't tip the teapot over and pour it out, how am I supposed to know what you're doing? You *are* short, so it was just you bouncing around like you OD'd on speed. I stand by the fact that a dancing gnome was a good guess."

"Well, I stand by the fact that you're an idiot."

Yeah... We were all a little too competitive to have anything remotely resembling a *friendly* game night. Unless friendly simply meant that no blood was shed, in which case we were golden. But when we reminded our baby sister of that fact, she wasn't hearing any of it. Said it would be good for everyone to get together. Good for Quinn and me to *practice.*

Which would've been fine and great, except for the fact that Beck and I had beat Quinn and Everly by a score of 3–2, and my wife was just as competitive as the rest of us. Hell, when it came to me, she was even more so. And now, she was giving me the cold shoulder.

I'd never been in a relationship long enough to experience this particular milestone, but I...didn't hate it. Especially when it was Quinn on the other end of that glare. I didn't know if it was our history or if it was just her, but her attitude got my dick hard every fucking time.

"Maybe next time we should all participate in a group meditation first to calm everyone down," Luna said from where she sat draped sideways across Brady's lap.

"Unless that meditation includes a fuck-ton of weed," Levi

said with a shake of his head, "I don't think it's gonna do much."

Aiden hummed his agreement. "Gotta go with Levi on this one. This is how we've always been."

"Is that true, Quinn?" Everly shifted next to Beck, glancing around my twin from where he had her tucked tight against his side.

"I'm actually not sure..." Quinn shrugged. "I didn't spend a whole lot of time around them when we were growing up."

Quinn had always kept to herself. People in school thought she was snobby, but I knew it was just because she was focused. She didn't allow herself to relax often. Or at all. Which meant if she wasn't striving for a goal, she wasn't interested. Through high school, that had kept her busy and hadn't allowed her the social life I'd had.

I'd always thought that was just who she was, but after learning more about her parents, hearing how her mother spoke to her, I wondered if it wasn't a product of her upbringing instead. What she felt she had to do to try to earn her parents' respect and approval. Something I now knew they'd never given her.

But I also knew that wasn't something she'd share freely, so I steered the conversation back to our history.

"She saved all her energy just for me. She was basically obsessed."

Quinn rolled her eyes. "That's a gross misrepresentation of our history."

"Kitten, you don't have to pretend around them. They already know you liked me well enough to marry me."

BRIGHTON WALSH

"Speaking of... What's happening here?" Addison asked, bouncing her finger between Quinn and me. "That's not how married people sit. Look at those four disgustingly in love fools." She gestured to our coupled-up siblings. "They're not married, but Luna's moved all her crystals and shit straight into Brady's house, and Beck and Everly are officially at the emergency contact stage of their relationship, so you two have to kick it up a notch."

I snapped my gaze in Beck's direction. "Wait, what? I'm not your emergency contact anymore? When the hell did that happen?"

Beck shrugged. "Couple weeks ago."

"A couple— What the fuck, man?"

"What?"

"They're living together," Aiden said. "What did you expect?"

What did I expect? I expected my twin would tell me when he was booting me out of the top spot in his life at the very fucking least.

There were six of us siblings, yes, but it had always been me and Beck. The two of us against the world. From day one, we'd been each other's person, and I wasn't quite sure I was ready to let that go.

Worse, this feeling felt a lot like...jealousy.

And I hated it. I wasn't a jealous person by nature. And I didn't begrudge Beck his relationship with Everly. If anyone deserved to be happy, it was him. As I stared at the two of them whispering quietly to each other, I realized this jealousy

238

wasn't over the fact that Everly had a part of him I no longer did.

It was that I didn't have what they did.

Which was quite the mindfuck since it was something I never thought I wanted, but now I couldn't help but wonder if I'd ever find it. Was anyone ever going to want that with me, considering everyone saw me as the good-time guy? Just a playboy only good enough to warm someone's bed? I was the guy girls dated before they found someone to take home. Like Chelsea said, I wasn't the one they *kept*.

Except, I was someone's husband now. Whether real or fake, in whatever circumstances it had come about, I wore Quinn's ring. Maybe I wasn't kept forever, but I was kept for now.

I glanced over at her, studying her features in the firelight. In the month we'd been doing this, we'd finally hit our stride. I knew when she had bad days, knew when she needed to blow off steam, when she needed to be left alone, when she needed a distraction. Likewise, she could tell from a glance if I'd had a challenging shift at the fire station, if Addison had me spinning my wheels with projects for the resort, if I needed a drink or a cupcake or a fuck. She'd started to read me as well as—in some cases better than—my twin could.

"*Hello?*" Addison snapped her fingers to get our attention. "Back to the issue at hand—you two aren't even touching. How do you expect this to pass as real if you act like this?"

Quinn made a show of looking around at the otherwise deserted beach. "I think that's a little overkill, don't you? There's no one here we have to perform for."

"And that's exactly the reason you *should* be performing. Get in some practice. Honestly, you guys need to get your heads in the game. We've got a lot on the line here—"

"We?" I asked, brow raised.

"Yes, *we*. I already told you I'm bringing every one of you idiots with me to my next doctor's appointment if I have to book it with Dicknose. If I have to suffer through, so do you. Now, focus! You've got Chelsea's wedding coming up, and you've got to be on point for that, so snuggle up. Pretend like you like each other enough that you just committed your lives to each other."

Well, I sure as hell wasn't going to say no to that.

Bracing myself back on one of my hands, I widened my legs and patted the space between. "She's got a point, wife. Time to snuggle up."

Quinn shot me an impassive look, but I simply grinned back at her. It was time for her to get over this little grudge. It wasn't my fault Aiden called the tie game for Beck and me rather than her and Everly.

With a long-suffering sigh, she stood and walked over, settling into the space between my legs. She relaxed back into me by degrees until she was soft and pliant against me, her hands resting on my thighs.

"See," Addison said. "Is that so hard?"

"Yeah, is that so hard, kitten?" I murmured against Quinn's ear before pressing a kiss there, knowing damn well she could feel exactly how much I loved having her this close.

It'd been two weeks since the Blueberry Fest and thus since beginning to fuck my wife on a consistent basis, but my dick still reacted to the scent of her shampoo like he was a starving man at his first feast. Like he hadn't just been inside her two hours ago, our impromptu not-so-quickie making us late to this little family night.

Quinn slid a glance at me out of the corner of her eye, her lips pursed to the side, proving just how unimpressed she was. But even through the flickering light of the bonfire, I could see the flush of her cheeks and the tight peaks of her nipples against the front of her T-shirt.

Yeah, my wife could pretend to be irritated all she wanted, but she loved knowing just how much she turned me on, and I was all too willing to remind her.

CHAPTER TWENTY-THREE

QUINN

MY PERIOD WAS unpredictable and didn't like to be confined to any kind of schedule, but when it hit, it hit with a vengeance. That wasn't true for everyone who suffered from PCOS—that was part of what made it so hard to diagnose... no two women's experiences were the same—but it was my reality and had been since I was eleven years old. In the past twenty years, I'd learned how to manage it. But *managing* it was about as good as it got.

Thankfully, Day One hit on a Saturday, so I wasn't needed at the clinic, and by some kind of miracle, Ford was working a twenty-four at the fire station, so I could turtle away without worrying about anyone else.

We'd been married for a little over a month, but since this was the first period I'd had since living with him, I didn't know what to expect. In my experience, men were either clueless, dismissive, or—worst of all—disgusted by women's bodies and the shit we dealt with. I wasn't sure I could handle if Ford was any of those, but especially the latter two.

Though maybe that would be better. Maybe if he was a jackass about something like this, that would help siphon off some of this...affection...I'd been feeling toward him.

Maybe that would help me stop falling for my husband.

But I was beginning to wonder if it was a losing endeavor. Between the sex and the laughs, the ease we felt when we were around each other, I was in over my head. More so than I'd intended. More so than I ever expected. And I had no idea where to go from here.

I'd spent yesterday curled in bed, bingeing *Emily in Paris*, and drugging myself with enough ibuprofen to kill a horse. Day Two generally wasn't much better, but I needed to put on a brave face and downplay how I was feeling because Ford would be home any time. I doubted he'd even considered this aspect of marriage when he agreed to be my fake husband, and who knew how he'd react to it.

Ford was a sexual guy, and since that night of the Blueberry Fest, we hadn't gone more than thirty-six hours without some form of sex. And only that long on the days he was scheduled at the station. When he was working, he'd fill his downtime by sexting me in preparation for pouncing as soon as he walked through the door.

Usually, I loved it. I'd never been wanted like this in my life, so I loved knowing that he was thinking about me while he was gone. Loved knowing that he couldn't wait to be with me again.

He'd tried the same yesterday, but I'd shut him down and

warned him my pussy was a no-go zone right now. He might have been able to talk me into sex on day five or six, but on day one or two? Not even his magic peen could get me to succumb.

I was in the middle of season three of Emily's exploits when the front door opened, and in walked Ford, carrying half a dozen bags. He sought me out immediately, his gaze running over me from head to toe, as if he could see beyond the piles of blankets I was burrowed under in our bed to verify I was okay.

"How're you feeling, wife?" he asked, dropping off the bags in the kitchen before walking into the bedroom. He braced his hands on either side of me and pressed a soft kiss to my temple.

"I'm okay," I said, lying through my teeth.

He made a disbelieving sound in the back of his throat. "Well, my beautiful little liar, your husband is finally home, and he brought reinforcements."

"You didn't need to get anything. I'm good."

"Are you kidding? This is my job." He strode into the kitchen, heading straight for the bags. "Actually, I was slacking. I should've had this shit already in the house."

I sat up in bed and leaned against the headboard enough so I could see straight to where he stood. He unloaded the bags onto the counter, and my brows rose with each item he pulled out. Jesus, when he said he brought reinforcements, he wasn't lying. Chocolate bars and truffles, potato chips, crackers, ice cream, popcorn, wine, pineapple juice... It looked like Main Street Market threw up in our kitchen.

"I wasn't sure if you usually craved salty or sweet, so I got both. I grabbed some chamomile tea, too, because I read that helps with cramps. I didn't read anything about pineapple juice helping, but it's your favorite, so it can't hurt, right? Same with the wine." He shot me a grin over his shoulder and went back to unloading. "And I didn't know if you wanted to just Netflix and actually chill or if you were bored with that, so I asked Everly for a couple of her favorite books. They're all romance, but if you're feeling stabby instead, I can swing by Brady's and pick up some true crime. The guy loves that shit. You can read them and I'll leave you alone, or I'll read them to you—whatever sounds good to you, kitten, okay?"

Thank God he wasn't actually waiting for an answer, because I could only stare at him, slack-jawed, as he continued pulling item after item out of the bags.

"The tricky part were the supplies. Holy fuck, I felt like I needed a goddamn PhD in tampons just to pick the right ones. I didn't know if you were feeling sporty today, and they didn't have anything for lounging—I honestly didn't even know they based them on your activity level—so I just got a few different variety packs in case you have a favorite. They also had this weird measuring cup-looking thing that said it was good for heavy flows, so I grabbed one of those, too."

The items were never-ending as he pulled one after another out of the bags—four different packs of tampons, two packages of pads, a box of pantyliners, and a menstrual cup—and I couldn't stand it anymore. I crawled out of bed and shuffled my way toward him, needing to be close to him.

Needing to squeeze him and tell him how much I appreciated this. No one—and I mean no one...not even my mom—had ever done anything like this for me. When I'd first gotten my period, she'd tossed me a package of pads, and I was on my own from then on.

In my years in the medical field—and, hell, just as a woman—I'd come to learn how uncomfortable people were with women's bodies. Most couldn't discuss any part of a woman's cycle without getting squeamish, and here Ford was, buying out the whole damn aisle just because. Because I'd told him I was on my period so he wouldn't come home expecting sex.

I'd spent my life learning over and over again that I was the only one I could count on. I was an island—by choice or by design, it didn't really matter. But in my short time with Ford, it had started to feel a little like maybe I wasn't so alone. Like maybe I could count on someone else once in a while.

"I didn't have a heating pad here, so I picked up one of those, too," he said. "And I read that these new patches can help with cramps, and they got really good reviews. I'm not sure if it'll work with your PCOS, but I figured it was worth a try. This article I was reading said—"

I wrapped my arms around him from behind, pressed my face into his back, and breathed him in. This man... *God*. If you'd have told me four months ago that my rival would be buying me tampons and tucking me into bed with a chocolate bar when I had my period, I'd have said you were out of your mind. And yet, here we were.

"Why are you out of bed?" he asked, turning in my arms

until he could wrap his around me. "I was going to bring in whatever you wanted."

"Thank you," I murmured into his chest.

"For what?" he asked, sounding genuinely confused, and that just made me adore him more.

"This." I tipped my head back to look up at him. I was a mess. I wasn't wearing makeup, my hair was half out of the ponytail I'd put it in that morning, and I was wearing one of his sweatshirts I'd stolen and a pair of pajama pants that had seen better days. But with the way he was looking down at me, brushing the loose hair from my face and holding me like I was...special, it was obvious he didn't care how messy—how imperfect—I was. "All of it. Just...thank you."

He pressed his lips to my forehead and squeezed me tight, then he pulled away and smacked my ass. "All right. Back to bed, kitten. I'll be there in five for a cuddle party. And I'll bring the goods."

IT'D ONLY BEEN a few hours, but I could say with absolute certainty that Netflix and actual chill—aka cuddle parties—with Ford was pretty much the best thing ever. We'd worked our way through season one of *The Good Place*, and I wasn't sure there was anything better than Ford chuckling into my neck, his chest rumbling against my back as he laughed.

How the hell had we gotten here? What had begun as a farce was starting to feel all too real. And I...didn't hate it.

He sat against the headboard, his legs spread for me to

settle between them. And all the while, he alternated between running his fingers through my hair and lightly tracing them over any exposed skin until I was basically a puddle in his lap.

"My mom used to do this when I was little," he said against the top of my head as he ran gentle fingers down my arm.

I shifted, tipping my head back to look up at him. He rarely talked about his mom—or his dad, actually—so he had my full attention. "She did?"

"Yep. Whenever we were sick." He laughed under his breath. "Sometimes I'd fake it just to have her tickle me. I'm pretty sure she was onto me, but she did it anyway."

I grinned, thinking of a sneaky little Ford trying to get more of his mom's attention. "That's sweet. I think I probably would've faked it, too. In fact, I might pretend to have my period again just for this."

"Maybe we can work out a swap. BJ for a tickle?"

Giving Ford a blow job wasn't exactly a hardship—the times I'd done it, I'd barely gotten started before he'd pulled me off him and fucked me into oblivion—so this was a no-brainer. "Deal."

We were quiet for long moments before I murmured, "You miss her?"

"Yeah," he answered without hesitation.

"Can I ask what's going on with your dad?" Any previous mentions of him had been short and unemotional—as if Ford were commenting on the weather—which only increased my curiosity.

"Not much to tell. He's like he's always been—absent. I don't know if you remember, but my mom handled everything when we were young. Ran the resort, took care of us kids. Took care of *him* when he was too drunk to take care of himself. Tried to cover for him with us, too. At least now we don't have to deal with that because we don't expect his presence anymore. Don't count on him to be around. Less disappointment for everyone that way."

"You don't ever see him?"

"Nope. Not since Mom died. Beck and I swing by and drop off things for him once a week, but he's never so much as acknowledged it."

"Does that bother you?"

"Only because it bothers Beck and my other siblings, but I've sort of accepted that this is how it is." He shrugged. "I don't like to dwell on shit like that, so I don't."

And here I'd spent the past however long thinking he'd had it easy. That his demeanor was because he sailed through life without a care. But his mom had died far too young, and his dad had abandoned him for all intents and purposes. Ford had never had it easy. He just hadn't let it define him.

There was so much more to him than everyone else saw... than he allowed people to see. But he'd shown me... Opened up in a way I wasn't sure he'd done with anyone else.

"It's hard to miss someone who was never really around, but I miss the idea of a relationship we'll never have, you know?"

"Yeah, I know." I knew all too well, having spent too much

time wishing for parents who would love and support me. Wishing for any other parents but mine.

"What about you? Your mom ever do anything like this for you?" he asked, tracing his fingers along my palm.

I snorted. "Uh, no. Nurturing wasn't really her style. Or my dad's. They focused more on tough love...minus the love."

Ford stiffened behind me, just the subtlest change in his posture. "How long's that been going on?"

"Let's see...my birthday's in September, so...almost thirty-two years?"

"Jesus, kitten. I never knew. I thought—"

I shrugged, swallowing the lump in my throat at the anger in his voice. Just knowing he cared enough to be upset on my behalf warmed something inside my chest. "No one did. And they worked hard to keep it that way. Narcissists are great at putting on a mask for the world. Pretending everything is fine —that they're the real victims, and *I* was the problem."

"How bad was it?" he asked, his voice strained as if he had to force the words out.

"Not...awful. They didn't physically abuse me."

He swore under his breath. "That doesn't make me feel any better. They hurt you?"

In sneaky ways...ones that were so hard to articulate. Ways that had taken me years with my therapist to fully realize.

"Nothing my therapist couldn't help me work through."

"*Kitten.*" It was a single word, but his tone said so much. *Tell me* and *Let me be here for you* and *I want to kill them* all wrapped up in two syllables.

I blew out a deep sigh. I'd never opened up like this with anyone in my personal life. Only my therapist knew these parts of me, and that had taken years of building trust before I'd felt comfortable sharing.

But somehow, it didn't feel scary with Ford. I didn't wonder if he'd believe me. If he'd make me out to be the bad guy like my parents were so good at doing. If he'd think I was overreacting. Didn't worry he'd see me as weak for striving to be better for them instead of myself. For not taking charge of my life sooner.

Somehow, I just knew he'd support me.

"I wasn't who they wanted me to be," I said. "Who they thought I should be. And I got really good at listening to what they were saying. So much so that I started to believe it. I was too fat, too tall, too driven, then not driven enough... Too smart, then too dumb. They found a way to criticize me for *everything*. And the trickiest part was they kept moving the goalposts. In one breath, they wanted me to dumb myself down so I could find a husband. And in the next, they told me I'd never make anything of myself if I wasn't valedictorian. And when I wasn't..."

"Fuck. No wonder you hated me."

"I didn't hate you," I said, meaning it this time.

"You didn't like me."

I shrugged. "It was just hard coming to terms with everything, especially when I'm still living with the repercussions of it."

"What do you mean?"

"All my plans hinged on my achieving that. So when I

didn't, I ended up at my sixth choice for undergrad because that was the only one that gave me a full ride, and I didn't get into Harvard Med. It was probably a pipe dream, but I kept thinking that maybe if I had gone there, my parents would finally be proud of me."

"They should be proud of you anyway," he said with a hard edge to his tone. "You're here, trying to buy your own practice."

"Only because a small-town medical clinic was the best I could do. But at least it'd be mine. Or it would be if Dr. Dicknose stopped fucking around and agreed to sell already."

"He's still dragging his feet?"

"He's refused to even look at the proposal I sent over." I took a deep breath and let it out slowly, finally voicing the thought that had been bouncing around in my head for weeks. "What if we did this all for nothing?"

"We didn't," he said firmly, his tone laced with something I couldn't name. "We still have Chelsea's wedding."

"Right." The whole reason he'd agreed to this in the first place. "I promise to be on my best behavior."

"What if I like you when you're not?"

"I can do that, too."

He hummed low in his throat, then said, "Your parents are complete shitheads."

It was so out of the blue that I couldn't stop the laugh from bursting free.

He shifted me so I was straddling his lap and wrapped his arms around me, holding me against his chest. "I'm serious. You don't have to put up with it. You *shouldn't*. In fact, next time they call, I'll answer the phone and tell them to fuck off."

"I can't just...stop talking to them."

"Why not? You're amazing, and they're assholes for making you doubt that. Why would you want to invite that into your life?"

"I don't," I murmured, but I didn't know how to tell him that part of me felt like I didn't deserve to be free of them. Part of me believed their lies. And part of me—the little girl inside still desperate for her parents' approval—still yearned for the kind of loving relationship I now knew they'd never give me.

Almost as if he could hear my thoughts, he said, "You shouldn't listen to anything they say, kitten. You're gorgeous and kind and so fucking smart. And if I have to tell you that every day for the rest of your life until you believe it, I will."

My eyes burned as I let his words sink into me. Could it really be that easy? To just...stop talking to them? Put up a boundary and cut off that part of my life—the part that only ever brought me pain and suffering—and be rid of them once and for all?

I didn't know. I wasn't sure it was something I could actually do, but knowing I had his support if I ever chose to lightened something inside me.

I snuggled into his chest, letting him hold me. Letting him comfort me after I'd been weathering this storm on my own for so long. He tightened his arms around me, dropping his head so his lips pressed against my neck. After long moments, I shifted to sit back, but he just squeezed me tighter.

"Not yet," he murmured into my neck.

Tears clogged my throat for an entirely different reason as I relaxed back into him, closing my eyes as I returned his embrace.

Had I ever felt this cared for...this loved...this precious...in my whole life? I didn't think so. In fact, I knew so. This was a first for me.

And how sad was it that I was finally feeling it now with the one person I wasn't supposed to keep?

CHAPTER TWENTY-FOUR

QUINN

TONIGHT WAS THE NIGHT.

Nothing had yet come of my offer to purchase the clinic. Dr. Dicknose was actively ignoring me, which meant next week, I was going to have to pull out the gives-no-shit tack again.

Because of that, it made Ford's ex's wedding feel even more important. Like the entirety of our marriage sham was riding on this one single night and what came of it—if Ford would get out of this marriage what he'd hoped.

The event tonight was the whole reason Ford had agreed to this in the first place, so I needed to fulfill my end of the bargain. I needed to get this right because I didn't want to let him down.

"Fuck me, you're gorgeous." Ford leaned against the doorframe of the bathroom, wearing an unbuttoned dark gray dress shirt, his black suit pants sitting low on his hips.

And *good God*. I wasn't sure I was going to survive this night in public with him.

He didn't try to hide the slow perusal he gave me, his gaze skimming over my red wrap dress, eyes lingering a little too long on the deep V showcasing my breasts. Before I could give him shit about it, he stepped up right behind me.

"I have a present for you, kitten."

I met his gaze in the mirror, one brow raised as I finger-combed through my curls. "Oh yeah?"

"Two, actually."

"What are they?"

He set two boxes on the vanity, then braced his hands there, caging me in. He ran his nose along the column of my neck and pressed a kiss to the underside of my jaw before brushing his lips against my ear. "Open them and find out."

I glanced down at them. They were both black and roughly the same size—small, though the one on my right was slightly bigger. I reached for that one, and Ford hummed low in his throat.

"Did I pick right?" I asked, lifting the black lid off the top but not yet peering inside.

"You're getting them both, kitten. But this one pairs well with your horny eyes, and opening it first just means we can have a little fun before we leave."

Well, now I was intrigued. I glanced down, finding a small satin bag nestled in the box, one of my favorite toy brand's logos stamped on it.

I lifted my gaze to his in the mirror as I loosened the drawstring holding the bag closed. "You got me a toy?"

"Don't be greedy, kitten. It's not just for you." He reached around, dipping his fingers into the satin bag and pulling out two pieces that were tucked inside. "*This*," he said, holding a small U-shaped black silicone toy between his thumb and forefinger, "is for you." He handed it to me, then held up something flat and cylindrical. "But this is for me."

I turned the vibrator over in my hand, looking at it this way and that. It was small, both in length and thickness—maybe three inches on the wider end, two on the side that was slimmer than my pinky...the part that'd go inside me—and there was no way this was going to do much of anything, especially when I was used to what he was packing.

But then Ford pressed something on his part of the toy, and mine buzzed to life, the sudden jolt nearly making me drop it into the sink.

He chuckled under his breath and brushed his hand up the outside of my thigh, beneath the fluttery hem of my dress. Then he reached around, slid his hand between my legs, and cupped my pussy. "Here's what's going to happen, kitten. I'm going to make you come right now to take the edge off. Then I'm going to slip our new little toy inside you, and we're going to have some fun tonight."

"But...we're going out. To your *ex's* wedding," I said, though my words lacked heat. Between his hand cupping my pussy and thoughts of us using the toy—of him having that power over my pleasure and my not knowing when it would happen—I was already getting wet.

"Yep," he confirmed, humming low as he massaged my pussy over my underwear. "But you and I will be the only ones who'll know what you've got tucked inside these pretty panties."

As he said the words, he slipped his hand beneath the material and slid a finger through my lips. He groaned against my neck when he found just how wet I already was.

"I fucking knew you'd like that," he said. "Knew when this sweet pussy squeezed the life out of my cock while I fucked you in front of that window that you'd love the idea of getting off in public."

He slid his fingers down, slipping two inside me and pumping deep. The slow grind of his palm against my clit made me gasp as I braced myself on the counter, my eyes locked on his.

"You do, don't you?" He brought his other hand up, pushing aside the top of my dress, pulling down the cup of my bra, and freeing one of my breasts. "Love the idea that I'll be able to make you come in front of everyone, and there won't be a thing you can do about it."

"Ford," I breathed, unable to take my eyes off our reflection in the mirror. At how...*hot* we looked together.

My hair fell in perfectly curled waves around my face, and my makeup was subtle and understated. But that was where the civility ended. That all went out the window as soon as Ford got his hands on me. My lips were parted, my cheeks flushed a deep pink, my breasts heaving—one cupped in Ford's hand—as I stood there and let my husband finger-fuck me to orgasm. All while knowing he was going to make me come at his ex's wedding in front of who knew how many people.

"Look at how gorgeous you are, riding my hand like that. Fucking beautiful. I could watch you all goddamn day." His cheeks were flushed, his eyes dark as his gaze darted over me in the mirror.

With his right hand between my legs, his left cupping my breast, he held me to him and ground his hard cock into my ass. I wanted—*needed*—to feel it, so I reached around to grip him, but before I could, he sank his teeth into my neck.

"Not yet," he murmured. "This isn't about me. I want to be so desperate to fuck you by the end of the night I can barely see straight. But don't worry, baby, I'm going to let you have this one. I'm not going to leave my wife's pussy needy. Not yet."

He pressed a kiss to my neck, lifting his eyes to meet mine in the mirror as he pumped his fingers inside me. "We'll save that for when we're surrounded by dozens of wedding guests. When you're standing there, looking so fucking beautiful, having a conversation with someone and pretending like you don't have a vibrator slipped inside your cunt. Like your husband isn't watching your every move and controlling your pleasure with a flick of his finger. Do you think you'll be able to hold it in, baby? When you're commenting about how good the dinner was or how nice the reception is and I turn this on, are you going to be able to stop yourself from coming all over what you wished was my cock?"

"Oh *God*," I choked out, closing my eyes against the picture he painted, but it didn't matter. I was already falling.

With his fingers buried inside me, his palm pressing insistently against my throbbing clit and his other hand cupping my breast, I came with Ford's scent surrounding me, his soft, whispered words of encouragement in my ear as I shuddered and shook in his arms.

"Just like that... That's my good girl. Jesus Christ, you look so fucking beautiful when you come for me." Ford rubbed me gently, drawing out every ounce of pleasure until he slipped his fingers from me while I tried to catch my breath.

And then suddenly, his hand was back, sliding something inside me as he pressed a kiss to the back of my neck. I snapped my eyes open when I felt the toy settle against my sensitive clit, and a shudder racked my body.

Ford slid my panties back into place, righted my bra and the top of my dress, then rested his hands on my hips, his eyes locked with mine in the mirror. "You want to try it now?"

I paused only a second before shaking my head. The anticipation of the unknown was almost better than the reality. Not knowing when he'd use it, or how it'd feel was a turn-on in and of itself.

His eyes heated, and he wrapped an arm around me, pressing his palm flat against my stomach. He tugged me back until I was flush against him, no mistaking how much he'd enjoyed making me come. "It's going to be so good, kitten. I'm going to give this pussy exactly what it needs."

I didn't doubt that. Ford was the most unselfish lover I'd ever been with—by miles—and I couldn't say I wasn't going to miss that whenever this thing between us was over. Whenever we went back to our real lives instead of playing pretend.

"One more," he said, grabbing the other box and holding it out in front of me.

"I'm not sure how you're going to top a vibrator, but good luck, I guess."

He chuckled lowly, his eyes locked on me in the mirror, and waited for me to open it. I pulled off the top to find a black velvet box nestled inside. My brows went up, and I glanced at him as I pulled it out.

"Don't look so surprised. I told you I ordered a ring. I was just waiting for it to get here."

Holding my breath, I lifted the lid of the velvet box, nervous of what I'd find inside. What if I hated it? But I shouldn't have worried. Ford seemed to be able to read me with ease...better than anyone else in my life.

Nestled in the black velvet was a simple rose gold band... exactly what I would have chosen if I'd been told to pick it myself. I pulled it out, ready to slide it on my finger, but engraving on the inside of the band caught my eye. I brought it closer, studying the words etched there.

No take backs

I stood frozen, reading the words over and over again, a lump caught in my throat. I was thrown right back to all the times he'd said those words before—the coin flip before the dinner that changed my life, as he'd drafted our contract, right before he'd kissed me for the first time as my husband...

"You like it?" he asked, a hint of uncertainty threading through his tone. "You can get something different if you—"

"No," I said too quickly, my voice shaky. Unable to lift my

gaze to his, I stared at the ring and swallowed down the knot in my throat. "It's perfect."

"Good," he said, relief clear in his tone. Then he pressed a kiss to my temple before stepping back and slapping my ass. "Then it's time to slide that on your finger, and let's go. I want to show off my wife."

CHAPTER TWENTY-FIVE

FORD

MY WIFE WAS the hottest fucking thing in this room, and I was seriously starting to worry about the side effects of walking around with a hard-on for hours on end.

We'd sat through the boring-ass ceremony, choked down a bland dinner, and now were suffering through part of the dance. And that entire time, I'd been playing with our new toy. Whether Quinn was sitting right next to me as she had been during the ceremony and dinner, or was across the room chatting with someone as she was now, it didn't matter. I'd lost count of how many times I'd turned it on. How many times I'd gotten her to the brink of coming, only to turn it off and leave her shaking with need.

I couldn't tell if she loved or hated it. Her horny eyes looked shockingly similar to her murder eyes, which was only making things worse for me because they both turned me the fuck on. Thank Christ I had a suit jacket to hide exactly how much I was enjoying this, because I really hadn't thought this through.

I should've known better. Should've known I'd be rock fucking hard witnessing Quinn's reaction to every flick of my finger. How she'd shift in her seat, stutter midsentence, or grip the back of a chair, head hanging, as if she was trying to hold herself upright. How her hand shook as she lifted a glass to her lips, her horny murder eyes locked on mine from across the room while I tormented us both.

But now... Now, the countdown was on. We'd put in our time, made our appearances, and I was ready to take my wife home and fuck her until we both tapped out.

Hell, I wasn't even sure we'd make it home.

Maybe we'd just get as far as the parking lot. She could ride me right there in the front seat of the Jeep. She'd be so wet from being edged all night that I'd be able to slide right in, even while she was wearing the vibe. With the added thickness it provided and the buzz directly against her clit, she'd be coming in seconds, and I wouldn't be far behind.

My cock throbbed at the thought, and yeah... It was time to drag my wife out of here, whether or not I'd actually spoken to Chelsea. I didn't even know if she'd seen me and Quinn tonight. And I found I just...didn't care.

Not when I knew exactly what the rest of my night was going to consist of. Not when I knew who was waiting to go home with me.

I started toward Quinn across the room, my steps only speeding up when that fucking groomsman sidled up next to her at the bar. Again. He'd already asked her to dance, which she'd politely declined. Then not-so-politely excused herself when I'd turned on the vibrator just to make a point. And now this fucker was back for more? Not on my watch.

I ignored calls of my name and those trying to talk to me, my attention focused solely on my wife. She had on her *I'm not interested in your bullshit* face—a face I fucking loved, by the way—and this guy wasn't taking the hint. Finally, after shaking her head three different times and saying no at least twice, she turned around and walked away while he was in the middle of talking.

Jesus Christ, I loved that woman.

My steps faltered as the thought slammed into me. I stood frozen in the middle of the reception hall, eyes locked on where Quinn had disappeared, my thoughts consumed by her. Though that wasn't anything new. I couldn't remember a time I hadn't been consumed by her, but this felt different.

Heavier.

Real.

Fuck me. I was in love with my wife.

Though was it really all that much of a surprise? Like Beck constantly reminded me, this thing between us had been building inside me for more than half my life. I shouldn't have been shocked that this was how it had manifested itself. Especially now when I'd spent these past several weeks learning her, inside and out.

Learning to love every single part of her.

That complicated things infinitely, especially when I had

no idea what she was feeling. No idea if this had become real for her, or if she was still pretending. I thought back over the past month, how she'd been with me...opening up and letting me in in ways I wasn't sure she'd ever done before. If she was pretending, she was a hell of an actress.

I needed to find her. Needed to look into her eyes and see if I could get a read on if she felt any of this, too.

But first, I had to make a quick detour.

"Hey," I said, leaning my elbow on the bar next to the asshat who wouldn't take no for an answer.

He glanced over, brows drawn down. "Yeah?"

"You know that woman who keeps turning you down?"

He snorted. "Whatever, man. She's a bitch. Acting like she's too good for me."

"Watch your fucking mouth when you talk about my wife." My voice was hard even as I smiled and nodded to someone who waved at me from across the room. "She *is* too good for you. And if you bother her again, we're gonna have a problem. She's a doctor, so she won't punch you right in your smug mouth, but I don't have any such hang-ups. We clear?" Without waiting for him to respond, I clapped him on the back—hard enough that he choked on his drink—and set off to find Quinn.

I strode down the hallway she'd disappeared into, slowing as I heard voices coming from around the corner.

"—can't believe he actually showed up. And he's *married* to her. Pathetic, especially when he could've had me." Snorts of laughter followed, and I'd recognize that nasally cawing anywhere. Fucking Chelsea.

Considering I no longer gave two shits what my ex had to tell herself about my marriage or what she thought about my being here, I was about to turn around and head in the other direction in search of my wife when her voice pulled me up short.

"God, you really are a bitch, aren't you?"

"Ex*cuse* me?"

"You're a bitch," Quinn said, like she was stating that two plus two equaled four. "I don't usually like to call women that, but I feel okay making an exception in your case. You were a mean girl in high school, and you're still a mean girl now. Is your life seriously that unfulfilling that you get this much pleasure from tearing people down?"

"Who even invited you into this conversation?" Chelsea snapped.

"Well, it's my husband you're talking about, so...you. And I'll save you the trouble of trying to figure out why Ford could *possibly* have moved on from you since I know brains aren't your strong suit," Quinn said, her voice saccharine sweet. "It's your personality, sweetie."

A few shocked gasps sounded, and I grinned, shuffling forward quietly as I peered around the corner, desperate for a peek at my wife, the badass. Quinn's back was to me as she faced off with Chelsea, who stood surrounded by her bridesmaids.

My ex's face was bright red, her lips pressed in a thin line. "Whatever. You can have my sloppy seconds. I moved on to someone better. Thank God I cut that dead weight back in high school because he hasn't amounted to anything. You're just too desperate to see it."

My jaw ticked, anger flooding me, but not for the reason I would've thought. Turned out, I no longer gave a shit what she thought of me, but I'd be damned if I sat back and let her talk about my wife that way.

But before I could take a single step forward and put an end to this, Quinn snapped back at Chelsea. "What I see is a washed-up prom queen who's mad her ex moved on and found someone else—someone who doesn't have to count using her fingers."

I watched as all the bridesmaids' mouths dropped open, and I had to smother a laugh. Damn. My kitten's claws were sharp tonight, and that shit was making me hard.

Chelsea fisted her hands at her sides, her face turning a mottled red. "You—"

"I'm not done," Quinn cut in, waving a hand through the air, the light glinting off her wedding band. "I'm going to try to explain this to you using small words so you can understand—Ford's a *firefighter*. That means he saves people's lives for a living. He's a literal hero. Your husband sells used cars, so how about we stop throwing stones when we live in glass houses, m'kay?"

I didn't know what was hotter—that Quinn had my back without hesitation or that she stood up for herself to a woman like Chelsea, who loved cutting others down. Someone so much like her parents. And if she could do it to Chelsea, maybe she could do it with them, too.

The entire purpose of our coming here—of my side in

this farce of a marriage—had been to show my ex I wasn't the man she claimed I was. But now that that time had come, I couldn't care less. Not when my wife stood there in that red dress, my ring glinting on her finger, and my cock hard as steel for her.

I couldn't wait a second longer and strolled around the corner toward them. "Evening, ladies."

All gazes snapped to me, Quinn's included, and God, she was so fucking beautiful, all anger and indignation on my behalf.

I was going to fuck her so hard.

"You don't mind if I steal my wife, do you?" I said, settling in behind Quinn and wrapping an arm around her waist. I dipped my head to hers, pressing a kiss to her temple and murmuring, "You about ready to come—I mean go—kitten?"

Before she could answer, I slid my other hand into my pocket, my finger hovering over the button on the remote. And then I pushed it.

Quinn's body jolted against me, and I bit back a grin. She placed her hand on top of mine, her nails digging into my skin, and I wasn't sure if she was telling me to leave it on or turn it off. Didn't know which I'd prefer, either. There would be some definite satisfaction from making her come like this. Right here.

But after the night she'd had—after the edging I'd put her through—I wanted to be buried deep inside her when she finally exploded, so I turned it off, and she sagged back against me.

"Ready," Quinn managed through a tight throat.

"Nice wedding, Chels. You and Gary deserve each other."

"It's Barry!" she yelled after our retreating forms, but I couldn't be bothered to even offer a wave, in too much of a hurry to get my wife...somewhere. *Anywhere.* Just as long as I could be inside her.

"Where are we going?" Quinn asked, breathless, her hand gripping mine as she kept up with my long strides.

"We're finding an empty hallway or bathroom or coat closet or whatever the fuck. I'm not picky."

"For what?"

"You know what." I pressed her hand to the front of my pants, letting her feel exactly what she did to me. "After watching you all night, and then *that*? There's no goddamn way I'm waiting."

"We can't have sex here," she said, though her voice lacked any firmness. She wanted this just as badly as I did.

"Don't tell me I can't fuck my wife wherever I goddamn want. Not after I've been tormenting both of us all night. Not after you walked away from that douchebag at the bar. Not after you told Chelsea off. And not after I watched you do it all while wearing *my* ring. So pick someplace, wife, because I can't wait another minute to be inside you."

We turned the corner into a darkened hallway, and she came to a sudden stop before spinning to face me.

"Here," she said.

The music from the reception hall carried to us, growing louder every once in a while when someone opened the door before quieting again. We were no longer in the main walkway, but we were still out in the open. Still near enough to the party that someone could walk by at any moment and see exactly what we were doing.

But I was too far gone to care.

I reached down and gripped her ass, tugging her up against me. "Wrap those gorgeous legs around me, kitten. This first one is gonna be quick, just to take the edge off. Then when we get home, I'm going to spend an hour with my face buried in your pussy and see how many times I can make you come."

"After what you've put me through tonight, you better."

I grinned and undid the fly of my pants, pinning her against the wall as I kissed my way up her neck. "Tell me how much you loved our new toy."

"I hate it," she said, her fingers fumbling as she tried to undo the buttons on my shirt before she groaned out a frustrated huff and yanked the sides apart, sending a button flying. "Need to feel you."

"Jesus Christ," I muttered, my cock throbbing with the need to be inside her. "You need this bad, don't you, kitten?"

"Yes."

"You think you can take me with it still in you?"

"*Yes.*"

My cock twitched at the thought...how tight she'd be like this, and I needed to get inside her or this was going to be over before it even started.

I reached under her skirt and groaned when I found her soaked panties. "Oh, fuck me. *Fuck me*, how are you so goddamn wet? These panties are ruined, aren't they, baby?" I

275

slid them to the side and pressed the toy against her clit as I thrust two fingers inside her.

"Oh God," she said, her head falling back to the wall, eyes fluttering closed. "Only because someone thought it was a good idea to tease me for three fucking hours."

"But it felt so good, didn't it?"

She bit her lip, glaring at me with her horny murder eyes and refusing to admit just how much she loved it.

"Don't worry. I'm going to make it feel even better because we're done waiting." I slipped my fingers from her and pulled out my dick, notching myself at her entrance. "I need to fuck you."

"Yes. *Now*." Her voice was breathy, need laced in each word, and all my self-control evaporated.

Without waiting another second, I sank deep inside her, groaning at how tight she was. How fucking wet. She was ready for me, all swollen with need, her cunt already pulsing around my cock.

"Oh my God," she breathed, eyes wide and locked on mine.

"You had me hard all fucking night, kitten." I gripped her ass in my palms, my hips slapping against hers with each punishing thrust. I couldn't keep this gentle or sweet or slow. Not now. Not after everything that had happened tonight. "Watching you fight off your orgasm. Knowing how bad you needed to come. But I wasn't going to let you until you had my cock inside you. Not until I could fill you up."

"*Ford*." She delved her fingers into my hair, pressing our foreheads together as she panted against my mouth.

"Don't even care that someone could find us. Someone could walk around that corner right now, but I don't fucking care. Let them see me give my wife exactly what she needs."

She slid her gaze toward the open end of the hallway, her fingers tightening in my hair and her pussy clenching even harder around me.

"You love that, don't you? Love the idea of someone finding you getting fucked against a wall. All because you made your husband so wild with need, he couldn't wait to have you. Couldn't wait to be buried in your perfect cunt. You feel how much I want you? How hard you make me?"

Quinn whimpered into my mouth, her lips parted, eyes glazed as she clung to me and nodded.

"My wife needs to come, doesn't she?"

"Oh God, yes. Please, Ford. *Please.*"

I groaned low in my throat, barely hanging on when her pussy was rippling around me and she was begging me to make her come.

"Then do it, wife. Come all over my cock so I can fill up this pussy." I slipped my hand into my pocket and pressed the button on the remote, the sudden vibration making us both groan. And that was all it took.

She moaned my name, her eyes rolling back as she came around me and took me with her. I captured her lips, slipping my tongue into her mouth as I spilled myself inside her, the overwhelming urge to say those three little words nearly choking me.

Instead, I swallowed them down and whispered how beautiful she was, how much I loved feeling her around me, what a good girl she was when she came for me. All the while hoping she could hear every underlying word I didn't say. The ones I *couldn't* say aloud.

Not yet.

Not when we were supposed to be temporary.

Not when this wasn't ever supposed to be real.

Not when I had no idea if she felt the same.

CHAPTER TWENTY-SIX

QUINN

FORD:

Make sure my dinner's warmed up when I get home.

QUINN:

Excuse me?

FORD:

Your pussy, kitten. Make sure your pussy's warmed up for me. I'm starving.

QUINN:

omg

A SMILE TWITCHED on my lips at Ford's last text, but even filthy messages from my husband couldn't make this day better.

I should have known Dr. Dicknose's stipulation was too

easy. That he would never agree to sell his practice if I simply showed up with a marriage license. Not with the way he viewed women as second-class citizens. He'd only told me that because he assumed it was never going to happen for me. So imagine his surprise when I'd taken it to heart and actually found a husband.

But our time was almost up. I'd tried not to think about it when Ford and I were together—especially when it had started to feel a little too much like it was real—but the expiration date Ford and I had set at that first dinner was days away. Which meant it was now or never.

After weeks of avoidance on my boss's behalf and an official offer on mine, I'd finally confronted him this morning. Told him I was tired of waiting. Tired of tiptoeing around what we both knew was the entire reason I'd agreed to come here in the first place. The entire reason I'd agreed to help him dig himself and this clinic out of the hole he'd placed himself in.

Sitting behind his desk with his hands folded neatly on top, that fucker had looked up at me with a pitying expression and told me point-blank he had no intention of fulfilling what he'd promised.

He didn't want a woman taking over his practice—married or not.

And that was it. End of.

Everything I'd worked for...my dream... Gone. In a flash.

The smart thing would have been to confront him at the end of the day, but since I had done it first thing this morning, I'd had to sit with this for hours, making my anger increase by the second. And I was certain it was written all over my face.

Thankfully, Ford had a shift at the fire station today, so he wouldn't be by to take me to lunch. It wasn't that I didn't want to see him. Worse was that I *did*.

I'd never had the kind of relationship Ford and I shared. Never had someone to confide in. Someone to count on. Someone who saw me for me.

Someone who took me as is, flaws and all.

Those were the good things my brain told me. But more often were the all too familiar whispers that had been with me my whole life. Telling me that I wasn't good enough. That the only reason he was in this with me in the first place was because of that contract. That he couldn't wait to get out.

But lately...I'd begun to wonder if maybe he didn't mind being married to me. Had begun to wonder if he might actually like it.

And now, somehow, I was going to have to tell him we'd done all this for nothing.

We hadn't needed to get married to attend Chelsea's wedding and show her Ford wasn't who she claimed he was. It didn't matter anyway—she'd thought what she wanted to, despite us showing up as a committed couple, but Ford hadn't seemed to care.

I'd known from the beginning that this was an unbalanced partnership, but I'd jumped in without thought. I figured he owed me, considering my entire life trajectory was off course because of him. But now, none of it mattered.

I wasn't going to get this clinic, whether Ford was my husband or not.

Which meant there was no longer a reason for us to stay married.

That thought pierced my stomach, sending it rolling. Where I'd once detested him—or more accurately, detested what he stood for because it was something I thought I could never have—now, I couldn't see my life without him. I didn't *want* to see my life without him.

In the short time we'd spent together, he'd become my best friend. And somehow, I'd done the dumbest thing in my life and fallen in love with him.

When we'd entered into this, I'd snorted when he'd suggested that I'd fall in love. But I'd had no idea the difference he'd make in my life. No idea how easy it'd be to fall for the man.

Well, the joke was on me, because I was well and truly fucked now.

I glanced at the clock, realizing it was fifteen minutes after closing time. Since I hadn't had any patients this afternoon, I'd shut myself in my office, trying to figure out how I was going to go home and tell my husband he no longer needed to be. That the expiration date on the contract we'd scribbled on the napkin didn't matter because this wasn't going to happen anyway.

I didn't want to tell him. I wanted to stay in this fairy tale a little longer.

But I couldn't avoid it forever. Eventually, Ford would come looking for me, wonder what was wrong—I'd never be able to hide that from him. The guy was more astute than he looked, and it would be better if this came out on my terms.

I gathered my things and grabbed my purse before heading out of my office. Walking down the hallway, I raised a brow at the light coming from Dr. Dicknose's office. Since he didn't like to stay two minutes past closing time, it was highly unusual for him to be here this late—especially when Alicia was already gone and all the lights in the rest of the clinic had been shut off.

With my luck, he'd stayed just to rub it in again before I left. One last dig at stupid little Quinn, who actually thought her father's oldest and dearest friend would welcome her into the fold with open arms.

Well, fuck him. I was going to walk by with my head held high and not even spare him a glance.

I knew this wasn't sustainable. I wouldn't be able to weather this for the next who knew how long. Because eventually, he would find someone to buy the practice, and I'd have to sit back and watch someone else living my dream all over again.

Maybe it was time to look for something else.

Maybe it was time to leave Starlight Cove.

Just the thought of that had my stomach twisting, an ache settling in the back of my throat. Growing up here, I hadn't loved it. I'd struggled to fit in. To find my place. Always feeling like an outcast, even with my peers. But now that I'd been back, I was beginning to wonder if that hadn't had more to do with my parents and what they told me—what I believed—than it did with the town. Than with me.

Because in the few short months I'd been back, it had begun to feel like home.

An image of Ford popped up in my mind, and I amended my thought. It wasn't Starlight Cove that felt like home. It was him. He was the one place I felt free to be unapologetically myself. He was my safe place to land.

And I was going to have to find a way to tell him we no longer had to be together without letting him in on the fact that I'd somehow, beyond all reason, fallen in love with him along the way.

Even though I swore I'd walk by Dr. Dicknose's office with my head held high and not spare him a glance, curiosity got the better of me, and I looked inside his office.

It took me long moments to register what I was seeing.

The man who'd been a constant thorn in my side since moving back...

On the floor.

His feet peeking out from behind his desk.

Body still and unmoving.

It was one of those split seconds that felt like an eternity. The moment at the beginning of an emergency when you had to decide the best course of action.

I didn't think. I didn't pause.

I dropped my bag, rushed over to him as I pulled my phone out of my pocket, and dialed 9-1-1. And then I dropped to the floor next to his still body and started compressions.

Ford

HEARING the clinic's address as the scene we were being dispatched to was one of the scariest moments of my life. I knew, logically, that Quinn wasn't the one who was having an emergency. It was a doctor's office, for fuck's sake, so needing emergency services there wasn't out of the realm of possibility.

But logic didn't have a place when I was in love.

And I would never admit it out loud, but when I'd stormed into the building, eyes scanning for her, and found her over Dinsmore doing chest compressions, I'd never been more relieved in my life. She'd been sweating, out of breath, and had looked up at me with a flurry of emotions in her eyes.

I'd taken over to give her a rest. But in the end, it hadn't mattered. He was gone.

I'd called his death—grateful I'd been able to do that for her—statements were filed, the body was removed, and then I took Quinn home.

My shift wasn't technically over for another twelve hours, but the chief had told me to take my wife home and take care of her. That she'd need me by her side as she decompressed from this.

The entire drive, I'd kept shooting her glances out of the corner of my eye. Her forehead had been pressed to the passenger side window, her gaze unfocused as she stared at the passing scenery.

There was a lot to be said about living in a small town.

Sometimes it was a pain in the ass, but tonight, I was grateful for it. Word had already gotten around about Don, which meant we had come home to a spread of food, courtesy of Beck.

Quinn hadn't been interested in eating much—okay, at all —but I forced her to have at least a little, knowing she'd need it.

And though I'd tried to engage her in conversation, she'd responded with one-word answers only. I hated seeing her like this. Hated seeing that fire in her eyes dimmed to only smoldering embers.

I wanted to help her come back to herself, but I didn't know how. She'd said no to a bath, a walk on the beach, and even an axe throwing competition. The one thing she'd agreed on was a cuddle party with season four of *Schitt's Creek* playing in the background.

So now we lay in bed, Quinn's body curled against mine much like that day weeks ago when she'd had her period. I ran my fingers through her hair, and I lost count of how many kisses I'd pressed against her temple, hoping my comfort was enough to soothe her.

She was always the strong one. She wore an armor with everyone, rarely allowing anyone to see beyond her defenses. But I'd watched her wipe away tears at the clinic. She was hurting. It couldn't have been easy losing someone on her watch, no matter how big of an asshole he was.

"So...today was a lot," I said against her hair.

"You don't know the half of it..." she murmured.

"You don't have to say anything, but I'm here if you want to."

She took a deep breath, then exhaled slowly. "Not right now."

I nodded against the top of her head. "Okay, I'll shut up, and we'll watch."

"Actually, would you just...talk? About anything." Her voice was low...raw. And I wasn't so sure that if she had asked me to reach into my chest, pull out my heart, and hand it to her, I wouldn't have done it. I was coming to realize that where Quinn was concerned, there wasn't much I wouldn't do. There wasn't *anything* I wouldn't do.

I hummed, thinking about what I could talk about and decided my siblings would provide nearly endless material. "I don't think I told you, but Harper came last week to do the follow-up interview for that article and almost ran into Levi at the diner." I chuckled under my breath, recalling how he'd scurried out the back door just to avoid any confrontation. "I've never seen him move so fast in my life."

"What's the deal with them? Didn't they used to hang out every summer?"

"They did, yeah, and I have no idea. Levi's not saying anything about it."

She hummed in acknowledgment and tightened her arms around me.

"And I can't believe it, but Luna actually got Brady to attend a protest with her last weekend." I pulled out my phone and thumbed to my photos, pulling up the one Luna had sent me. Wearing sunglasses and a scowl, Brady stood in a crowd of people, holding a sign Luna had clearly made. I tipped the phone toward Quinn and said, "Rumor has it, he almost punched another cop for trying to touch Luna, but that's coming from Mabel, so who knows how accurate it is."

She laughed softly, her body shaking against mine, and I exhaled a sigh of relief. I'd keep talking for the rest of the night if it lifted her spirits.

"Oh, this will make you laugh. Aiden was traumatized at our last little league game."

"Why?"

"One of the single moms came up and not so subtly hinted that her kid didn't have to be the only one to call him Daddy. And by not so subtly hinted, I mean she flat-out said that."

"Oh my God... What'd he do?"

"Pretended he got a call and then just walked away. No idea how he's going to handle that at the next practice. And God help him, but Addison's never gonna let him live it down. The woman who said it graduated high school with her."

"He should just be glad Mabel didn't hear about it."

I snorted, thinking about the fun she'd have with that tiny tidbit of information.

"What else?" she asked, her voice soft.

I hummed, thinking back over the past week. "Everly wanted to adopt a friend for Chuckanut, but Beck swore up and down one dog was his limit. I give it a month before they have dog number two."

"You ever want one?"

I shrugged. "Maybe. For now, I'm satisfied doggy-sitting

for Chuck once in a while. Speaking of, I ran into Mrs. McCaffrey a couple weeks ago when I was walking Chuck at the park. You remember home ec with her?"

Quinn hummed lowly, but that was her only response as her body sank deeper into mine, relaxation finally settling in. I slipped my hand under my T-shirt that she wore, running my fingers lightly up and down her bare back.

"I fucking hated that cake-baking unit. I didn't want to fail in front of you and give you any more ammunition to flay me alive, so I forced Beck to make it with me four times that week."

"And it was still awful," she murmured.

I laughed into her hair. "*So* awful. And it definitely gave you ammunition."

I blew out a heavy sigh and shook my head, thinking back to those years when I'd done just about anything to get her attention. Didn't matter if it was the wrong kind or not. If she was paying attention to me, I called it a win.

"The shit I used to make Beck do back then... We had this whole stretch of empty beach, but I'd still drag him downtown to the park to toss around a football, just because I knew you'd be studying in the gazebo." I chuckled under my breath. "God, you'd get so mad at me whenever that ball landed anywhere near you. Say it was distracting you and that *some* of us actually cared about our grades and our futures. We'd argue for five minutes, then I'd go back to playing catch with Beck, only for it to happen all over again. And then I'd dissect the interaction all the way home and force Beck to weigh in on it."

I let the words hang in the air for a moment before I took a deep breath and admitted, "That's probably why he thinks my agreeing to get married to you was a bad idea. Made it unbalanced... Because I've pretty much had a thing for you since we were fifteen. Beck says I'm obsessed, but I stand by the fact that I'm not at that level of creepy. I never Edward Cullen'ed it and watched you in your sleep or anything. Just basically jacked off to thoughts of you three or four times a day. So...not much different from when you moved back."

I chuckled softly, but only silence greeted my confession. Shit. Had I gone too far? I hadn't come right out and told her I loved her, but I might as well have. And I'd done it when her emotions were already high. When she was already feeling a loss...already overwhelmed.

I held my breath, waiting for her response. *Hoping* for her response. When it didn't come after long moments, I shifted and glanced down at her, only to find her fast asleep.

CHAPTER TWENTY-SEVEN

QUINN

I FELT like I was waking up from the worst hangover I'd ever had. Even though I'd only shed a couple tears last night, and only because of the grief that came from losing someone under my care, my body felt like it'd been put through a blender, and I was still tangled up in knots.

I didn't know where to go from here. Had no idea what the next steps would—or should—be. No idea what this meant for my job. For my dream.

Or for my marriage.

Last night, I'd lain with Ford's heartbeat under my cheek, his soft, soothing voice lulling me into sleep. The last thing I remembered was him mentioning that awful cake he'd made in home ec our junior year. I'd been the guinea pig who'd had to suffer through that monstrosity because through some cruel twist of fate, we'd always been partnered together in our classes. It had been one of the reasons I'd hated him so much because it had given me a front-row seat to him slacking off and still somehow earning straight A's, while I busted my ass for the same.

We'd definitely come a long way from high school rivals to what we were now. I'd been mad at him for so long, so certain that if things had only gone differently, I would've been happier. My parents would've been happier. They would've actually been proud of me...accepted me.

But I knew now there was no way that was ever going to happen. My parents would never be satisfied with anything I did, and I was done trying to appease them. Had stopped answering their calls. I hadn't yet gotten up the nerve to block their numbers, but at least I was taking baby steps.

As for me... Well, I might not have gone to Harvard Med School like I'd wanted, but this life I had wasn't so bad.

I reached out, brushing my fingertips over the arch of Ford's brows, down the straight slope of his nose, and around his perfect, full lips, parted in sleep.

Talk about a twist of fate... Somehow, this man was mine.

I had him. Now I just needed to figure out a way to *keep* him. Needed to figure out if he even wanted that.

I was more grateful than I could say that he'd spent last night filling my head with something other than the anxious thoughts that had consumed me since leaving the clinic. He'd looked after me. Taken care of me. And after a lifetime of having to protect myself from those who were supposed to do just that and did the opposite, this had become a welcome reprieve.

But today was a new day. And for the first time in my life, I didn't know what the hell to do. Had no idea where to go from here because none of this was part of my Plans A through Z.

What I did know was that I had to get up. I had to get out of bed and do...something. I'd been in enough therapy and had enough experience to understand my triggers, and high stress...high emotions tended to send me down a path of negative self-talk. So that meant I had to pretend like this was just another day or I'd spiral into what-ifs and worst-case scenarios, and neither was a good place for me to be.

There were appointments on the schedule...patients to be seen. And now that Starlight Cove was down to one doctor, that meant everything landed on my shoulders. Even if the clinic wasn't mine.

With one last look at my husband, I slid out from under his heavy arm and made my way into the bathroom to get ready. Once I was showered and dressed, I headed back into the bedroom, finding Ford still sleeping soundly. The sheet was pooled around his waist, revealing his bare back and teasing the upper curve of his ass. A mouthwatering sight, without a doubt.

Half of me wanted to slide right back under the covers with him. Wanted to forget yesterday. Forget today or tomorrow or next week. Forget that our expiration date was a giant red X looming on the calendar. Forget everything but what I felt when we were together.

What I'd begun to hope maybe he felt, too.

But the other half of me—the half that was in charge...the half that always did the right thing—knew I couldn't. People needed me today, and I was the only one who could help.

Ford had been up just as late as I had—later, even—so I didn't want to wake him. I'd let him sleep, and we could talk tonight. Figure things out. Maybe...maybe he felt the same as I did? Maybe we could actually turn this fake marriage into something real. Maybe I could somehow make him love me as much as I loved him.

I glanced around the kitchen, looking for a blank sheet of paper or an envelope to jot a note for him on, letting him know where I went. Peeking out from under Ford's keys was a white napkin. Not ideal, but it would do. I pulled it out and grabbed a pen, but before I could scrawl my note, writing on the other side caught my eye. I flipped the napkin over, and my breath caught when the words registered in my brain.

It was our contract, with our expiration date circled.

That red X on the calendar that I hadn't wanted to think about—that I'd thought...hoped...maybe he'd forgotten about—stared back at me. I hadn't thought about this stupid napkin in weeks, but it was clear that wasn't the same for Ford. Had he had it with him last night with the intent of... what? Showing me? Reminding me our time was up and he had better things to get to? That he'd done what he could to help me, but he was finished with the marriage? That he was finished with *me*?

My chest ached at the thought. That while I'd been falling in love with him despite my best efforts not to, he might've been counting down the days till the end. Just biding his time until he could get on with this life and go back to how things were before we'd said our vows. Before he'd called me his wife.

I braced myself on the counter and hung my head between my shoulders, closing my eyes and taking several long, deep breaths. That was my negative self-talk speaking. I had no proof that Ford thought that way. The reason this napkin was on the counter could be something totally innocuous. Maybe it was—

His phone pinged with a text, and my eyes popped open, automatically going to the message on the screen. I blinked, the words not quite registering at first, but when they finally did, my heart sank.

The napkin might not have meant much on its own. It could've been there for any number of reasons. I could've been blowing it completely out of proportion.

But this... This was harder to excuse.

JENNY:

It's been too long. I'm in town and missing you. Tell me when the coast is clear and we can hook up.

I stood frozen, swallowing repeatedly as I tried to force down the lump that had lodged itself in my throat. I knew I shouldn't be, but I was still shocked that he'd move on so quickly. That he was ready to toss away what I thought had been special.

I'd thought what we had was different...for both of us. And I felt like an idiot for even entertaining the thought.

As of the moment Ford had called Don's death last night, the contract became irrelevant. There was no longer a need for Ford and me to be married. And he was, apparently, ready to get out of it as soon as possible so he could get back to business as usual.

My stomach churned, and the negative voices in my head that my parents had fostered my entire life and the ones I'd worked for years to overcome weren't whispering anymore. They were screaming.

What did you expect?

This was all just a game.

None of it was real. Certainly not the way he made you feel loved.

He's seen all of you, your good and bad, and he didn't choose you.

Of course *he didn't choose you.*

He can't wait till you're gone so he can move on with his life.

He's just biding his time until he can be rid—

"Kitten?"

I jumped, dropping the napkin on the counter and spinning to face him. God, he was gorgeous. Standing there in those damn gray sweatpants with rumpled hair and pillow creases on his face, his cheeks the dark pink they always were when he first woke up.

An ache bloomed in my chest over the thought of losing this man when I'd only just gotten him. When I'd only just finally opened my eyes to who he was instead of who I *thought* he was. When I'd only just gotten a glimpse of what it felt like to be his...even if it wasn't real.

"Why're you dressed?" he asked, his voice low and rough as he scratched at the scruff on his jaw. He walked to me and gathered me in his arms, pressing a kiss to the top of my head.

I stayed stiff in his embrace, not allowing myself to sink into his warm body, even if I desperately wanted to. I wanted to forget what I'd seen. Pretend I didn't know he was planning to hook up with a random girl. That he wasn't counting down the days until he was free of me. But that would only make this worse in the long run. It was best to pretend this was what we both wanted. That I was just as ready to be rid of him as he was of me.

When he relaxed his hold on me, I stepped back, averting my gaze. I cleared my throat, hoping my voice came out even. "I'm heading into work."

"*What*?"

"I'm going to the clinic."

He stared at me, brows pinched as if he couldn't understand what I was saying. "Don't you think you should take some time after what happened? I don't think it's a good idea for you to go back this soon. It's barely been twelve hours."

I blew out a frustrated breath, sidestepping him as I gathered my things. Irritated that after everything, he had the gall to pretend like he actually cared.

I needed to get out of there. The past twenty-four hours had been too much, and I was at my breaking point. But I refused to cry in front of him. Not when the inevitable tears were his doing.

"It doesn't really matter if you don't think it's a good idea. Not all of us can take off whenever we want to, Ford. I'm the only one here to do this. If I don't go in, sick patients aren't going to be seen. People need to be taken care of."

"*You* need to be taken care of," he said, a hard edge seeping into his voice. "That's what I'm trying to do here."

"Why?"

"What do you mean, why? Because I'm your husband, and that's what husbands do."

I forced out a laugh. "I think we can probably cut the act now. Seems pretty pointless, doesn't it? Chelsea's wedding is over, and there's no one left to fool at the clinic. No more fake marriage needed. Bonus was that you got out of it a little early, so you can start bed-hopping again whenever you want."

He was quiet for long moments, and I finally lifted my gaze to his. He stared at me, eyes hard and jaw bunching, his entire body stiff. "Thanks for thinking the best of me," he said flatly.

Oh, he had a lot of balls to say that while he had a booty call invitation on his phone from Jan or Judy or whatever the hell her name was.

"It doesn't matter what I think," I said. "Your track record speaks for itself."

"Yeah? What does it say?"

I stared at him, at the eyes I'd grown to love, and felt that hole in my heart expand. The pain seeping into every inch of my body, weighing me down.

I'd never really thought about how this would end. Never concerned myself with it. But I knew, without a doubt, this was it.

We were done.

And there'd be no going back.

"You and I both know you're not forever," I said, the words tasting bitter on my tongue. "*We're* not forever."

Ford's eyes shuttered, his body going rigid, and I wanted to take the words back as soon as they left my lips. Not because they weren't true—that was exactly what we'd said this entire time...that we were only temporary—but because I so desperately wished they weren't.

"And here I thought the ring on your finger said differently." His voice was hard, but there was no denying the thread of hurt woven into his words.

But I'd already been fooled once by him. Tricked into actually believing this had been real. I'd be damned if I'd let it happen again.

I glanced over at his now-darkened phone, recalling what the text had said, and a fresh wave of pain rushed over me, reminding me exactly what this wasn't.

"We both know the ring didn't mean anything. You're the one who put an expiration date on this and said we should get our first divorces out of the way. It's obvious that's what you've been waiting for, so let's just get on with it. Consider this my notice. Go ahead and tell your friend you're free tonight."

CHAPTER TWENTY-EIGHT

FORD

GO AHEAD and tell my friend I'm free tonight? What the fuck did that even mean?

I stared out the window as Quinn drove off, wondering how this morning had become so fucked so quickly. Last night, when she'd fallen asleep in my arms, when I'd finally admitted how long I'd wanted her, I'd hoped it was the start of something real. Where we didn't have to pretend anymore.

And then I woke up to this, and I had no idea where the hell it was all coming from. She was obviously feeling the stress, and who could blame her after the day she'd had?

I didn't know where I'd gone so wrong that she assumed I couldn't wait to get out of this marriage. I thought I'd done a pretty fucking good job of showing her exactly how much I wanted her. But apparently not. And that was something I was going to have to rectify, because I'd be damned if my wife didn't know exactly how fucking much I needed her. Exactly how much I loved her.

But we could talk about everything tonight when she got home. Set things straight. I'd lay it all out on the line and tell her where I was coming from.

As much as I hated that she was already going back into work—especially after the trauma of yesterday—I knew she felt a huge responsibility to the people of Starlight Cove. I just wished she felt that much of a responsibility to herself and her own well-being, because what I said would only go so far.

She was headstrong and stubborn, and they were two of my favorite traits of hers. Seeing her in her element, being strong and confident, turned me the fuck on. But her bullheadedness meant I could push her as much as I wanted, and in the end, she could still decide to dig her heels in. If she didn't want to do it, nothing I could say would make her change her mind.

So it would've been a lost cause trying to stop her from heading into the clinic if that was what she felt she needed to do. But tonight, we were going to talk. Whether she wanted to or not. I wasn't going to roll over without a fight. Not after I knew what it was like to have her as mine.

She thought we weren't forever? By the time I was done with her, she'd know forever wasn't nearly long enough when it came to the two of us.

Scratching my stomach, I strolled over to the kitchen counter, my brows bunching when I found our napkin contract on top of my phone and keys. I normally kept it tucked away in my pocket, along with a hair band she'd flicked at my forehead shortly after she'd moved here, just like she used to do in high school. They were my daily reminder of when she'd come back into my life...when she'd finally become mine. But last night, I'd been in such a hurry to get her settled in and figure out what I could do to help her that I'd emptied my pockets without care.

I picked it up and reached for my phone. The screen lit up, showing a text from Jenny, someone I'd hooked up with a couple times in the past.

JENNY:

> It's been too long. I'm in town and missing you. Tell me when the coast is clear and we can hook up.

Apparently it wasn't just a small-town issue that people from forever ago still had your number, because she wasn't even from around here. Jenny had wanted things as uncomplicated as possible, which had suited me just fine. She didn't do families, so whenever she was in town, she'd text to make sure the coast was clear of mine before we'd get together.

I'd have to tell her she was out of luck and was going to have to find another partner to fill her night with because I'd be busy with my wife.

I glanced at the time the message had come in—right around the time I'd woken up and come in here to find Quinn standing right where I stood now. I snapped my gaze out the window to where she had retreated, the pieces clicking into place. Her total one-eighty, her sudden hostility...

Tell your friend you're free tonight.

"Motherfucker."

I didn't have to be a genius to realize she'd seen the message from someone I hadn't been with in more than a year—someone I'd never reached out to. Someone I'd delete without a second thought... She'd seen it and assumed the worst of me. Assumed I was ready to toss her aside and move on to the next woman. In typical Ford fashion.

She thought I was still that guy.

Not the one I had shown her every day for the past two months. Not the one who couldn't keep his hands off her, who was clearly...obviously...head over fucking heels in love with her.

Instead, she saw me the same way the entire town did. Saw nothing more than the façade I projected, the one no one cared to see beyond.

Never mind that I hadn't looked at another woman since Quinn and I had been married. Hell, I hadn't even been remotely interested in one since she'd stepped foot back in Starlight Cove, well before she'd been mine.

That thought only further twisted the knife in my heart because I thought she'd seen me for me. I thought, after everything we'd been through, that she'd begun to see me as something more. As the man I actually was...

Hers.

Instead, she saw nothing more than the man everyone else in this town saw me as. Just a playboy. Good enough for one night, but not good enough for forever. That was what she'd said, wasn't it? I wasn't forever. *We* weren't forever.

And the irony was, she was the only one I wanted to give my forever to.

I DIDN'T THINK. I got dressed, grabbed my keys and my go bag—a duffel I kept stocked with essentials—and headed to my Jeep. I couldn't be there anymore. Couldn't walk around my home that she'd made hers and see pieces of her everywhere I looked—her hair bands on the table, her bras hanging in the bathroom, her lotion on the nightstand—and not hurt even more with every glimpse.

I needed to get away. Needed to go...*somewhere*. I wanted to escape to Peru or Budapest or fucking Antarctica, but that wasn't in the cards right now.

So instead, I went to the one place I'd always gone when shit got rough. I didn't usually like to dwell in those kinds of feelings for long—in my mind, life was too short to focus on the bad shit—but when things got too heavy, I needed to escape and be by myself for a while until the emotions could settle. Needed to process whatever happened and do so without the well-meaning intrusion of my siblings.

I drove to the forest preserve that bordered the resort's property, traversing the familiar path to the farthest back corner. My favorite spot was an alcove off the beaten path, near the cliffs that overlooked the ocean. I hadn't been back here in years. Hadn't needed to.

It was quiet. Peaceful. And far enough away from any other campsites that it felt like I was the last person on earth.

Which was exactly why I loved it so much. No one ventured out this way because there wasn't a flat surface to be found to place a tent. Good thing I didn't need one.

I parked a dozen yards from my destination—as far as my Jeep could get—grabbed my bag and the hammock I kept stashed in the back, and made my way over.

Going through the routine motions of setting up my site was soothing in a way I'd forgotten how much I loved. The repetitiveness of it...the rhythm... It allowed me to forget for a little while the entire reason I was out here in the first place.

But by the time I lay in the hammock, swinging back and forth to the sound of the waves crashing against the bluffs, it all came back with a vengeance.

Quinn's eyes as she looked at me as if she didn't know me. The cold tone of her voice as she tore down what we had to something she could swat away as easily as a fly. Something she could leave behind without a backward glance.

But what hurt the most was how she'd immediately jumped to conclusions and thought the worst of me. She saw me the same as everyone else did. Even after I'd shown her who I really was. After I'd stripped away every false piece of me and showed her my true self. After I loved her every one of these past fifty-four days.

And, still, she hadn't seen me for me.

It had always been different with Quinn—all the way back in high school. She made me feel things I hadn't been ready for. Fighting with her, egging her on just to have her fury unleashed on me...to have her undivided attention, was the same high I got playing sports or rock climbing or jumping off the cliffs into the ocean. It was an exhilaration that was damn hard to replicate.

But I'd tried.

After she'd left for college and I'd stuck around, I'd tried. I'd pursued women, chasing that thrill I'd always gotten with Quinn. And when the nameless women couldn't fill that void, it was on to the next. A never-ending cycle where I was searching...always searching for something I couldn't find.

I was desperate to feel everything she'd brought out in me —that rush that I experienced around her. The hum under my skin that had made me feel like I had met my counterpart...my match...my perfect equal.

It had taken me more than a decade to realize I'd been searching for her all along.

It had always been her.

But clearly, that had been one-sided. It had to be when she was so willing to throw away what we had, all because she saw me just like everyone else did.

Even though what we had wasn't supposed to be real, it *felt* like it. And every second had felt real to me. Enough to make my chest ache with regret and longing for what we'd never have.

CHAPTER TWENTY-NINE

QUINN

YESTERDAY HAD BEEN a shitshow from start to finish.

After fleeing the cottage in the morning, I'd been distracted all day, providing less than stellar care to the full schedule of patients I saw thanks to the fact that I was now the only doctor in Starlight Cove.

I didn't know what the future of the clinic would be, and I certainly didn't expect Mrs. Dinsmore to already know what her plans were when her husband had just died. And after my fight with Ford, it was the last thing on my mind. At one time, it had been my sole focus. My only goal. But now, I couldn't even muster up the bare minimum of interest in what the future might hold.

Not when my heart was cracked and bleeding, and the only person I wanted to go to for comfort was the one who'd hurt me in the first place.

I'd had all day yesterday to come to terms with what had happened. With my overreaction and my failure to let Ford explain. Worse was that I hadn't even *asked* him to. I'd jumped to conclusions and fled. I'd known the circumstances had made it ripe for me to spiral, but knowing it and being able to do something about it—being able to *stop* it—were two very different things.

Last night after work, after I'd had time to calm down and ignore those voices in my head, I'd gone back to the cottage with the intention of talking to him and getting everything out in the open. Figuring out where the hell we stood and where we went from here. Because real or not, we were married, and that meant deciding our future wasn't going to be easy.

I'd stayed up until 2 a.m., sitting in the chair in the living room and staring out the window, waiting for his headlights to shine through. Only, his Jeep never pulled up in front of the cottage. He never stepped inside. We never talked.

Because Ford never came home.

I'd been called an old soul more than once in my life, but I was certain that descriptor had less to do with my soul and more to do with the childhood I'd somehow survived. In my experience, old souls were just people who'd lived more in their short lives than most did over the course of decades.

And in *my* short life, the lesson I'd learned over and over again was that people didn't love me the way I needed to be loved—with confidence and assurances and unwavering loyalty... I'd learned that people didn't choose me.

Ford had just reiterated what I already knew.

No matter how many therapist visits I'd gone to, or how many years had passed since I'd become aware of those negative thoughts and actively worked against them, they were still my default, especially in times of high stress. Still the whisper in the back of my mind that reminded me of all my faults. Of all the reasons Ford wouldn't stay.

Of *course* he wouldn't stay...

I didn't know where he'd spent the night, and I couldn't bring myself to ask Beck, too scared of what he'd say. That Ford was with that other woman. That I'd finally pushed him away. That he'd realized I wasn't worth the trouble.

That none of this had been worth the trouble.

So, I'd avoided. I'd barely slept and had left before the sun had even risen. I'd taken a sunrise yoga class with Luna on the beach, then headed into town with the sole purpose of keeping my mind occupied all day. It was Saturday, so the clinic was closed, which meant I couldn't even fall back on work to fill my time.

Instead, I swung by the café on Main Street, picked up a latte and a muffin, and headed to the gazebo in the park. Maybe not my best idea since I had a front row view of the firehouse from here, but Ford wasn't on duty today, so at least I didn't have to worry about seeing him.

Climbing the steps and settling onto the bench that wrapped around the interior of the gazebo felt like déjà vu. In high school, this was the place I'd escaped to when I'd been avoiding going home.

And there had been a *lot* of nights I'd avoided going home.

I'd loved the peace of it here, with the distant lullaby of the ocean and the hum of Starlight Cove residents as they wandered the streets of downtown. But mostly, I'd just loved that my parents weren't there. That I didn't have to listen to their thinly veiled insults tearing me down. Reminding me I wasn't good enough. That I'd never be good enough.

It had always been quiet and serene here... Or it had been whenever Ford hadn't been nearby, which he'd tended to be with alarming frequency. Of all the times I'd wanted to strangle him with my bare hands—and I'd wanted to do that a lot—at least half of them had happened right here. Where he'd argued with me about absolutely nothing while playing catch with his brother. One time, he'd debated me for fifteen minutes about the pen I'd been using on my homework, as if it had caused him personal distress.

How sad was it that I wanted to have those stupid arguments with him again? Wanted that low-level hum of competition that always radiated between us. Wanted the safety, the familiarity our relationship had been providing me for years, even before this fake marriage.

I couldn't stop the tears from filling my eyes, but I bit my lip to keep them from falling and swallowed down the lump in my throat. The last thing I needed was someone showing up and asking why I was crying. So I put myself back together, sorting everything I was feeling about Ford into a neat little box and closing the lid tight.

When I finally had control of my emotions, I took a sip of my latte and stubbornly pretended I'd been successful at shoving Ford out of my mind. I could do that all day.

"Well, I thought that was my previous tenant out here!"

I turned my gaze toward the voice. Mabel waved, strolling toward me wearing a leopard tracksuit and a matching visor.

I forced a smile to my face even as my stomach churned and dread filled me. Had word already spread about what had happened with Ford and me? God, was Mabel here to interview me for a Live? Ask me about my fake marriage and what I thought about my husband hooking up with some random woman already?

I wasn't sure I'd survive it.

But one glance at her empty hands, free of any recording device, had me exhaling a deep sigh of relief.

"Hey, Mabel."

"Hey yourself!" She climbed the stairs before taking the seat next to me and giving my knee a pat. "How are things going with that hunky firefighter husband of yours?" Before I could answer, she continued, "Really damn good, I imagine." She elbowed me in the side and waggled her brows as if I hadn't caught her meaning. "Is he at the firehouse today?"

"No, he's...with Beck." I hoped she didn't catch the stumble in my words or pick up on the fact that I was lying through my teeth. Because, no, I *didn't* know where my husband was.

She hummed in acknowledgment and shot me a bright smile. "I'm so happy for you both. After knowing you since you were babies... Well, it makes this a whole lot sweeter. You left for college before you could really settle into yourself— and thank God for that...gave you a chance to get away from your parents for a bit and blossom into the amazing woman you are..."

I snapped my gaze to hers, trying to read in her expression if she'd meant that how it had sounded. My parents had always put on a show for everyone else and had no problem making me out to be the issue. They were so good at it, so convincing, that I hadn't stopped to question if maybe not everyone had believed them.

Before I could ask her anything about it, she continued, "But I was lucky enough to watch your husband grow up into the man he is. Watched him wander around, too," she said wryly, "trying to figure out what it was he was searching for. But I think we both know it was you."

I blew out a humorless laugh. "I'm not sure I'd go as far as to say that."

"Oh, honey. That boy's been smitten for *years*. Might've been too dumb to say anything, but sometimes we women make them stupid. And there's no doubt that man is stupid in love."

"I'm not—" I cut myself off before I could finish the rest of that sentence, because what could I say? That I wasn't who he wanted? That he didn't love me? Even if those statements were true, I was his wife in the eyes of everyone in this town. From their perspective, of course he was in love with me.

"Well, I've gotta run." She patted my knee again and pushed to stand. "Would you mind letting your husband know the picture he wanted should be delivered to you soon?"

"Picture?"

"Yes! He didn't tell you? It's your first kiss as a married couple. The one from the front page. Boy, let me tell you, when he cornered me after that was printed, I thought for sure he was going to tear me up one side and down the other." She clucked her tongue. "Could've knocked me over with a feather when he said he just wanted a copy—one for his phone and a print for the cottage—and if I got him both, he'd let my stalking slide and wouldn't mention it to Brady. Heaven knows I don't need any more trouble with the sheriff..."

My brows furrowed as I registered everything she'd said. "Ford asked for that?"

"Sure did." She grinned then gave a slow shake of her head. "I never thought I'd see the day Ford McKenzie voluntarily displayed a picture of himself and a woman on his phone for the whole world to see, but here we are. He enjoyed sampling the wares, if you know what I mean. Nothing wrong with that! I did a little of it in my day. But as soon as George and I had our first date, that was it. I'm not surprised Ford was the same. As soon as you came back into town, it was game over for him. But of course, after the crush he had on you in high school, that's to be expected."

"Crush..."

"Oh sure, like you didn't know." She smirked at me. "And it was no surprise that continued, especially when you've grown into such a gorgeous, kind, intelligent woman that anyone with half a brain cell would be proud of. He didn't stand a chance, now did he?"

That damn lump was back in my throat, and I worked overtime trying to swallow it down. Trying to make sense of what she'd said, but everything was getting jumbled up, too much information at once. Ford hadn't had a crush on me in high school... He'd driven me to the brink of insanity, and I'd been downright cruel to him. And the picture he wanted? That didn't necessarily mean anything. Of course he'd have proof of his wife when we were trying to make this ruse a reality to everyone around us. Of course it wasn't real.

"Oh, and I forgot to tell you that I ordered more of that strawberry lube. I'm sure you two've already gone through what I gave you..." She sighed, a dreamy, far-off look on her face. "I remember when George and I couldn't keep our hands off each other in that honeymoon stage. But don't you worry—my supply should be restocked lickety-split."

And then, before I could tell her there wasn't any lube use in our future, she took off, leaving me staring after her, my thoughts chaotic.

Ford...crushing on me in high school? Ridiculous. And absolutely not true. It couldn't be...

But before I could focus more on that, my phone pinged with an incoming text.

LUNA:

I think you left your water bottle down at the beach this morning. Purple?

"Dammit," I muttered before typing a response.

QUINN:

Yeah, that's mine.

320

LUNA:

I thought so! I'll leave it at the main inn for you.

QUINN:

Thank you. And thanks for the class this morning. I had a lot of fun.

LUNA:

Anytime. I mean that.

There was no way Luna had known what had gone on with Ford and me, but she'd been extra gentle with me this morning, shooting me concerned looks whenever she thought I wasn't looking. So I definitely looked like a mess. And I had no interest in seeing Ford yet if my pain was written all over my face.

But I needed to pick it up, and at least doing so would occupy my mind for a little while. After I grabbed it, I could go for a walk on the beach. Let it soothe me in the way it always did.

And the chance I'd run into Ford at the main inn when he wasn't working today was slim to none. That made it a safe bet in my mind.

CHAPTER THIRTY

FORD

THE PLACE I had always escaped to was losing its charm because I didn't feel even a tiny bit better the following morning. Normally, after an entire day to myself with nothing but my thoughts to keep me company, I would've worked my way out of my funk. Would've gotten over whatever was bothering me and gotten back to the status quo.

Instead, I still felt like shit. Still felt this ache in my chest, this emptiness that had Quinn's name branded on it.

And I had no idea what the hell to do about that.

I sat in the hammock, my legs hanging over the side as I stared out at the glittering path the sun made on the surface of the ocean. It wasn't long before the sound of shoes crunching over the forest floor reached me, and I didn't even have to turn my head in that direction to know who it was.

"Aren't you supposed to be at the farmers market?" I asked as I swung back and forth, not bothering to lift my gaze to his.

"Made an exception this week."

"How'd you find me?"

Beck walked up and took a seat in the empty space next to me, the hammock halting its rhythm until he got settled and pushed us to swing again. "It wasn't hard. If you're hiding, maybe don't go to the same place you always do when shit gets too real." He scratched his jaw. "And also not a place Brady drives through every night for welfare checks. He sent me a text last night to let me know you were here."

I blew out a frustrated breath. I loved my siblings. Didn't know what I'd do without them. But Jesus Christ, they irritated the shit out of me sometimes. Couldn't they ever leave well enough alone?

"I figured my coming out here was a big enough hint to stay away."

He shrugged, his shoulder brushing against mine. "I gave you till the morning."

"How generous of you," I said flatly.

"I'm going to go out on a limb and say you're not out here because the asshole doctor died."

I breathed out a humorless laugh. "Not exactly."

Although, in a roundabout way, all this pain was his fault. If he hadn't made his stupid stipulation and Quinn and I hadn't gotten married, I could've gone on living in blissful ignorance, chasing a high I didn't know I'd found in her, all while my dick ignored every other woman in existence. It would've been a lonely life, but at least it wouldn't have been painful.

"What's going on?" he asked, all teasing gone from his tone.

I didn't want to tell him. It wasn't like he'd be able to fix it anyway. And I didn't want to admit it. Didn't want to voice aloud that it was over. Because maybe if I didn't say it, it wouldn't be true...

He jabbed an elbow in my side. "Well?"

I shrugged like what I was saying wasn't a big deal. Like the two words weren't tearing me up inside. "We're done."

"You're...done."

"Yep."

"Are...you gonna tell me any more? Or do I have to guess what the hell is going on?"

I blew out a frustrated breath. "She said I wasn't built for forever. That *we* weren't forever, then she stormed out of the cottage like her ass was on fire. Like she couldn't get away fast enough."

"I thought you *weren't* forever. Wasn't the whole point of this idiotic plan just to be temporary?"

"Thanks for reminding me I was an idiot."

"No problem."

I shook my head. "You and I both know the whole temporary clause was a crock of shit. I was all in from the beginning. You knew it, and I refused to acknowledge it. But I'm not in the mood for I told you so."

"Good because I wasn't going to say it."

I cracked open one eye and glanced over at him. "Why not?"

"Why would I? I'm not an asshole." He paused, then said, "Not *all* the time."

"No, but it's the truth. You called this from day fucking one. Said I shouldn't go through with it because I was already in too far. You were right."

"I didn't want to be."

"Doesn't matter. You were. I was in too deep, and she wasn't in nearly deep enough."

"I find it hard to believe it's over just like that. Have you tried—oh, I don't know—actually talking to her?"

"It wouldn't matter even if I did. She already made up her mind about me."

"What do you mean by that?"

"She saw our contract on the counter, and then she saw a text from someone and assumed the worst about both."

"The contract's not usually out?"

"No. Usually, it's tucked away in my pocket because I'm so fucking gone for her I act like some kind of love-sick idiot. But I was in such a hurry to make sure she was all right last night that I emptied it out of my pockets along with everything else."

"That seems reasonable. A little weird, but reasonable. Who was the text from?"

"Jenny."

"Who the fuck is Jenny?"

I blew out a humorless laugh. Yeah...exactly. The woman hadn't even ranked in importance enough for me to tell my twin about her, which was to say she wasn't important at all. "Someone I hooked up with a while ago."

"Obviously pre-marriage…"

"Try pre-last year."

"And?"

"*And* Quinn thought I was…I don't know. Cheating on her? Or I was going to? I have no fucking idea."

"So what? You obviously weren't, so just tell her that."

"So what?" I asked incredulously. "*So what*? So I opened myself up to someone other than you for the first time in my entire fucking life. I cracked my heart in two and laid it at her feet…showed her who I am—who I *really* am and not who I project to everyone else. I showed her *me*, and she either didn't care enough to see it or decided she didn't like what she saw. So that's *what*."

Beck blew out a long sigh and shook his head. "Look, man, I don't know how things are between you two behind closed doors. And I don't know what her history is or what kind of baggage she's got, but we've all got shit. I'm going to hazard a guess and say she felt like she was backed into a corner. And people don't always think rationally when they're backed into a corner." He gestured to our surroundings. "Case in point—your dumb ass out here because you're scared."

"I'm not scared."

"No? Then you're hurt. Or you're just being an idiot. Or you can't figure out how to own your shit and come out and tell her you love her. Take your pick."

"I never said I loved her."

Beck rolled his eyes so hard, I could've sworn I actually heard them. "I'm not going to dignify that with a response.

But I'm guessing if she's feeling insecure enough about your relationship that a random text from another woman was sufficient to set her off, you haven't bothered to tell her that you've been obsessed with her for half your life."

"For the last fucking time, I'm not obsessed with her. Jesus, you make me sound like a stalker."

"*Fine*...you've been *into her* for half your life. Better?"

No, that wasn't fucking better because that made this even worse. Made this loss hit all that much harder. Because she was all I wanted. All I'd wanted for *years*, and it'd taken me until recently to realize it.

To realize it, only to lose her in the end.

"You're being an idiot," Beck said.

"Awesome," I said flatly. "Great pep talk. Thanks for that."

"You want a pep talk? Fine. This is crunch time—which you should know, based on the number of romances you steal from Everly—"

"I don't steal them!"

"—when the two idiots in the book can't figure out their shit and they break things off because they're too scared or too stupid to talk it out. Except this isn't a book. This is happening in real life, in real time. And you've got to decide if you're going to be the dumbass who buries his head in the sand and lets the best thing that's ever happened to you slip through your fingers, or if you're going to pull your head out of your ass and actually fight for something for once in your life."

He pushed himself out of the hammock and stood in front of me, blocking the sun's glare as he stared down at me.

"This isn't going to be handed to you, man. Not like everything else in your life has been. If you want this bad enough, you're actually going to have to fight for it."

———

IT TOOK me all of twenty minutes after Beck left to come to my senses. My twin was a man of few words, which meant the ones he used generally held weight and should be listened to. So, I did.

And...he'd been right.

No two ways about it. Hadn't I said the same thing to Cassidy at little league practice? That we all had off days, but the point was to show up and try again. That you didn't give up if it was something you loved. And instead of loving Quinn like I needed to—like *she* needed me to—I'd been ready to give up. Ready to shove my head in the sand instead of facing things and putting in the work.

I was so used to things coming easily for me that I didn't know what to do when I was presented with an actual challenge. And my wife was nothing if not a challenge—I loved that part of her. And she was a challenge I would gladly face every day for the rest of my life.

First, though, I had to make sure I had the rest of my life with her. I just had no fucking idea how to go about doing that. Not when I'd already been loving her every day of the past nearly eight weeks. I didn't know how else to show her that.

But I was going to have to figure that shit out because I

wasn't going to lose her now that I'd finally gotten her. Not after spending fourteen years searching for everything she gave me.

I tossed my hammock and bag in the back of my Jeep and then climbed into the driver's seat, intent on heading to the resort to do...something. I wasn't sure what my next step was, but I knew I wasn't going to find it out here.

Before I could pull out, my phone buzzed with an incoming text. I couldn't stop the hope from rising, but it was quickly squashed when Addison's name flashed on the screen.

ADDISON:

You've got a package at the main inn

Come pick it up because I'm not your fucking courier

FORD:

Calm down. I'm heading that way now.

Have you seen Quinn?

ADDISON:

This morning at yoga

Why?

Shouldn't you know where your wife is?

What's going on??

FORD:

Relax

ADDISON:

Say that to my face

Um, I'd pass on that because for being such a tiny thing, she could throw a punch like...well, like she had five older brothers who'd taught her how to throw a punch.

ADDISON:

I don't have time to sit around and wait for your slow-ass, old-man texting skills

I'm showing some guests to their cottage

Aiden's doing a supply run

Don't touch anything except the package while I'm gone

I mean it!

I'll know if something is out of place

I rolled my eyes but tossed my phone on the seat and drove toward the inn, my fingers drumming on the steering wheel. I wanted to see Quinn now. Wanted to tell her all the things I loved about her while I was buried inside her, kissing away every one of her insecurities.

But it wasn't going to be that easy, and I still had no idea how to approach this. And since I had absolutely zero impulse control, I took a roundabout way to avoid driving past our cottage because if I saw her car there, I'd be tempted to stop and go in half-cocked without a plan.

Instead, I drove the long way. Most of the cottages were occupied now—a far cry from only a few months ago—but it'd been a relief to the whole family. It was more work for us —Aiden and Addison, especially—and I wasn't sure how long we'd be able to continue on with just us running the show. But for now, we made it work.

By the time I pulled into the parking lot in front of the main inn, I still had no idea what to do about Quinn. No idea how to go about winning her back. But I shoved that aside as I parked next to a rental car in front of the main inn. A *Be Right Back* sign hung on the inn door, but I knew from experience it wouldn't be locked, so I made my way inside.

It was quiet, unsurprisingly since both Addison and Aiden were gone. She didn't tell me where she'd stowed the package, so I headed to the check-in counter first, my steps faltering when I saw someone standing there.

"Can I help—" I started, my words cutting off when the man turned around to face me.

Quinn's father stood in front of me, a too-bright smile on his face. It was the first time I'd seen him since Quinn and I had gotten married...since she'd shared the devastating stories from her childhood, with him featuring as one of the villains.

Where once I would've seen an overly polished man who was obsessed with his appearance—his perfectly groomed hair, freshly shaven face, and name-brand items from head to toe—now all I saw was her abuser. What he'd done to her might not have been physical, but his words had hurt her just as badly as a blow would have.

"Mr. Cartwright," I said, my voice cool.

"Oh, I think we're probably beyond that, all things

considered." He winked at me, like we were both in on a secret. "You can call me Brock."

"I don't think so. What can I do for you?"

He sniffed, clearly not used to people not fawning over him, and shifted on his feet. "Well, I'm hoping you can help me find my daughter. She hasn't been returning my or her mother's calls, and we're worried about her. Since she wouldn't pick up the phone, I had to take some time out of my schedule to fly up here and make sure everything was okay. You know how she can get..."

I folded my arms over my chest and leaned back against the counter. "No, I don't think I do. Why don't you enlighten me?"

He rolled his eyes. "Oh, you know. Always so dramatic. Making a bigger deal out of everything than it is. She does *love* to play the victim."

This motherfucker...

"You think *she's* the one who plays the victim," I said, tone flat.

He blew out a long-suffering sigh and shook his head. "Afraid so. She's been doing it since she was little. Her mother and I have tried to get her to stop—honestly, it was embarrassing. Well, I'm sure you know what that's like now. Being—" he cleared his throat, giving me a once-over "— married to her."

"Oh, I know exactly what she's like."

Beautiful and kind and strong and stubborn and committed and determined and soft in all the perfect ways and loyal and giving and a million other qualities I couldn't even detail.

"Exactly, so you know she's—"

"I'm not sure what you think is going to happen here," I said, cutting him off. "Or if you thought somehow I'd be stupid enough to take your words at face value... As if my wife hadn't confided in me all the awful, fucked-up things you've been doing to her for years. But I—"

"Whoa, whoa. Now wait just a minute." He held out his hands, as if that would be enough to calm me down, his face a mask of concern that was pure bullshit. "I don't know what she's told you, but you have to take what she says with a grain of salt. Girls like her say whatever they need to to get the attention they aren't going to get otherwise because...well, you know."

"No, I don't know."

"She's—"

"You think I'm just going to let you stand here and insult my wife?" I pushed off from the counter and stepped toward him. "Go ahead. Try it again."

He held up his hands in placation, the corners of his mouth turned down. "Look, I'm sorry if you were offended by what I said. I just want to talk to my daughter. I haven't seen her in months, she's not answering our calls, and then last night, I find out my best friend died at her hands." He shook his head, his façade cracking for a moment as anger overtook his features. "Well, it wouldn't surprise me if she just let it happen. She's always hated him, even when he gave her a handout so she could work at his clinic. God knows he could've found a dozen other more qualified physicians to take her place."

"Get out," I said, my voice hard as I pointed to the front door.

"Excuse me?"

"Get the fuck out, get back in your rental car, head to the airport, and fly home. If you think I'm going to let you within breathing distance of Quinn, you're out of your mind. I don't want you here, and it's obvious neither does she, so I'm not letting you anywhere near my wife. Not now, not ever. Not when I'm around."

"You can't stop me from seeing my own daughter."

"The fuck I can't." I stood to my full height—I had a couple inches on him and quite a bit of muscle, and I was damn well going to use it—and stared him down. "If she says she wants to see you, then I'll support her, but that hasn't happened. So it's time for you to get out before I call the sheriff and let him know you're trespassing on our family's property."

He breathed out a forced laugh. "You can't be serious."

"Can't I?"

"How am I supposed to talk to her if she's not answering?"

"Maybe take that as the hint it is—your daughter doesn't want to speak to you anymore."

"Well, she can't just—"

"She can, and she did. And it's about fucking time because you've been abusing her for too long. Don't contact her again. If she wants to be in touch with you, she will be. Do we understand each other?"

His demeanor changed so fast, it was almost like a switch being flipped. One minute, he was all confusion and remorse, and then next, he was glaring at me, his eyes hard and jaw tight, hands clenched at his sides.

But I wasn't moving. In fact, I wished he'd take a swing at me so I could lay him out. He could try to intimidate me all he wanted, but it wasn't working. This waste of space thought I was going to let him within a ten-mile radius of Quinn? I didn't fucking think so. Not when he was only going to pile more stress on her shoulders. Not when his only intention was to tear her down.

When he finally realized I wasn't budging, he sneered at me. "You can keep her. She's been nothing but an embarrassment from day one."

The only thing that kept me from decking this asshole was the fact that if I were in jail for assault and battery—and there was no way this motherfucker wouldn't press charges— I wouldn't be able to find Quinn and make things right between us.

"I'll gladly keep her. For the rest of my life, if I'm lucky."

Finally, he spun on his heel and stormed out of the inn, his tires screeching in his quick retreat. What an absolute piece of shit. I felt like I needed a shower after that ten-minute interaction just to wash off the slime. And Quinn had put up with that for more than thirty years. Put up with it and somehow still turned into the woman she was. The woman I loved.

I made a quick detour to the back office in search of the package, finding the small box on Addison's messy desk.

Without reading the label, I opened it to find a small black box inside, shock registering as I lifted the lid and pulled out what was inside. I stared at the item for long moments, turning it this way and that, a tiny detail making me shake my head as hope swept over me for the first time.

CHAPTER THIRTY-ONE

QUINN

I DIDN'T KNOW how long I stood there, frozen to my spot around the corner from the check-in counter. It'd taken me longer than it should have to realize what was happening, but my dad's voice had stopped me dead in my tracks, that all too familiar pit opening up in my stomach, my nerves in overdrive at just the thought of having to interact with him.

But then Ford had stood up to him. For *me*. And not just that, but he'd parked himself in front of me like a ten-foot brick wall, refusing to let anything harmful come my way, including my father. *Especially* my father.

Ford hadn't waffled for even a second. Not when my dad had pulled out his usual tricks, all his old standbys. Not when he'd spewed lies and overexaggerations about me. Ford hadn't believed a word of it. Without wavering, he'd trusted me...believed me.

Protected me.

He'd done what no one in my life ever had. And the fact

that he'd done so after everything I'd said to him yesterday morning? That he'd done it thinking we were done? That I was through with him?

I swallowed repeatedly, trying to shove down my emotions. Park them in the neat little box I'd created for them so I could keep a lid on it. So I could be the strong one, too tough to be torn down. Never letting people see my soft underbelly. But it was no use. My eyes burned, my nose stung, and my throat tightened as the tears came unbidden.

I cried—truly cried, not just a tear or two, but a deluge of them—for the first time in a long time because I stood there, rooted in place, as I finally realized what I'd thrown away. What my insecurities had made me toss aside.

Ford's love.

I wasn't sure how I'd never seen it... How I hadn't realized it was there. Not when he'd shown me all along. He was unwavering in his focus on me, in his support of me, in his care for me. He was the only person I'd ever been able to count on. The only one I trusted enough to share the deepest, darkest parts of myself with. My rival at one time, and now my best friend.

And I'd walked away from him because I was scared. Because I believed the old voices in my head—the voices my parents had cultivated in me—instead of his. I'd thought the worst of him solely because of my insecurities. I'd slotted him into the safe space outside of my heart so I wouldn't get hurt, and instead, I'd hurt him.

Swiping at my tears, I forced myself to move, making my way into the inn and listening for any signs of movement. I'd only been inside this part of the resort a couple times, so I wasn't overly familiar with it, but I rushed room to room, hoping I'd find Ford in each one.

But room after room was empty until I'd searched them all. He was nowhere to be found. At some point in my searching, he must've gone outside and I'd missed him, like sand slipping through my fingers.

Knowing he had to be close and needing to find him, I pushed through the front door, nearly colliding with Addison in my haste to leave.

"Whoa, what's the rush?" she asked. "Late for a date?"

"Um...kind of. Did you happen to see Ford out here?"

"No..." she said, drawing out the word. "But Ford was looking for you earlier. Did you guys lose each other today, or what?"

"Kind of." Lost our way, definitely.

She narrowed her gaze on me. "Why are your eyes all red? Are you two fighting?"

"I just...really need to find him," I said, praying a new wave of tears wouldn't choose now to rush forward. "Do you have any idea where he might be?"

She studied me for several long moments, her lips pursed as if she wasn't sure if she wanted to push me on the subject or not. Eventually, she said, "He was here picking up a package that was supposed to be delivered to your cottage. He's probably headed there—"

"Thank you!" I said without waiting for her to finish the sentence.

I'd walked over here because I wanted the fresh air, but

now I was wishing I had my car because it'd get me to Ford a hell of a lot faster.

By the time I made it to the cottage, I was really regretting my stance to only run if a murderer was chasing me because I was out of breath and a little sweaty, and I wasn't sure I wanted to reunite with my husband this way.

But as I tore through our front door, my gaze scanning the inside of the cottage, I realized it didn't matter.

Because Ford wasn't here.

Ford

WITH MY THOUGHTS A JUMBLED MESS, I walked straight from the main inn to the diner. I strode inside—glad to see it was empty save for my twin and Everly—and jerked my chin at them both.

"Hey," Everly said, her eyes warm and concerned. Beck had clearly filled her in on what was happening—how much, I wasn't sure. But I could use a female perspective, so I was glad she was here.

"I see you're back in the land of the living," Beck said, setting a giant strawberry spinach salad in front of Everly. "Does that mean you pulled your head out of your ass?"

"Kind of. I mean, mostly. I was all set to figure that shit out, but then I got a text from Addison and had to swing by the inn before she castrated me. And then I ran into Quinn's absolute shithead of a father—I told him to never come back, by the way, so if you see him around, call Brady. Or me, because I wouldn't mind landing him on his ass. After that, I picked up the package Addison wasn't going to deliver because she's not my fucking courier—her words, not mine —and I found *this*."

I slammed the box down on the counter and raised my brows at him.

Beck looked at it, then at me, then at it again, before shifting his gaze to Everly and then back to me. "I want to ask about the whole dad thing, but I feel like you're really pushing this box on me. Did you buy me something?"

"No." I took off the lid, pulled out the black metal ring that was nestled inside, and held it up for him and Everly to see. "It's for me. I think. Probably. Well, I'm pretty sure. Okay, I'm like ninety-nine percent sure..."

Everly laughed as Beck said, "Awfully certain of yourself..."

"My deduction skills say I'm right."

"Why's that?"

"Well, first, it was addressed to our cottage. Second, it's basically a replica of this one." I held up my hand where I wore the black silicone ring Quinn had put on my finger the day we'd gotten married. "Except it's metal. And third, it's engraved with this..."

Beck and Everly both leaned forward as I held out the ring to them.

"*No take backs...*" he murmured before glancing at Everly, then me, brows up. "Are we supposed to know what that means?"

"No, but *I* do. It's... It's like mine and Quinn's thing. I said it right before we got married... Had it engraved on the inside of hers."

"*Aww.*" Everly leaned on her elbow, sliding closer to me, and I swore her eyes actually turned into hearts. "That doesn't sound like something a *fake* husband would do. In fact, that's book-boyfriend material right there. Did she love it?"

"Um..." I scratched my temple, thinking back to when I'd given it to her. Maybe doing so after slipping a vibrator inside her pussy with the intent of making her come in public had been the wrong move. "I don't really know. She didn't say too much when I gave it to her."

"She does seem like the strong, silent type," Everly said with a nod. "But I bet she was squealing like a schoolgirl on the inside."

"So she got this for you, huh?" Beck said, arms crossed over his chest. He looked like his typical grumpy ass, but there was also relief in his posture. Like her doing this had settled something inside him. I wish he'd share with the class, because I had no clue.

"Well, what does it mean?" I asked.

"What do you mean, *what does it mean*?" Beck stared at me with a furrowed brow, and I was pretty sure he'd have smacked me upside the head if I were within reach. "It means you're a dumbass for leaving, and you're a dumbass now because you're in here talking to us instead of hunting for your wife."

"I think I'm done with you calling me a dumbass today."

"You don't want me to call you a dumbass? Stop acting like one, dumbass."

Everly reached out, placing a hand over Beck's, and said, "I think what your brother means to say is that this shows she is clearly as into this as you are. And that you should probably find her and talk out your issues."

Beck pointed a finger at Everly and nodded. "I mean, if you need to be coddled, then yeah, what she said."

I blew out a deep sigh, scrubbing a hand on my face. "Okay... But what do I *say*?"

"When you see her, you'll know what the right thing to say is," she said.

"And what if I don't? What if it doesn't magically come to me?"

Everly shrugged, shooting me a smile. "Then you tell her you love her. That you never want to live without her. And then you actually talk about the issues that pushed you apart in the first place, so this doesn't happen again. Because I kind of love the idea of having her as a sister-in-law."

I shot my gaze between the two of them, then down to Everly's bare left hand, before settling on my brother's shocked face.

Everly rolled her eyes. "Oh, don't look so surprised. Is that not where this is going?"

Beck cleared his throat. "No, it is. I just figured it would be more of a surprise than you casually dropping it like it's no big deal."

"Well, you've basically peed a circle around me every day for the past two years, and we're building a house together on your family's land. I don't think marriage is going to be a surprise to anyone, sweetie."

"I mean, she's right," I said. "You *have* been super obsessed with her that whole time. Like, disconcertingly so."

Beck shot me a glare. "Why are you still here?"

That was a great question. I snatched the box off the counter and placed the ring back inside before offering them a two-finger wave. Then I hustled out of the diner, ready to find my wife, that beautiful little liar, and put to rest any uncertainty she had over exactly how I felt about her.

CHAPTER THIRTY-TWO

QUINN

I HAD no idea where to search for Ford, but starting by asking Beck was probably my best option. I was sure he knew everything that had happened between my husband and me —he and Ford didn't keep many, if any, secrets. Which would mean he'd know how I'd jumped to conclusions and left. He'd know all the hurtful things I'd said to Ford. He'd know that I'd let my insecurities get the better of me and hadn't seen Ford for the amazing man he was.

But that was something I was going to have to deal with, something I needed to face head on. I didn't want to go another night without my husband. Didn't want another *hour* to pass without telling him everything I was feeling. And if I had to spill my guts to Beck in order to find his brother, so be it.

I stepped out of the cottage and into the late-summer sun. Giving myself an internal pep talk, I locked up before smoothing my hands down my sundress. Beck wasn't a scary guy—okay, he kind of was. But only in that he was protective of those he loved, and the only person he loved more than his twin was Everly. What I had to tell him was probably going to be a hard sell, but I was going to do it. I'd make him see exactly how much Ford meant to me.

Exactly how much I loved him, and exactly how sorry I was for everything.

With my head down, I took a deep breath and spun around on the porch, intent on making my way to the diner to spill my guts. Hopefully Beck was in a good mood today. Hopefully he was feeling generous. Hopefully he—

"Hey, kitten."

I jerked my head up at the sound of Ford's voice, all throaty and rough, and there he stood. He wore jeans and a gray T-shirt, his hair in disarray as if he'd been running his fingers through it without thought. As if maybe this separation had been just as hard on him. God, had it really only been a day since I'd last seen him?

As I looked my fill of him, it took me several moments to realize what he'd said...what he'd called me, and I snapped my gaze to his, my voice caught in my throat as hope bloomed in my chest.

He slowly walked toward me, ascending the stairs of our front porch, until suddenly, he was standing in front of me. He ran his gaze over me, his eyes cataloging all my features, running over every inch of my body. And I had no idea how I'd never seen this before. How I'd questioned this man's feelings. How could I when he looked at me like that?

"I was looking for you," I said, finally finding my voice.

He studied me, his eyes holding an apprehension I wasn't used to seeing with him. Normally, he jumped in headfirst. Doubt didn't register in his thought processes. But there was no denying it was there now. No denying I'd been the one who put it there. "Why?"

I bit my lip, wondering how much I should say. Wondering where to start... "I heard what you said. To my father."

He froze, his entire body going stiff as he stared down at me. As he tried to read more into my posture. Into my words. "I'm sorry if I overstepped and—"

"You didn't," I said, my words already coming out shaky. "I can't even tell you what it felt like to hear you do that for me. To support me. Even after..."

He made a gruff sound in the back of his throat, his hand lifting toward me before falling back to his side. "I'll always support you, kitten. Always protect you. No matter what."

"I know that now." I shoved aside my nerves, forcing myself to say what I needed to. What he deserved to hear. "And I'm sorry I didn't see it sooner. I'm sorry for not seeing *you* sooner. Seeing the man I know you are. The man I'm in love with."

There was a beat of silence, and then Ford's mouth dropped open, his gaze locked on my face, wide eyes darting to every inch of it as if he couldn't believe the words I'd spoken. That was my fault, for not making him feel seen or heard. A mistake I hoped I'd get the chance to work the rest of my life not to make again.

I swallowed, trying to force down the tears, but it was no

use. They clogged my throat and filled my eyes, spilling over as they ran down my cheeks. "Me lashing out yesterday and immediately going to the worst-case scenario was more about me than it ever was about you."

Ford let out a low, rough noise as if my tears physically pained him and shifted to step forward, but I held up my hand, holding him back. I needed to get this all out in the open so we could hopefully start over. Start fresh and build something permanent. Something real.

Something forever.

"You know how I grew up," I said. "The things my parents said to me—hell, you got to witness it firsthand."

His expression hardened, his posture growing stiff as he clenched a hand into a fist. "I don't know how you lived with that, kitten. It just reiterates how strong you are."

I shook my head, ready to bare myself in a way I've never done with anyone before. "I don't always feel strong. Getting down on myself is a daily struggle. And that sort of conditioning doesn't just suddenly go away, as much as I wish it did. Those negative voices are in my head constantly, repeating all the lies they told me. It's something I have to actively fight against. Most of the time, I can. But sometimes... Sometimes I can't, and they get the better of me. Like yesterday, after I saw the contract and the text."

My bottom lip quivered as I sucked in a deep breath, recalling the sharp pain that had exploded inside me.

"They didn't mean anything. Or they didn't mean what you assumed." Ford reached into his pocket and pulled out the napkin, holding it up between two fingers. "I've carried this in my pocket every day since we made it."

"Why?"

"Because it was the day you finally became mine," he admitted, his low voice wrapping around me like a blanket. "And as for the text..." He pulled out his phone and thumbed to his messages before turning the screen toward me.

The woman's messages were still there, but they weren't what snagged my attention. It was Ford's reply. Two little words—*not interested*—sent with an image of his left hand, wedding band on display.

"I can't erase my past, kitten. Just like you can't. But no one—and I mean *no one*—means more to me than you do. I don't ever want you to doubt that."

I let his words crash over me, soothing all the raw and vulnerable places inside me. But I'd been living this life long enough that I knew it wasn't going to be that easy. He wouldn't magically be able to erase a lifetime of insecurities with a few words.

"I'd like to tell you it's never going to happen again, but that would be a lie," I said, needing him to know exactly what he was getting into if we actually made a go of things. "It *is* going to happen again. Probably many times. And for this to work between us, I need to know that you're not going to bail. That you're not going to run away and leave me when things get tough. I need to know that I can fall apart, and you're still going to catch me."

This time when he stepped closer, I didn't stop him.

He reached out, brushing my hair back from my face

before sliding his hand down to wrap his fingers around my nape. Leaning down, he closed his eyes as he pressed his forehead against mine. "I will always catch you, kitten. I was an asshole to walk away from you when you were hurting. I promise—I *swear*—I won't do it again."

I reached up, gripping his forearms. "I know my need to feel like I've earned your love is something that I have to work on, but it's always a whisper in the back of my mind, and it's not going to go away anytime soon."

He pulled back enough so he could stare into my eyes, his thumbs swiping away at the tears that continued to fall. "You don't have to *do* anything for me to love you. That's not something you have to earn. It just *is*. Like the sun rising every morning and setting each night. It's there whether you achieve all your goals or you Netflix and actually chill all day instead. It's there when we fight and when you pull away, and it's sure as fuck there whether or not you feel it, too."

"I feel it," I said, my voice choked as I nodded.

He exhaled a deep breath, his entire posture relaxing. "I love you. So fucking much."

"I love you, too," I whispered.

The words were barely out of my mouth before Ford's lips covered mine. He cupped my face in his hands, his mouth slanting over mine as his tongue slipped inside. He kissed me like he was afraid I was going to float away. Like he was worried he would lose me again. And that only made me grip him tighter, knowing that fear all too well. Knowing it was something we could overcome together.

It didn't take long for our kiss out front to turn heated and then downright indecent, and we fumbled with the lock before stumbling our way into the cottage. Ford's hands were everywhere, divesting us of our clothes in record time. And I had no idea how I could be so hungry for him when we'd only been apart for a day. But I was coming to expect that was just the norm where he was concerned.

Whenever we were together, whether in competition with each other or boosting each other up, we burned brighter... hotter...than we ever did alone.

Ford pushed me back until my knees hit the bed, and I yelped, falling onto the mattress with a bounce. His eyes heated as he raked them over my naked body. At one time, that would've made me uncomfortable. I would've had the urge to cover up, hide away from his assessing gaze. But there was absolutely no denying the hunger as he looked at me, his eyes darting over every inch of me. Hunger he had for *me*.

"It's been too long, kitten. I need to be inside you. Need that sweet pussy to remind me who I belong to. But first, I want you to come on my tongue."

Without waiting for me to respond, he dove headfirst between my legs. He wasn't gentle, wasn't soft or sweet. He was a starving man at his first feast, affixing his mouth to me, his tongue not leaving an inch of my pussy untouched. He worked me up into a frenzy with startling ease, sliding two fingers deep inside me as his tongue tormented my clit with tight circles.

"Come on, wife. Give it to me. Come for me like a good girl, and let me taste how much you've missed my tongue on your pussy," he said, his voice gruff, his words sending me even higher.

As soon as he reached up with his other hand and cupped my breast, brushing his thumb over my tightened peak as he stared up at me with lust in his eyes, I broke. With a sharp cry, I came against his tongue, my hips rocking against his mouth as the waves washed through my body.

"Need to be inside you," he murmured against me. And before I could even nod my assent, he stood to his full height, jerked my ass to the edge of the bed, and settled himself between my spread thighs. And then he sank inside with a groan. "Need to feel you come on my cock."

My mouth dropped open, the air expelling from my lungs at that first deep thrust. Even though I'd gotten used to his size, that first moment always took my breath away, as did every time his piercing rubbed against that magical spot inside me. I might've just gone off against his tongue, but I knew a second orgasm was on the horizon, already building as Ford stared down at me. His expression was intense, and at one time, I would've thought it was unreadable. But now that I knew how he felt, I could see it as clear as day.

It was love. It had been all along.

He draped himself over my body, capturing my lips with his as he ground himself against me, rubbing my clit with every shift of his hips. Linking our fingers together, he stretched them out above our heads. Then he pressed them into the mattress, silently telling me to keep them there as he stood back so he could see all of me, spread out before him, my pussy stretched around his thick cock.

"Jesus, look at you," he said, his voice low and gravelly and filled with awe as he ran his hands down my body. Cupping my breasts before passing over the swell of my stomach, the stretch marks on my hips. "Look at your perfect tits bounce every time I slide inside you. My wife's body is insane. So fucking gorgeous."

For once, I let his words wash over me and didn't immediately try to push them away. Didn't try to brush them off as nothing or counteract them with the negative words that I'd grown used to. Instead, I let them sink inside me, settling deep in my bones.

For once, I let them build me up instead of knocking them aside so I could tear myself down.

He rested his hand on my lower stomach, his thumb slipping down to strum my clit. "Come all over me, wife. Show me whose pussy this is. Show me what's mine and claim what's yours."

His thrusts grew shallower as he dragged his piercing over that spot inside me, and I gasped. Even though he'd wanted me to keep my hands over my head, I couldn't. I needed to feel him against me. Needed to tug him down and have him as close as possible. Chest to chest, mouth to mouth, heart to heart.

He didn't hesitate when I tugged him down, resting his forehead against mine as he ground his cock into me and my body tightened around him. "There it is, kitten. There you go. Fuck, you feel so good. You're gonna make me come. Gonna make me fill up this perfect little cunt."

"*Ford.*" My body arched into his, my mouth open in a

silent scream as his thrusts tipped me over the edge and my second orgasm crashed over me.

Ford captured my lips with his, groaning into my mouth as he thrust twice more before settling deep and spilling himself inside me.

After we'd both caught our breath, he slipped from me before padding to the bathroom. He came back with a warm washcloth he used to clean me off and then scooped me up and settled into bed next to me.

With my head resting on his bare chest, his fingers playing in my hair, I asked something I'd been wondering for a while. "Did you really agree to this marriage just because of Chelsea's wedding?"

He shrugged under me. "That was part of it."

"And the other part?"

"Besides getting to marry the woman I jacked it to during my teenage years, you mean?"

I snorted. "Stop."

"You think I'm lying? Ask Beck how infatuated I was."

I shifted to sit up, pushing against his chest so I could see his face. As I stared at him, I recalled what Mabel had told me earlier today—that Ford had had a crush on me in high school, but I hadn't believed her… "Wait…seriously?"

"Yes, seriously. Especially when you used to wear that yellow sundress. You remember the one? I'm pretty sure that's where my obsession with you in them came from." He closed his eyes and groaned. "Christ, I'd rub one out three times after school on those days."

I breathed out a laugh. "You're lying."

He grabbed me by the hips and pulled me over to straddle him, allowing me to feel exactly what the memory did to him, even though he'd just come inside me less than ten minutes before.

With wide eyes, I said, "Oh my God, you're actually serious."

"Yep."

"Why were you such an ass all the time?"

He smirked up at me, that playful glint in his eyes I loved so much. "Would you believe me if I said I wasn't trying to be? I was a teenage idiot. And it was pretty much the only way you'd talk to me."

"I'd yell at you, Ford. Oh my God, I was so mean to you."

"Probably why you scowling at me now only gets my dick hard."

I breathed out a laugh and shook my head. "We sure took a roundabout way to get where we are."

"Maybe, but I wouldn't change it." He rested his hands on my hips and stared up at me, earnestness in his gaze, all teasing gone. "All of it, including valedictorian…"

My breath caught, worried whatever he said was only going to dredge up old memories…the grudge I'd held for so long. "Why is that?"

"I want to say I'd go back in time and do it differently because of how much it meant to you back then." He swept his thumbs over the bare skin of my hips, his eyes locked with mine. "But I'd be lying. If I could do it all over again, I'd do it exactly the same because it's the reason you moved back to

Starlight Cove. It's the reason you came back to me. And I wouldn't change that for anything."

Tears brimmed in my eyes once again, and I realized he was right. If things hadn't happened how they did...if my life hadn't been altered in that way...we might not be here right now. I might never have known what it felt like to be his.

I leaned over him, lowering my face until I could press my lips against his. "I love you."

"I love you, too, wife," he said. "And in case it wasn't clear, I don't want this marriage to be fake. I don't think I ever did. I want to tell off fuckers who can't take no for an answer and carry your bags when we run errands and have cuddle parties with you when your period makes your life miserable. I want to go to bonfires with my family and beat you at charades."

"Watch it," I said, though my voice lacked any heat.

"So, is it cool with you if it's a little longer before we get this first divorce out of the way?"

"What do you mean by a little longer?"

He shrugged, then reached down to grab his jeans from the floor, pulling a small box from his pocket. Lifting the lid, he pulled out a black ring from inside and held it up between us.

I recognized it immediately as the one I'd purchased for him. The one that had the same inscription on the inside that mine did.

"I was thinking forever," he said. "How does that sound?"

"That sounds like a long time..."

"You think so? It doesn't sound like nearly long enough to

me. But I want you to think long and hard before you agree to this."

"Why's that?"

"Because when you do?" He slid off his silicone ring and set it on his nightstand before slipping the metal band into place. "There's no take backs."

A smile spread across my face as Ford gripped my nape and tugged my mouth to his. The kiss was slow and sweet, both of us saying without words exactly what we needed to. That we were in this, together. Forever.

No take backs.

EPILOGUE
FORD

I DIDN'T KNOW if it was a blessing or a curse that our first little league play-off of the fall season was against my wife's newly sponsored team. No matter where Quinn and I stood —whether it was a good day or a challenging one—one thing that never changed between us was that competitive streak we'd had since we were kids. Us being officially—not fake... and definitely not temporarily—married didn't change that.

"When we beat you today, are you going to take it like a big girl, or are you going to give me the silent treatment like you always do?" I asked, brushing my lips up the column of Quinn's neck, barely restraining myself from pinning her against this wall and fucking her, to hell with the onlookers. We were *technically* out of sight. And, really, how many people came to buy concessions during a little league game? We could probably get away with—

"When *we* beat *you*, are you going to take it like a big girl or pout like you usually do?" she shot back, eyes narrowed.

"Kitten. While I've definitely got the big part down, I think we both know there's nothing girlish about me." I gripped her hip, digging my fingers into her soft flesh as I pressed my dick against her.

I'd known I wouldn't stand a chance of making it through this game without getting a hit of my wife first. Not when I hadn't seen her since she'd left for work that morning, leaving me blissed out in our bed. So, as soon as she had strutted from her car across the field toward her team's dugout, that fucking sundress swinging in the breeze as she went, I'd told Aiden I'd be back. Then I'd intercepted my wife, tugged her behind the field house and kissed her within an inch of her life.

I could admit it hadn't been my smartest move since I was now sporting a huge fucking erection, and we were surrounded by—if out of sight from—a bunch of kids. But I didn't make too many smart moves where Quinn was concerned. She reduced me to a puddle of nonsense and need on a daily basis, and today was no different.

"Quit rubbing your dick all over me," she murmured against my mouth, but her words lacked heat, and she held me to her with two fistfuls of my shirt, like she was just as needy for me as I was for her.

And I was here for it. Here for those public declarations... and the private ones, too. There was no more pretending between us. No more concealing our true feelings or hiding behind a history we couldn't change but one we'd both grown grateful for. How we loved each other was on display every day, in private or not, arguing or not, competing or not...

without fail. Loving each other through the ups and downs... *Staying* and working through them was new to us both, but we were learning. Together.

While it was pretty fucking obvious how I felt about Quinn, we'd come clean to my family and told them there was no longer anything fake about our marriage. That we were in it for the long haul. My brothers all nodded their congrats, but that little dictator Addison had only grinned smugly, as if she'd had a hand in Quinn's and my fake-turned-real love all along.

I stared down at my wife, a heavy gratefulness washing over me not for the first time. This gorgeous, smart-as-hell, hot-as-fuck woman was *mine*. For the rest of our lives.

"If you don't want me to rub my dick on you, wife, then quit wearing these goddamn dresses." I pinched the hem of it between my fingers, desperate to tug it right off her. To flip up the skirt and get an eyeful of those panties I'd seen her slipping into this morning. To sink inside all that perfection between her thick thighs and fuck her until neither of us could breathe. "All I have to do is see one laid out on the bed, and I'm fucking hard."

She hummed low in her throat, leaning into me for the briefest moment, before straightening and pushing away. Narrowing her eyes, she pointed a finger at me. "I know what you're doing, husband. And it's not going to work."

First of all, her calling me husband was doing fuck all for the beast in my pants, desperate to be inside her. And second, I was certain she didn't have any idea, because what I was doing was trying to stop myself from saying fuck it and dragging her into the bathroom to have my way with her, play-off game be damned. Aiden could figure that shit out on his own. Brady was in the dugout to help. Those two bossy assholes would be fine.

"What am I doing?" I asked, voice rough.

"You're trying to distract me so you can win." She braced her hand on my chest as she stood on her tiptoes, her lips brushing mine with every word, her eyes sparking with challenge. "But it's not gonna happen."

Then she nipped my bottom lip and patted my chest twice before taking a step back, out of my reach.

I had to force myself not to grab her around the waist, tug her back into me, and kiss the hell out of her, just for a little while longer. Like...maybe another hour or two. We wouldn't be missed during that time, would we?

I had no idea when I'd stop craving my wife every goddamn second of every goddamn day, but if history was anything to go by, the answer to that was never.

I'd never get sick of calling Quinn mine.

I huffed out a pained laugh, hanging my head as I willed my dick to calm the fuck down. "The last thing on my mind is this game, kitten. All I'm thinking about is getting you naked as soon as fucking possible. When will that be, by the way?"

She bit her lip, her eyes heating for a moment as she stared at me, and I thought I had her. Thought she was going to tip her head toward the bathroom and drag me inside to let me have my way with her. But instead, she spun around and headed toward the field. Over her shoulder, she said, "How about the winner gets to decide our evening activities?"

"By evening activities, do you mean how I'm going to fuck you?" When her only answer was a raised brow at me, I laughed lowly and swiped a thumb across my bottom lip, my eyes glued to the sway of those luscious hips as she walked away from me. "In that case, you better be ready to lose, wife, because I already know exactly what I'm going to do when I win."

And it involved her naked and bound to the bed while I tormented her with the new toy that had arrived in the mail today.

So, yeah, there was no fucking way our team was losing.

Even if this was the first play-off for the clinic's team. Even if I was so fucking proud of her, I couldn't bear it. Going easy on her wasn't what she needed from me. Wasn't what our relationship had ever been about. We'd pushed each other from the beginning—forced each other to strive for more—and that wasn't going to stop now. Even as I smiled, watching my wife greet her team, the kids sporting jerseys that proclaimed *Sponsored by Dr. Quinn McKenzie*.

Because yeah...that shit was permanent.

Where she'd once balked at taking my last name, it had ultimately been an easy decision for her once we'd decided this was forever. She'd wanted a clean break after cutting her parents out of her life, and keeping her last name would never allow her to do that.

Quinn had looked into sponsoring a team as soon as she'd purchased the clinic—a purchase that had been far easier than either of us had anticipated. It turned out not even Don's wife liked the jackass, and the poor woman had been married to him for forty years. She'd reached out to Quinn barely a week after his death to discuss my wife's offer that, apparently, had been tossed in his trash can.

No one had been more shocked than Quinn when Mrs. Dinsmore had not only agreed to sell her the clinic, but to do so at a much lower price than what Quinn had offered. But the biggest surprise had come when she'd told my wife she'd sold it to her specifically *because* Don had fought so hard against it.

Yep. My wife had been rewarded for putting up with that asshole every day for months by getting his practice in the end, all because he hadn't wanted her to have it in the first place. And if that wasn't karma, I didn't know what was.

I strolled down to the dugout, grin on my lips as I figured out how we were going to win this game. Normally, Aiden was on that—focused to a fault when it came to...well, everything. But today, he was distracted. And not quite as surly as he stared out at the kids on the field practicing their throws. He also hadn't yelled at me once, even for sneaking away to fuck off with my wife. He didn't—

My mouth dropped open as I eyed him from head to toe. He stood there in his usual uniform of gray dress pants and a white button-up, the sleeves rolled up, his eyes focused on the kids practicing on the field. But there was something different about him. He had an air to him that only came from—

"Holy shit," I said, splitting my gaze between him and Brady, who sat on the bench in the dugout. "You got laid."

Aiden snapped his head in my direction, the briefest

flicker of shock registering across his face before he wiped it clear of any expression. "I don't know what you're talking about."

I barked out a laugh and shook my head. "Sure you don't. There's no use trying to deny it. I can sniff that shit out like a bloodhound. Can't I?" I asked Brady, gesturing with my chin toward our lying brother who most *definitely* got some action last night. And it was about fucking time.

"You do kind of have something going on there," Brady said, circling his own face as he stared at Aiden. "Is this because of the woman you told me about?"

His gaze shot to Brady. "Dude. *What the fuck.*"

"Oh, this is too good. What woman?" I asked, rubbing my hands together. "Tell me more. Tell me *everything.*"

But instead of saying anything, Aiden just split a glare between Brady and me, his arms crossed over his chest as if that would protect him from my interrogation.

Not fucking likely.

"Was it the *I can call you Daddy, too* single mom? Is that why you don't want to talk about it right now?"

Aiden's jaw ticked, and he didn't even glance over at me as he said, "No, it wasn't with that woman. I know better than to get involved with someone who would make my life difficult. And I don't want to talk about it right now because A) we're surrounded by a bunch of little kids and their parents—"

"One of whom is desperate to call you Daddy..."

"And B) it's none of your fucking business."

"Oh no. You're the one who showed up at this game with your *I just got laid* face on, thus making it my business." I shrugged. "I could also make it Addison's business if you wanted... She'll be here any minute."

"You're such a dick."

My smile only grew, because I could see his façade cracking, and I knew I had him.

Finally, after way too damn long, he let out an annoyed sigh and scrubbed a hand down his face. "It was no big deal, all right? I needed to blow off some steam, so I went to One Night Stan's, had a one-night stand, and that's it. She didn't leave her number, and I don't even know her name—"

Brady cut in, "Just that she's a redheaded smokeshow with a penchant for—"

"Would you shut the fuck up?" Aiden hissed at him. Then he cleared his throat and rolled his shoulders back. "Anyway, she's not from around here, so it's done."

"What if she was?" I asked.

"What if she was, what?"

I raised a brow at him. "From around here?"

Something passed over his face, but it was gone too quickly for me to name. "Doesn't matter, because she's not. And we're done talking about this."

"If you actually want to be done talking about it, you better do something about your face, because Addison's on her way over here..."

Aiden glanced behind me to where our baby sister walked toward us through the crowd, slipping past people with someone on her heels. Then, his entire body went rigid.

I glanced back to Addison, my brows shooting up when I registered the woman next to her. She looked to be about

Addison's age, with a bright smile and a laugh loud enough to draw everyone's attention. And a waterfall of red hair that shone in the sun.

Holy shit.

"Hey..." I said, brows up as I glanced between my sister and this newcomer who might or might not be—but probably definitely was—the "smokeshow" Aiden had seen last night.

"Surprise!" Addison said, holding out her hands toward the other woman as if she were presenting her on a game show. "This is Avery, my college bestie! Thanks to my impressive persuasive skills, I've managed to sweet-talk her into working at the resort for three months so you can stop being such a grump all the time, Aiden. *You're welcome.*"

Holy. Shit.

"Avery, meet Aiden," Addison continued, completely oblivious to the way the two of them were frozen, staring at each other in shock. "One of my brothers and your new boss. Isn't this gonna be *great*?"

ACKNOWLEDGMENTS

Eternal thanks to the following people for helping to make this book what it is:

Christina, the best Plot Whisperer and alpha reader in the world who I get to call bestie. For being a sounding board, idea bouncer, and cheerleader. And for knowing when I need an active participant or someone to sit silently on the other end while I work out my shit through extensive word vomit. Thank you for loving these characters and this world as much as I do.

Becca for understanding that Communication needs to talk shit out but Responsibility doesn't like to ask for help in order to do so and presenting me with a solution to satisfy both. I've loved our weekend Zooms and am grateful for the chance to talk my way out of any issues before they even arrived while helping with yours. Thanks for getting my certain brand of...eccentricity.

The Emerald Elite—my Thursday night crew who are always there to talk shop, brainstorm, or commiserate when needed. From trope butter lists to dissecting a popular book, we rock it all. Our weekly chats are one of the very few things I'm grateful to the 'Rona for.

Annika, for our morning accountability calls and helping

me work through little stumbles so I don't spend all day fretting over the dumbest thing I could've talked through in five minutes. Let's face it...if it weren't for these calls, some days I'd just fuck around on Facebook all morning, so thank you.

Molly O, Lisa H, and Patricia E, for offering suggestions and guidance to ensure I portrayed Quinn and the personal and medical challenges she faced with sensitivity and care. Thank you for your insight and experience!

Lisa Hollett for wielding a red pen like a goddamn pro. I appreciate you, even (maybe especially) when you tell me to remove one of my 2512 beloved em-dashes. (That's an over-exaggeration. Probably.) And for sending me serious notes wondering if Ford wants to refer to his dick with a neutral pronoun or continue with personification. You're the real MVP.

My readers and those in Brighton's Brigade for anxiously awaiting Ford and Quinn's book and understanding when physical limitations forced me to push back this release. You're truly the best.

Last but never least, the menfolk I live with. My husband for still being impressed AF when I finish a book, even after dozens, and my boys who don't see what the big deal is. Thanks for building me up while keeping me humble. I love you.

OTHER TITLES BY BRIGHTON WALSH

STARLIGHT COVE SERIES

Defiant Heart

Protective Heart

Fearless Heart

Reckless Heart

————

HOLIDAYS IN HAVENBROOK SERIES

Main Street Dealmaker

————

HAVENBROOK SERIES

Second Chance Charmer

Hometown Troublemaker

Pact with a Heartbreaker

Captain Heartbreaker

Small Town Pretender

————

RELUCTANT HEARTS SERIES

Caged in Winter

Tessa Ever After

Paige in Progress

Our Love Unhinged

————————

STAND-ALONE TITLES

Dirty Little Secret

Season of Second Chances

Plus One

ABOUT THE AUTHOR

Award-winning *USA Today* and *Wall Street Journal* bestselling author Brighton Walsh spent a decade as a professional photographer before taking her storytelling in a different direction and reconnecting with her first love—writing. She likes her books how she likes her tea —steamy and satisfying—and adores strong-willed heroines and the protective heroes who fall head over heels for them. Brighton lives in the Midwest with her real life hero of a husband, her two kids—both taller than her—and her dog who thinks she's a queen. Her boy-filled house is the setting for dirty socks galore, frequent dance parties (okay, so it's mostly her, by herself, while her children look on in horror), and more laughter than she thought possible.

www.brightonwalsh.com

tiktok.com/@brightonwalshbooks

instagram.com/brighton_walsh

facebook.com/brightonwalshwrites

Printed in Great Britain
by Amazon